Kow

AFTER CLARE

A Selection of Recent Titles by Marjorie Eccles

THE SHAPE OF SAND
SHADOWS AND LIES
LAST NOCTURNE
BROKEN MUSIC
THE CUCKOO'S CHILD *
AFTER CLARE *

* available from Severn House

AFTER CLARE

Marjorie Eccles

Severn House Large Print
London & New York

This first large print edition published 2018
in Great Britain and the USA by
SEVERN HOUSE PUBLISHERS LTD of
Eardley House, 4 Uxbridge Street, London W8 7SY.
First world regular print edition published 2012 by
Severn House Publishers Ltd.

British Library Cataloguing in Publication Data
A CIP catalogue record for this title is available from the British Library.

ISBN-13: 9780727893291

Severn House Publishers support the Forest Stewardship Council™
[FSC™], the leading international forest certification organisation. All
our titles that are printed on FSC certified paper carry the FSC logo.

MIX
Paper from
responsible sources
FSC® C013056

Typeset by Palimpsest Book Production Ltd.,
Falkirk, Stirlingshire, Scotland.
Printed and bound in Great Britain by
T J International, Padstow, Cornwall.

Prologue

The Leysmorton yew still stood by the old wall on the boundary of the estate, its silhouette stark against the skyline, an ancient landmark for travellers, as it had stood for hundreds, maybe thousands of years, centuries before the house and its habitation. It could have arrived there as a seed on the wind, or been dropped by a bird, Anthony said. More likely, the first inhabitants of the village had planted it on one of the prehistoric ley lines, in a spot regarded as holy, in the belief that the properties of this sacred tree would ensure protection.

Do not disrespect the yew, he warned, aroused to unusual talkativeness. It is amazingly long-lived, a magical tree worshipped by the Druids for its mystical properties, for healing and as a means of communicating with the dead. It's a tree of duality – tight-grained and tough, its wood was once highly valued for practical purposes, for wheels and cogs, bowls and spoons; long ago, our nation's famous victory against the overwhelming forces of the French army at Agincourt was due to the use of the longbow, made from springy English yew. Its medicinal qualities are powerful, for those skilled enough to know how to employ its parts, all of which, however, are poisonous if used wrongly. Don't play with the loose, scaly bark, children, or the needles. Never on any account eat its scarlet berries.

1

Was it all too fanciful then, to believe that the tree, keeping its secrets and its dark magic to itself, was, like the house and its garden, waiting? As they had waited for nigh on fifty years – through occupation by strangers and four devastating years of war, through loss and sorrow. Waiting for everyone to reassemble . . . for secrets to be revealed?

One

Of course it was fanciful, ridiculous. She would not entertain the notion. All the same, the vibrations were so strong, so inimical, Emily almost turned and marched back the way she had come. It was a mistake, I should not have come home, she found herself thinking, chilled.

That in itself was an extraordinary admission, given that she had yearned for this moment for decades. She was not in the habit of doubting herself or her decisions – although this particular one had taken years to mature, and in the end had only been carried through on the back of her determination to return for the wedding; she alone knew how painfully brave that was. This self-doubt was new, as dismaying as that first glimpse of the beloved old garden.

How her father would have hated this! Anthony, that big, shambling figure in his baggy old pepper-and-salt Norfolk jacket, its pockets full of bits of string, seeds, clippers, notes to himself – though he rarely needed to be reminded of where every plant was situated, what jobs needed to be done.

Where once flagged paths and clipped box hedges had defined its proportions, where fountains had played and roses had flourished so

3

lavishly abundant, where lawns had been kept immaculate by men with scythes or a Ransome mower, where she herself, almost as soon as she was old enough to wield a trowel, had helped her father to weed and dig, and had learnt how to plant out precious seedlings, now there was . . . not desolation, precisely, but rather abandonment to a rampant air of disorder, almost indecent in a way, as if Nature in reclaiming her own had tossed up her skirts, shamelessly taken charge of her own destiny, and put Man firmly in his place.

At that heretical thought Emily drew herself up to her full height, and though it was not very considerable, looked rather magnificent. She was Lady Fitzallan, and had no intention of being put in her place.

'It's certainly a pity,' Hugh was saying, pacing alongside with his hands clasped behind his back like a royal consort, thin, correct and upright as ever, 'but the Beresfords didn't take much to gardening. Birds of passage. Liked the thought of a country house garden but hadn't much idea how to go about it.' He, too, looked glumly at the prospect before them. 'At least they kept the house in some sort of order.'

'There were clauses in the lease about that,' Emily reminded him, a shade crisply. Sharpness had not always come naturally to her. It was a habit she, like other expatriate women, had fallen into, with servants in India and other faraway places who expected to be spoken to in that way by English memsahibs, and if not, thought them soft and often found subtle ways of not obeying. 'And for that matter, clauses that the garden should be maintained.'

'And so it was, after a fashion. Not as it was in your father's day, mind. Petunias in pots, I'm sorry to say. It only got like this when the soldiery came.'

By this he meant the time during the war when the house had been taken over as an army convalescent home. While Emily, longing for damp English summers, lush green grass and soft, clouded, changeable skies, for Leysmorton and its roses, had been far away in places where gardens of the only kind that could legitimately be considered gardens in her view were non-existent. Too much sun, of course. Paddy revelled in the heat, it suited his temperament, but it had wilted her. Yet she had endured without complaint. And now she was here, with the sight of it disconcerting enough to reduce her almost to tears. And there was still the house to face.

When the war came, the four men once employed to help her father in the garden had all joined the army on the same day, pals enlisting together, as men did, to fight the Germans, and they had all four perished together, in the midst of the slaughter that was the Battle of the Somme. Emily had been told there was an old man from the village who came in now, and no doubt did the best he could, but it would be quite unrealistic to expect him to cope alone with a garden of this size.

'I dare say,' Hugh said, picking up her thoughts and adroitly sidestepping the wicked thorns of an untamed berberis that threatened to clutch at his trousers, 'I dare say I could get hold of more men for the garden if you wished, Emily. The state the country's in, there's plenty looking for employment, God knows.'

5

Emily was sure he could. Hugh Markham was a man who got things done while other people were still talking about it. Decisive and sensible, a man one relied on, as he always had been. For all of his working life he had been the lynch-pin of the Peregrine Press, having inherited – and improved upon – a flourishing family publishing business of nearly 200 years' standing. Now he merely sat on the board, advising on occasions, an asset to his son, Gerald. Tall, spare, elegant, well brushed and spruce, his iron-grey hair precisely cut and his fingernails manicured. Urbane and ironic, age suited him.

'I would take it as a great favour if you could, Hugh.' She laid a brief touch on his sleeve. He nodded and said she could leave it with him.

Waves of scent rolled towards them as a turn of the path brought them to the Rose Walk. Roses had always been the beating heart of Leysmorton, its greatest attraction, and they were everywhere, here on the Walk most of all. Punctuating the neglected herbaceous planting in the long border were great mounds of the old-fashioned roses Anthony Vavasour loved all his life long: the Damasks and Bourbons, the Musks, the Old Velvet Mosses. At the back, exuberant climbers scrambled up the pink brick walls that buttressed the terrace above. Emily saw that since her father's death – it could not conceivably have been before – many treasures had grown lax and undisciplined, some of them perhaps irrecoverable. Yet within their tangled framework, beauty and perfection might still lie. Roses, Anthony had taught her, were incredibly tough, and the lavish display all around

6

provided ample evidence of it. Held in the warmth soaked up by the brick wall behind them, their combined scent had always been brought out by the hot sun. Today it was very nearly intoxicating.

'I feel so guilty, Hugh. I should have come home before, not left it all to the agency people to manage.'

'Only if you felt able to.'

Maybe he was right.

Here, at the flight of mossy steps which bisected the terrace wall, were the two recesses built either side of it, narrow domed apses, each with a stone seat roomy enough for three at the most. Sentry boxes, Clare had called them, too narrow in proportion to the wide steps. Emily should have been prepared for them, but was taken aback by a shaft of memory so keen it flashed through her like a knife. Her eyes closed in an involuntary reflex and she reached out for support to the pretty little dolphin fountain, now dry, its basin cracked, ridiculously situated in the centre of the flagged path for what reason no one had ever been able to work out. A piece of the dried, velvety moss encrusting it came off whole, and as she felt it crumble in her tightening hand, she blinked and forced herself back to her senses.

The moment had been too brief for Hugh to have noticed anything, she was sure. Then he said, 'All right, m'dear?', and the controlled note of concern in his voice told her that of course he had noticed.

'Yes, thank you.' She let the moss fall and rubbed the fingers of her cream kid gloves together. 'I nearly missed my step, that's all.'

'It happens, sometimes.' She was grateful that he did not add, *at our age*.

7

He, too, must remember that other June night – the heat, the drenching, swooning scent of roses as they sat close together on the stone seat in one of the apses, as she turned her face guiltily away and looked anywhere but at him, while outside the little fountain made its music in time with her thumping heart.

But she could not bear to remember just now. She turned away, and with her foot on the first of the steps to the terrace, paused.

And there was the old house, the Vavasours' ancestral home. *Her* house now, its long lattice windows touched to gold by the late afternoon sun, warm and hospitable despite the tenacious cloak of Boston ivy which clung to its rosy bricks, frowned over the window lintels and threatened to engulf it entirely.

Leysmorton was very old. An ancient manor house, lowish and crooked, full of secret twists and turns, odd flights of steps, dim corners and small, extra windows here and there throwing light in unexpected places, its charm lay in the tranquillity the years had settled on it rather than any architectural felicities.

Her throat constricted with emotion. 'Hugh . . . do you think, perhaps . . .?'

'You would like to go in alone?'

Bless him for his understanding. 'If you wouldn't mind.'

'Of course not. I'll see you at dinner, then. Shall I send the motor?'

He had already met her train at the station with the Daimler and brought her to the gates of Leysmorton, and when she had said she would like to walk up

8

through the gardens, had sent the chauffeur round to the front of the house with her bags.

'No, no, there's no need for that. Thank you, Hugh, I'll walk over with Dirk.'

His home, Steadings, where they were all to dine tonight, was only a few minutes' walk away, if you took the path which generations of impatient Vavasours and Markhams had trampled out in order to avoid taking the marginally longer way round by the road, until eventually it had become the accepted route between the two houses.

'I must see you alone,' he said suddenly. 'Properly alone, I mean, with time to talk.'

'Hugh—'

'We haven't been alone,' he reminded her, unnecessarily, 'since Paris.'

'My dear, would it be wise?'

'Wise?' Shaken out of his composure, he laughed shortly. 'Wise? That's one thing we no longer need to be, not now.'

Their eyes held, and with sudden surrender, she reached up – she had to rise on tiptoe – and kissed him very gently. 'We will then, Hugh, we will. But not just yet, it's too early to make decisions. Give me time to get my bearings.'

'I can wait. I've learned how to, Lord knows.'

He watched her go. She had broken her journey in London on the way here and evidently done some expensive shopping. The young Emily he had known – eager, impressionable, loving, with a carnation flush to her cheeks and large, soft eyes that could still light up with mischief – had become a poised and elegant woman. The plump prettiness of her youth had gone, to be replaced

9

by something more interesting. Her features had fined down and she had gained dignity and presence, despite the ragamuffin, vagabond existence he considered her life to have been.

From behind, the neat figure in cream silk poplin and matching straw hat could pass for the young woman he had once loved to the point where he had thought it might not be possible to carry on, after she had left him. But they had both gone on, survived for another, unbelievable, four – no, nearer five – decades. Unbelievable? Where Emily was concerned, nothing was unbelievable to Hugh, even this wholly unexpected return. There had always been an element of unpredictability about her, which was one of the things he had loved her for, and still did, despite the pain it had brought. But she had steadfastly coped with Paddy Fitzallan for more than half a lifetime – and that said all that needed to be said, as far as Hugh was concerned.

Halfway up the steps, he saw her falter and stop. Having no wish for her to turn round and see him still standing there, he moved away. She was here at last, he thought, as he walked back towards the trees that hid Steadings from view, feeling twenty years younger. She was here.

Emily mounted the last few steps. It was only an upstairs curtain that had twitched, although for a heart-lurching moment she had almost imagined it was Clare at the window. But whoever had moved that curtain, it wasn't Clare.

She stood for another moment, uncharacteristically hesitant, before the solid, venerable door that was grainy and weathered to a silvery grey, this

10

door to the garden side of the house which had rarely ever been closed. Then, even as she hesitated, it opened and there was Dirk.

'Welcome home, Cousin Emily.'

Two

'What makes you think I've changed my mind?' Poppy asked. 'Naturally I shall go – and so will you, of course, Val.'

Valentine shoved his hands into his pockets and raised an eyebrow. 'There's no of course about it. Dee Markham isn't *my* best friend, Sis.'

'She isn't mine at the moment, either, ducky, if it comes to that, but the invitation includes you. She couldn't *not* invite either of us, really, since we're almost family, and it's going to be such a splash.'

He thought 'almost family' was stretching it a bit. The Drummonds and the Markhams were cousins at least twice, if not three times removed, but the wedding invitation, embossed gold on thick cream card, certainly held both their names. It stood prominent amongst the other announcements on the mantelpiece – notices of exhibitions by unknown artists in obscure galleries, a gaudy postcard from Antibes, an invitation to the opening of a new nightclub of the sort that Poppy considered it smart to frequent – all propped against the pewter vase that held a single, vibrant purple iris.

He watched her as she took a comb from the brocade vanity bag on her wrist and turned her head sideways to examine her hair in the mirror over the mantel, though her smooth, square-cut black bob with the ends curving towards her face

12

needed no attention. Val moved to stand behind her, a little to one side so that he could see her face in the mirror as he spoke, and saw his own as well. The same sweep of the eyebrows, the Drummond chin, but there the resemblance ended. He was an untidy, windswept young man with stormy grey eyes, he forgot to get his hair cut, and he wore a corduroy jacket that Poppy deplored.

It was she who spoke first, the jacket no doubt reminding her. 'You'll have to wear proper togs for the wedding.'

He laughed shortly. 'Apart from my demob suit, what do you suggest? The one bought when I left school? Since when my measurements have altered considerably.' Which was true enough. Although he was not tall, his shoulders were broad, and in the last few years he had become muscular and athletic.

She began to apply more lipstick to her already vivid mouth, as poppy-red as her name, startling against her white skin and black hair. She was dressed for the evening in a narrow, waistless number in sea-green and silver, her skirt short enough to show several inches of leg above the ankle, silver shoes with a double strap and a three-inch Louis heel, shiny nude stockings and a silver slave bangle set with glassy green stones high on her bare, rounded upper arm, others circling the opposite wrist. It was a get-up alto-gether too studied and sharp, too contrived, Val considered, remembering the warm, spontaneous little sister she had been not so long ago.

'Well?' She turned and he let his hand fall from

13

her shoulder. He threw himself down on the sofa and put his feet on the canary-yellow lacquered coffee table.

'Weddings are not my forte. Especially big ones, like this.'

'Not so very big. It's only a country wedding, after all.'

'Big enough.'

'Archie Elphinstone's going to be best man. He'll give us a lift down there, and as for a morning suit . . .' Calculation sharpened her features as she thought about ways one might be obtained for him at this last minute. She had not told him that she had already sent an acceptance for both of them.

He chose not to answer, but lifted his eyebrows and squinted at the invitation again: *Diana Margaret (Dee) Markham, daughter of Mr & Mrs Gerald Markham . . . to Hamish Erskine, son of Sir Trumpington and Lady Erskine of Kinmoray, Scotland . . . St Phillip's church, Netherley, Hertfordshire . . . June seventeenth . . .*

'I wouldn't have thought Gerald could afford such a do. The Markhams must be as hard up as all the rest of us nowadays.'

'Maybe, but he can't let it be seen that he isn't up to providing the necessary for his daughter's wedding to old Trump's son either, darling. Besides, Hugh will be doing most of the paying, I dare say. He's very fond of his granddaughters.' She laughed in the tinkling way she had adopted lately, then said, with stubborn intent, 'I really *want* to go, Val.'

Green was not a colour she should wear; her

eyes, grey like his but paler and cool, had taken on a greenish cast from the dress. They narrowed like a cat's as she watched him.

'One of life's hard-earned lessons, my dear, is that we don't always get what we want.'

'I don't know about that. I generally manage it, don't I?'

It wasn't always as true as she might like to think but, courageous and daring, she'd always had a knack of manoeuvring things her way. Yet how happy was she when she'd achieved her aim? Like all her friends, Poppy projected a relentless brightness and glitter – but happiness?

He lit a cigarette and leaned his head back on the sofa, more comfortable than the lumpy one in his own seedy bedsit, to which he must presently repair. They each had their own place; there was no room for two in this tiny, one-bedroom flat, and their lifestyles were too dissimilar, anyway, for either of them to want to share. For the moment, however, Val was happy enough to loll back on her sofa, feet up, head back against the cushions.

Through half-closed eyes he noticed that where the palest of grey walls met the ceiling of the same shade, Poppy, who was clever and artistic, had recently stencilled a geometric border in mauve and purple, with the same motif repeated around the grey-tiled fireplace, the colours echoed in the curtains. The paintwork was smart navy blue and there were touches of canary yellow here and there. She and a woman called Xanthe Tripp ran a little interior decorating shop in Knightsbridge, to Val pretentiously and incomprehensibly named *XP et Cie* (X for Xanthe, P for

Poppy and Cie for Company) – 'so French, so chic!', said Mrs Tripp.

They were not, however, making much money. Their clients were mostly friends, or friends of friends, and paying bills was not high on the list of their priorities, especially when they came as high as Mrs Tripp's bills did. She was a divorcée in her forties with a racy lifestyle, and was consumed by the necessity to get enough money for its upkeep. Valentine had met Xanthe Tripp only once or twice and had no desire whatsoever to meet her again, and although Poppy seemed happy enough with the set-up for the time being, he gave it another six months at the most and was not unduly perturbed at the prospect of its demise. Poppy might be upset at the failure of yet another venture, but not unduly, he hoped. Where once it had all been 'Xanthe this, Xanthe that', now when her name was mentioned it was sometimes followed by a slight pause or a frown.

Although at the moment he devoutly wished her way of life different, Val did not like the idea of Poppy being unhappy. They were alone in the world, poor as church mice, and he felt responsible for her. As for himself, he didn't see how anyone who had spent two years in that hellish show over the Channel could have a right to expect true happiness ever again. A company officer leading his men over the top, a young sprig straight out of school, by the skin of his teeth he had missed being killed, or even injured, not once but several times. He had gained a reputation for bravery, when he knew it was sheer luck – and plain fear of being seen to be in a funk. Luck had followed him most of his

16

life – apart from the disaster that was their parents. Lucky Val Drummond: scraping through his exams, batting the winning innings at the inter public school cricket match in his last year; lucky to be the brother of Poppy Drummond, many of his acquaintances would no doubt say.

Lately, however, that luck seemed to have deserted him. He was recently down from Oxford, where he had gone straight from the trenches because he couldn't think what else to do in the sombre hiatus, the anticlimax after the last dark, adrenalin-fuelled years, when all the world had teetered on the edge of catastrophe. He had easily obtained one of the many places available – all those young hopefuls gone west – and in the same haphazard way had chosen to read English. He hadn't yet lost the wild air of the undergraduate, and was apt to wear a college scarf wound around his neck, even when it was not strictly necessary.

This train of thought brought him back to the wedding. Oh, God! Bad enough being seen as the poor relations, but there was another, even more cogent reason he did not feel inclined to go. Reading English had given Valentine literary aspirations, but no one, it seemed, wanted to publish, much less read, the kind of novel he had recently surprised even himself by producing: angry, declamatory, accusing. They said everyone had had enough of that kind of angst; amusement was what the world wanted now, this fast and light-hearted world determined to forget the recent past and its horrors in the hectic whirl of nightclubs, fast dancing, jazz music, cocktail drinking – and perhaps more – as Poppy and her friends did.

If he went to the wedding he would have the embarrassment of facing Gerald Markham, who in his professional capacity had just turned down his novel. Gerald, conscientious and well-intentioned Gerald, whose own war had been spent at the War Office, was once more running the Markham Press, while old Hugh, who had emerged out of retirement to fill the breach for the duration of his absence, had gracefully stepped back into it once more.

Poppy picked up her black figured-velvet wrap with its white swansdown collar. 'You can stay here for a bit if you wish, Val, but I don't want you camping out on my sofa all night. For one thing, my landlord wouldn't like it.'

He swung his legs to the floor. 'No fear, I'm off now. Where are you going?'

'I'm not sure.' She avoided his eyes. 'Maybe the Blue Bird. With Xanthe and a few others.'

'Don't do it, Poppy.'

He'd heard of the Blue Bird of Happiness and what went on there. He caught hold of her wrist to emphasize his point. Her bracelets jangled. 'Let go, you're hurting me,' she said pettishly. 'I know what I'm doing, I am not a *child*.'

No use telling her not to act like one, then. There was no coping with Poppy lately. He dropped her wrist and picked up his scarf. Before he could say anything else, she added, 'By the way, Dee tells me Lady Fitzallan is coming home for the wedding.'

'What, the Female Fitz? After all these years?'

'The *rich* Female Fitz.' Shortly before he died, their father, Jack Drummond, had extracted a promise from his older friend, Sir Patrick Fitzallan,

18

to keep an eye on his boy, should anything untoward happen. A reluctant promise, Val was sure, for he and Sir Patrick had never met, although he had sometimes received gifts at birthdays and the like which he suspected had not come from him – or not without prompting.

Now, remembering this generosity, he felt ashamed of using the absurd nickname he and Poppy had once thought so amusing – why, he could not now recall.

'Paddy Fitzallan did promise to look out for you, remember, even though he seemed to find it convenient to forget more often than not,' Poppy reminded him, 'so you see why I think we might even have to consider hiring a suit for you, dear brother, so that you can be at the wedding. Just a jog to the memory.'

'You are the giddy limit sometimes, Sis.'

'Well, since he died without seeing fit to leave you anything – or scarcely anything . . .'

'Maybe he hadn't anything more to leave?'

'But she has, hasn't she?'

His expression as he stared at her turned to pity. It hurt Poppy more than it hurt him to be poor. What, in the ultimate, did it matter, as long as you ate and had somewhere to sleep? But sometimes he thought Poppy would do anything to be free of the worry about money. He said softly, 'Don't be like this, Pops. It's twisting the way you are, as if you didn't care any more, though I know you do.' He paused. 'You'll have to get over him some time, you know, but this isn't the way.'

'I don't know what you mean,' said Poppy.

* * *

Rosie stood in the middle of Dee's bedroom for her last fitting, feeling a fool in pale primrose crêpe-de-Chine. Yellow – it *was* yellow, whatever Dee liked to call it – was positively the *last* colour she would have chosen for herself, though she felt there was probably nothing else that would suit her either, not with this gingerish hair and pale skin. She was certain it would make her look washed-out, or jaundiced, and cruelly emphasize the band of freckles across her nose.

'Do pull your shoulders back, for goodness' sake, Rosie,' her sister said impatiently. 'It doesn't make you look one inch shorter to hunch up like that.'

Rosie tried to do as she was bid. It was Dee's wedding, after all, and she knew that it was useless to try and make herself look inconspicuous, since that was something she would never achieve, however hard she tried. Having been told decisively that no, she could not wear flat shoes, she was going to tower even more over them all, especially over Dee, who took after their mother, and not after their father's side of the family, the tall Markhams. But yellow! It was all right for the other five bridesmaids, most of whom came in varying shades of brunette, and it was, of course, all part of the colour scheme, everything designed to complement the bride's flaxen hair and Dresden-china complexion. Not that *Dee* would be wearing primrose – ivory slipper satin for her, orange blossom circling her brow and holding down Great-grandmother's cherished Valenciennes lace veil, a single string of pearls round her neck, her bouquet a sheaf of pale roses

20

and lilies, dripping with maidenhair fern and, tucked in for luck, a sprig or two of Scottish white heather. The white heather would also feature in the flower arrangements around the church, as a gesture to all the Erskines who would have made the long journey down from Scotland. There was going to be a lot of tartan, too, at this wedding. Rosie suppressed a giggle at the thought of Hamish with bare knees and a kilt.

For the bridesmaids, there were to be posies of cream moss rosebuds, a fillet of gold leaves across their brows, buckled black satin shoes and the black and gold enamelled pendants the bridegroom was going to give all of them, and of course the wretched primrose dresses.

'Ouch!' Rosie winced as a pin stuck into the fleshy part of her hip.

'Sorry, Miss Rosie, but you'll have to stand still while I mark where this seam needs a little – er – *release*. Just a teeny-weeny little bit, that's all it needs.'

That meant she hadn't lost the five pounds she'd been determined to shed before the wedding, even though Miss Partington from the village, who was making all six of the bridesmaids' dresses, was notorious for erring on the generous side with regard to measurements. Her usual customers were robust country ladies, not the fashionably thin clients of the London couturier who had made Dee's dress, an extravagance dear old Dad hadn't batted an eyelid over. Gerald had even offered to pay for Dimitri to make Mother's outfit for the occasion as well, but she had raised her eyebrows and said no thank you, she would go to the same

21

little woman in London who always made her clothes, an impoverished Frenchwoman who sewed beautifully, entirely by hand. Well, who could blame Stella for not wanting to change? Her clothes were never anything but a perfect, immaculate fit.

'There, that should do,' Miss Partington said, rising triumphantly and flush-faced to her feet and standing back to allow Rosie to admire the effect in the long pier glass.

Maybe she hadn't done such a bad job, after all. Apart from the colour, Rosie was surprised at how well the dress looked. Perhaps she was a few pounds thinner. She still wished she had won the battle over the shoes.

Miss Partington, who wore a handkerchief scented with Phul-Nana tucked into the vee of her brown moiré silk dress, a little pincushion strapped to her wrist with elastic and a tape measure around her neck, watched her walk across the room and then darted in to mark another 'teeny-weeny release', plus an adjustment to the handkerchief points of the skirt. Rosie sighed, but she knew that the dress-maker had put her heart and soul into this most important commission of her life, working her fingers to the bone for weeks so that there would be no room for supercilious comments from any of the London guests. 'Thank you, Miss Partington, that looks really lovely,' she said, and Miss Partington blushed a dusky red, captivated, as everyone always was, by Rosie's smile.

Dee sat at the dressing table applying nail varnish while all this was going on, making the most of it while she could. Whatever she wanted, she wouldn't be allowed to walk down the aisle with painted nails – or lips. Mother, so chic, never behind the fashion herself, was adamant about that. 'No,' she had said, and because Stella so rarely bothered herself to forbid anything, Dee knew there was no room for argument. Mothers had to be especially vigilant nowadays – no one wanted to be left with spinster daughters on their hands, which was more than a possibility when so many young men, eligible or otherwise, had been lost forever – and Stella was not about to allow anything to mar this brilliant marriage one daughter at least was about to make.

Dee herself was euphoric at having caught the eye of the heir to a Scottish whisky fortune, especially one who was not mean, as Scotsmen were reported to be. Freezing to death in a dreary old castle or tramping about in the damp heather, eating nothing but porridge and making babies to continue the Erskine dynasty didn't appeal much to her. But that wouldn't happen until old Trump retired (an event not likely in the foreseeable future) and Hamish became head of the Erskine whisky-distilling firm, rather than just managing its London affairs as he did now. Meanwhile, Hamish was prepared to give her anything she asked for, and more. She already had a twenty-one diamond bracelet, a fabulous fur and the divine little house just off Sloane Square, furnished in the very latest style on the advice of Poppy Drummond and Xanthe Tripp, and just waiting for them to move into.

Oh yes, Poppy.

Dee picked up the guest list and saw that she had accepted, after all. So she hadn't taken the huff at not being asked to be a bridesmaid, though she was supposed to be one of her best chums and an old school friend. Dee felt a tiny twinge of remorse about that, but with Poppy's looks . . . well, she would have been a fool to risk having her thunder stolen on her big day, wouldn't she?

Three

He was a virtual stranger to Emily – Dirk, this cousin who was more than twenty years her junior. Unknown to her apart from that short, very surprising visit he had made to her in Madeira, the year before the war, and by the few brief letters which had since passed between them.

It was the spectacles, though, that made him virtually unrecognizable. Heavily horn-rimmed, with thick lenses, they drew attention to themselves and disturbed her almost as much as the exaggeratedly careful way he walked. She followed his tall figure into the library where he said tea was waiting, and once there, he slumped clumsily into a chair. He couldn't be drunk, surely? At five o'clock in the afternoon? She thought not; his speech was in no way slurred when he introduced his stepsister Marta – a name evidently more acceptable to English tongues than Maartje, the one she had been given at birth – and he was taking his teacup from her easily, heaping jam onto a scone without any trouble.

Emily's aunt, Florence Vavasour, had not married until late in life, after accepting a proposal from a prosperous Dutchman called Kees Heeren, a widower with a young daughter. She had gone off with him to Holland, expecting to live happily ever after, but her hopes had been brought shockingly to a halt by his sudden and unexpected death after barely two years. The shock was not lessened by finding he had not been the well-to-do man he had led her to believe. She was left alone in Utrecht, with very little money, to bring up both his daughter, Maartje, and her own child, Dirk, who was still little more than a baby, whereupon her brother, Anthony, had invited Florence and the children to move back into Leysmorton, her childhood home. It would alleviate his own lonely existence – his wife dead, Emily already married and beginning to live that new, peripatetic life in various distant parts of the world. While as for Clare . . . it was best not to speak of Clare.

The Heeren children, then, had grown up in England, cared for by his housekeeper, once his daughters' old nanny, and becoming to all intents and purposes wholly English. It had never occurred to Emily, when she became the house's owner on her father's death, that she should not allow them to stay at Leysmorton, occupants and custodians, for as long as they wished. She was still living abroad, with no reason to believe she would ever return. Every reason indeed why she should stay away.

But when Dirk had decided to pursue his career in London and Marta, evidently unwilling to live at Leysmorton alone, had joined him, the house was left alone for the first time in its history. With some trepidation, Emily had agreed to it being leased, furnished, to the Beresfords. It had turned out to be a short-lived tenancy, though their eventual departure fortunately coincided with the taking over of the house by the army for use as a convalescent home for wounded soldiers.

She had been puzzled by Dirk's initial reluctance, when the war was finally over, to move back to Leysmorton. It had, after all, been his home for most of his life, and since Emily, the last of the Vavasours, was childless, the house, not to mention her fortune, would eventually come to him. Perhaps he had not wished to appear too eager to let it be seen he had an eye on his inheritance. In the end, though, he had returned, bringing Marta, still unmarried, with him.

Now, observing the ease with which he sat in a chair that was obviously 'his', Emily wondered what he felt about her return, and was relieved when he broached the subject himself.

'It's good to see you here,' he began, when the small talk languished somewhat. 'I hope, Emily—' and then he stopped, uncharacteristically hesitant, fiddling with those spectacles, an annoying habit he seemed to have. 'I wouldn't like you to think that I – we – don't still regard Leysmorton as your home, you know, and if you wish to come back and live here, Marta and I would leave—'

'My dear Dirk, don't be absurd! I have no plans for that.' Indeed, when Paddy had died, she had stayed where she was, unwilling, or perhaps afraid, to leave her island home. 'In any case, do you think I would dream of turning you out, as long as you're content to stay here?'

But he did not know her well enough to know what she might do, any more than she had insight into his wishes on the subject. That one time when they had met she had felt he was something of an unknown quantity, and now she was not sure whether it was relief or something else that showed on his face at her reply.

Her young cousin had succeeded in carving out a place for himself as an established author, reinvented as Dirk Stronglove. 'Heeren won't do, these days,' he'd remarked then, with a touch of cynicism. 'Could be German, as far as most English folk are concerned, and being thought German is hardly a thing to encourage in view of the feelings against the Kaiser and his countrymen at the moment.'

She knew he was right. The suspicion, if not downright antagonism with which the British regarded anything German had reached them even in Madeira; it was all part of the simmering cauldron of European politics that was boiling up in countries with unpronounceable names, and would soon disrupt the peace of the whole of Europe.

'At any rate,' he had concluded, attempting a lighter tone, 'the name Heeren wouldn't help to sell the books – not the sort I write, anyway.'

They were popular novels, set in exotic places, eagerly bought and read by men and women alike. Fast-paced adventure stories with a spice of romance and plots that often stretched credulity, they made no pretence to great literature, but they were easy reading, not too long, had colourful jackets and extravagant blurbs and featured an author photograph on the back flap that was not unlike the heroes of the books – dark and somewhat brooding, hinting at masterful, perhaps arrogant, tendencies. No doubt women still fell at Dirk's feet – especially when he chose to use that disarming, totally charming smile. He smiled at her now, and she smiled back, but she had learnt to be wary of charm.

'More tea, Lady Fitzallan?'

'Thank you, I believe I will.'

Marta Heeren was clumsier with the teapot than Dirk was with his cup and saucer, and left a slight splash of tea on the cloth, which she did not seem to notice. Nerves – though what had she to be nervous about?

She was older than Dirk, well over fifty. Already faded-looking, with that sort of fairish hair, frizzed by nature or design, which always looked dusty to Emily. A woman of few words, self-effacing, polite, she was strongly built, with a round Dutch face and a square Dutch body, dowdily dressed in a dismal grey blouse and a shapeless skirt, as though she had decided she wasn't worth the effort. She pressed Emily to take a slice of Dundee cake she did not want, or another scone and some elderberry jam which it appeared Marta had made herself.

'It's very good,' Emily said politely.

'I don't do all the cooking. Nellie Dobson from the village comes in for that, but I grow all the vegetables and herbs and make cordials and remedies, occasionally jams,' Marta remarked diffidently, and after that lapsed into silence, her round, rather protuberant pale eyes downcast.

Awkwardness like hers might be due to shyness, but it was contagious, making conversation difficult. Judging another few minutes would fulfil polite requirements before she might decently excuse herself, Emily enquired about Dirk's current book.

29

He reached again for his spectacles and put them on, the hugely thick lenses masking his expression. He offered her a black Russian cigarette and when she declined, lit one himself, filling the room with rich smoke, still not replying. Fair enough. She knew authors were often reluctant to talk about work in progress, but after a moment he shrugged. 'Oh,' he said discontentedly, 'the political climate has hardly been auspicious for travelling of late.'

It seemed to her that that had never prevented him from using foreign backgrounds for his previous books. Like Paddy, he knew that such situations could be used to advantage, though rarely, in Paddy's case, with conspicuous success.

'Things will be different soon,' she said. 'One day we shall have put all this behind us.' We, she thought, and again felt herself consumed with guilt that she and Paddy had not been here, in Europe, to share the suffering, even though she knew they had both been too old – and Paddy too ill – to have made any contribution.

And she could not help thinking of the London she had passed through on her way here, the frenetic gaiety amongst its young people, a determination to forget the last years; she had also been shocked at the level of unemployment, beggars on the streets, newspapers predicting strikes and lockouts – in a nation which had sacrificed so much, nearly bankrupted by the war.

Evidently this was something Dirk did not wish to discuss. He shrugged and she took the opportunity to escape. 'If you'll forgive me, perhaps I should rest before this evening.'

Marta jumped up. 'I'll show you to your room.'

30

'Please don't trouble. I believe I might still be able to find the way.'

Without returning the smile, Marta insisted. 'I'll just make sure you have everything you need.'

The house had always wrapped its own distinctive but indescribable aura of relaxed comfort around one as soon as one set foot in the door. Yet now, walking up the twisting stairs on carpets that were in places worn nearly down to the threads, Emily received the odd impression that Leysmorton was not at ease with itself.

To make room for beds during its time as a hospital, furniture must have been banished to join the centuries' old accumulated confusion of unnecessary objects previously consigned to attics and cellars. It was a well-known fact that for generations no Vavasour had ever thrown anything away, and pieces Emily remembered as being discarded had now reappeared, with bewildering results. Furniture stood in awkward juxtaposition: an ill-advised Victorian monstrosity of a chiffonier was totally out of place and occupying too much room; there were pictures in all the wrong places; a cherrywood bureau, her mother's most prized possession, had been shoved into a corner. In the library, Emily's critical eye had already noticed the chair covers, which could not possibly be the same ones she had known – ye Gods, yes, they were, still holding together, but only by a prayer – had moved onto the scuffed paintwork and curtains frayed at the edges, the old wallpaper above the panelling, darkened with age, and registered that something needed to be done. More money had evidently been needed than she had regularly provided for upkeep. She chided herself for not thinking of this.

Marta had apparently taken on the role of unpaid housekeeper. As if sensing criticism, she murmured, 'You must find things very changed. I know there are things that should be done, I really do, but . . .' It seemed she was not cut out to be decisive enough to take the initiative and ask, and Dirk, manlike, had most likely never noticed anything amiss.

Emily merely smiled and pushed open the door to her old room. Behind her, Marta immediately began to fuss. That Emily had asked to use this room had evidently put her out: it wasn't set up as a guest room, she said – kept shut up for years, of course . . . Aware she'd made a gaffe, Marta looked down at her feet, then rushed on. She was afraid it would be draughty, but at least she had made sure the bed wasn't damp. But are you certain you wouldn't rather have had the blue room, Lady Fitzallan?

The blue room. Silk curtains and a four-poster, no less. Everything needed for the comfort of a guest. The blue room was not where Emily wanted to sleep. 'No, no thank you, Marta. And I think it had better be Cousin Emily – better still, just Emily – don't you?'

She wished Marta would go. She wanted to be alone in the old, familiar room she had shared with Clare. Yet an eerie feeling of having stepped back in time sent an unexpected chill down her spine. She might even have shivered involuntarily, because Marta immediately said, 'I should have had a fire laid. The nights can still be cold.'

She meant well, no doubt, but her excessive politeness only succeeded in being irritating. The idea of a fire was ridiculous: the big space was warmed by the June sun, heat was trapped in the heavy hangings and the walls. It smelled as it always had, of old, dry wood, beeswax and pot-pourri. The room, with its odd, shadowy corners, had been well prepared for a guest: Emily's luggage had already been unpacked, her silver-topped toilet bottles and jars ranged on the dressing table and her clothes hung in the huge French armoire, whose doors still had to be wedged shut with a fold of card, due to the uneven floorboards. The sheets on the bed would no doubt be scented with lavender – the big double bed where as children she and Clare had lain close together like spoons, whispering and giggling until they fell asleep.

'Well, if you're sure you have everything . . .' Marta fiddled with the soap dish, ran a finger over the polished surface of a chest, found no dust. Leysmorton was well looked after, though there were no live-in maids now, only women who came in from the village. She opened her mouth to say something, changed her mind, then it came out in a rush: 'I – I think there's something you should know. About Dirk . . .' She stopped, and swallowed.

'His eyesight?'

'Oh.' Surprised, but clearly relieved. 'You noticed then?'

'I didn't think,' Emily said gently, 'that he wore those heavy glasses from choice. Was it some war injury I haven't heard of?'

'Dirk was never in the fighting, his duties lay

behind the lines.' She put a hand up to her dusty hair and Emily saw it was trembling.

'Do sit down, Marta.'

But she remained standing in the middle of the room, stocky, plain, ill at ease. 'It's all very difficult. He won't talk about it. But someone is bound to tell you and it might as well be me. Everyone knows he is losing his sight.'

'What? I am so sorry. When – when did he find this out?'

'Not definitely until about a year ago. He was beginning to have difficulties with seeing before the war, and that's why they wouldn't let him fight, but it's grown worse.'

'Is there nothing that can be done? An operation?'

'He has eye drops to dilate the pupil. And those spectacles . . . they help a little, but shapes and colours are still distorted. It makes writing and reading very difficult and he gets serious headaches. And yes, his ophthalmologist has recommended surgery, but he has warned that there is a poor outcome. There's every possibility that he could lose his sight altogether.' She sounded so worried, so fiercely protective, that Emily forgot her irritation and put out a hand.

Marta did not seem to see it. 'He's refusing to see the specialist any more. But I shall get him there, I'll make him see sense,' she went on, with a sudden air of confidence and authority that made Emily feel she might have underestimated Marta Heeren. 'Well, that's how it is. I suppose it may still all come right.'

'Pray that it will.'

Marta nodded, a full stop to the conversation,

as if she had regretted speaking. She turned to go, saying they would leave for dinner at Steadings at about seven. Emily finally watched her stump to the door. It closed very quietly behind her and Emily was left alone at last.

After she had washed her hands and face and tidied her hair, she stood for a moment in the bay window overlooking the garden, thinking about what she'd just heard. She recognized now the unfathomable look in Dirk's eyes when he'd taken off his glasses as the dark anguish of a man who fears he is going blind. Her own preoccupations seemed suddenly slight.

She leaned against the casement and the soft, scented air laid a caress on her cheek as she let the old, well-remembered scene work its own particular soothing alchemy.

Vavasours had lived here for centuries, land-owners and local squires, but her grandfather, Henry, had also ventured successfully into business and made a great deal of money. Too busy to care about maintaining many acres and several outlying farms, he had sold them off piecemeal. By the time Anthony inherited, as a very young man, the estate as such had dwindled to the extensive gardens surrounding the house, a small area of woodland and a few fields, which was, however, enough for Anthony. He did not ask for more than he had: his garden and sufficient funds to live the leisured life of a wealthy gentleman.

Leysmorton lay before her, its Rose Walk, its lily pond, and there, right at the end of the garden, by the high brick perimeter wall, the great yew Clare had named the Hecate tree. Beyond the wall was a meadow and the narrow, mouse-brown ribbon of the River Ley; hardly a river, not much more than a slow, shallow stream, overhung with willows. They had dragged it all the same when Clare had disappeared.

A rainy afternoon in the library. The two little girls are hugging their knees before the fire, listening to the story of the polished wooden drinking cup that stands in the recess above the stone fireplace in the hall, a most precious possession, they have now learnt. It's called a chalice, Anthony tells them, and has been made from the richly red heartwood of the yew, and is so old it might possibly have been used by those Druids who worshipped the tree for its magical properties.

'Go on. Please, Papa, go on.' Clare's hands are clasped together, her wide, green-gold eyes are fixed on Anthony, fierce and compelling, begging for more.

Slightly alarmed at the intensity of feeling he has induced, even Anthony, who will normally allow Clare to wheedle him into anything, looks sorry now at what he has started. 'No, that's enough.'

Not for Clare. She pesters for more stories and when he refuses, she later rummages among the old books on the library shelves and finds out for herself. '"The tree has powers of perpetual renewal, for it goes on living, and expanding in girth, to an inestimable age," ' she reads

36

out, thrilled, to Emily, who is by no means thrilled.

'"It used to be associated with death, yet—"' Emily, not naturally a timid child, shivers and wants to clap her hands over her ears, but Clare goes on, '"—yet its powers of healing and regeneration come through its exceptional ability to regrow and rejuvenate itself. This most ancient of trees is often known as the death tree, sacred to Hecate, the dark goddess of both rebirth and death,"' she finishes in sepulchral tones. But she goes on to inform Emily that the yew must have been planted where it is because of the two old paths which cross nearby. Hecate was the goddess who stood with her torch at the crossroads to the Otherworld, to guide travellers through the darkness, as she had guided Demeter through Hades to find her daughter, Persephone.

'Stop, Clare, I don't like it!' cries poor Emily. 'Please!'

'There, I've frightened you, little Em, though I didn't mean to.' Clare takes pity on her little sister and finally shuts the book.

But some days later she insists they perform a ceremony with some small, pearly white stones she has found in the pebbly shallows of the river, stones which she says are magic, which will tell whether it is auspicious to give the giant yew in the clearing the name of Hecate. Apparently it is, but the idea of naming any tree after

Hecate makes Emily's skin goose pimple and she feels really frightened, a different kind of feeling than the delicious terror that comes when Miss Jennett, to pay them back for some naughtiness, reads them the scary tales of the Brothers Grimm.

Even now, childhood left so very far behind, the tree succeeded in projecting its own menace. Despite the warm ambience of the beloved old room, Emily fancied she felt touched by its cold, distant fingers. She turned quickly from the window and, in doing so, caught a gleam of sunshine on the wall, touching the small framed pencil drawing almost hidden in the corner. The unexpectedness of it sent her heart to her mouth in a suffocating leap. Who had put that there?

It was framed in narrow gilt. The cream-laid paper it had been drawn on was warm-toned, fine, even-grained, a little foxed by now, but the drawing had lost none of its appeal. Two young girls, heads almost touching, their long hair dressed in the fashion of the day, waving to their shoulders, each with a fringe and a bow at the side. It was one of two their mother had asked that young man who was there for the summer to draw, and he had managed to catch, even in monotone, their singular differences and likenesses, though truth ended there. Sisters, obviously, the younger one vividly dark, but shown to be more conventionally pretty than ever her lively nature and mobile features allowed; the other ethereally fair, touched with grace, as if too good for this world. They had laughed at the idealized drawings, their

38

mother too, but she had loved them all the same. 'You could always try to live up to them!' she smiled, putting her arms around their shoulders, drawing them close. In one sketch, the girls were turned slightly to the right; in its companion they faced left. Leila had hung the drawings, facing each other, on the chimney breast of the fireplace in her bedroom, opposite her bed.

If she lifted the frame from the wall and turned it over Emily knew she would see, written on the back in their mother's extravagantly looped handwriting, 'My dearest girls: Clare and Emily.'

She stood rooted to the spot, unable to take her eyes from the image of Clare, the evening sun making a nimbus of light around her, surrounding her with mystery. Clare looked fairy-like – even fragile sometimes, but those who knew her had been all too aware of that core of something dark and inflexible running through her, like a vein of iron through marble.

'What happened, Clare?' she whispered at last. 'What happened?'

But Clare was not there to answer. There were only shadows, the curtain swaying gently in the breeze, the reflection of the room in the big glass, and the mute drawing of the two little girls as they had been then, half a century ago.

Four

'Yes, it's all going to go splendidly on the day, I'm sure, but arranging a wedding is simply *too* exhausting,' remarked the mother of the bride-to-be at the Steadings dinner table that evening. 'So enervating. So much to do.'

'Is that why you're looking so pale?' Dirk asked her in an urgent undertone. 'Are you unwell?'

'Of course not. It must be the hot weather,' Stella replied, flashing him a social smile that held a warning. 'Perhaps we might have the window open wider, Benson?' As the manservant attended to it, Stella cast a glance towards her husband, but Gerald, genial as always, was being the attentive host, keeping an eye on the guests' wine glasses, ensuring they were filled, whilst politely trying to make headway with Marta Heeren.

Marta, never much of a conversationalist at the best of times, was feeling more than usually dumbstruck under the eyes of Lavinia, Hugh's late wife, a stately beauty with magnificent Edwardian shoulders and a pearl choker round her neck, who seemed to be looking down her patrician nose at Marta from her portrait on the wall, demoralizing her further every time she looked up. I am fifty-four years old, an old maid, she thought, and though I am only one spinster among countless numbers nowadays, it does not make me feel any better, nor any more attractive. I am becoming stout. Neither do I know how to dress.

Her maroon cloqué, though nodding vaguely to fashion, had somehow missed the mark, and compared with the matriarch in the portrait, and with Stella, thin and chic as always, not to mention her daughter, Dee, she knew only too well how frumpy she looked. Even Lady Fitzallan – perhaps especially Emily Fitzallan, in her sixties, put her in the shade. Although more than her clothes, it was something else that made people light up when Emily was around. Marta had never been like that, or perhaps once, when she had been in love. Long, long ago, when a young itinerant man on his way to nowhere, playing the fiddle to earn his bread as he did so, had been brought to the house to tune the piano. When he had finished, he had taken her out into the garden, across the stepping stones and into the buttercup field . . .

She barely allowed the memory to enter her mind nowadays, and tried to think of some sparkling witticism to engage Gerald's attention, but he and Hamish had begun an amiable debate on the relative merits of single malt and blended Scotch whisky. Marta silently polished off her mutton and accepted more potatoes.

Steadings was a relatively modern house compared with Leysmorton. It was only a hundred or so years old, and Stella, its present chatelaine now that Hugh had turned it over to Gerald, had been allowed to bring it up-to-date. She had rid the house of its red plush and mahogany, the pampas

41

grass and palms of the last decades, and introduced modern wallpapers and white paint – except for the dining room, where Hugh had requested that nothing be changed. In here remained the chairs designed for weighty Georgian gentlemen, a seven-foot-long sideboard and a table which would, its leaves extended, seat thirty or more. Markhams long dead eyed each other across the walls, as they had over sumptuous meals taken here for generations.

This meal, however, was simple compared to those interminable, gargantuan, pre-war feasts, merely a memory now. But there were still candles on the table, pretty flowers, a manservant to wait on the guests, an attentive host and excellent wine.

A wondrous raspberry pavlova appeared, crisp, light, fluffy and topped with whipped cream. 'Delicious. But I really must pass on this,' Emily murmured. The mutton, though tender, had been filling. The asparagus soup had been enriched with cream. But it was not that which made it impossible to eat any more, rather the inappropriate, disconcerting recollection which had come to her suddenly, out of the blue, of the hollow-cheeked, one-armed ex-serviceman selling bootlaces who had accosted her in London. She had bought half a dozen pairs of laces she didn't need, and in addition had pressed a pound note into his hand. He had looked at her with contempt, as if he might have thrown it back, but he had taken it.

She pushed the unsettling memory away and watched the ruin of the culinary work of art as it went round the table. 'I see the war hasn't deprived you of a splendid cook, Hugh.'

'Oh, Stella's very particular about the food she serves.'

'To other people, perhaps? Her little dog seems to be getting more of her dinner than she is.'

'Nasty, spoilt little brute. Chu Chin Chow! Ought not to be allowed at table.'

'I suppose not.' Emily was not enamoured of the pop-eyed, snuffly little Peke either. 'But he seems content to stay out of the way—'

'Lose the use of his legs, he will, one day – if he hasn't already – forever on her lap or tucked under her arm.'

Emily laughed and turned to her other neighbour, that nice child, Rosie.

Rosie was saying, 'I don't suppose I should have had any of this, either, but raspberries are absolutely my favourite thing. My mother says I'll get fat, which is true because I do like food, and it would be just another burden.'

Another burden? At her age? Emily hid her smile. Rosie was still at the age when such things mattered tremendously, when one is often at a loose end with life, uncertain of oneself and what to do about one's future. She appeared to be convinced at the moment that she was neither clever nor pretty, and Emily suspected neither her mother nor her sister made much effort to disabuse her of this. From what she had seen of Rosie so far, however, she believed that she might be too much of a Markham to allow it to develop into an inferiority complex.

Dee was a little minx, just now concealing her boredom and looking as if butter wouldn't melt

43

in her mouth, blonde and petite in her pale, modestly-cut frock, appropriate for a bride-to-be, with no pre-wedding nerves, or any that showed. Her fiancé couldn't take his eyes off her. Hamish Erskine was a tall, raw-boned Scot with ginger hair and eyebrows, a big nose. Unprepossessing looks, but an amiable disposition – money, too, which must have been an added attraction.

The conversation had returned inevitably to the wedding – there was less than a week now before the great day – and if they could possibly hope for a continuation of this marvellous summer weather. Rosie, who was trying not to dwell on primrose crêpe-de-Chine, jumped as her father said across the table, 'Never mind, you'll be next, Rosie-posy.'

'Dad!' He seemed to have forgotten that his childhood name for her was absolutely forbidden, but she forgave him. 'No one will ever want to marry me. I shall probably end up learning shorthand and typewriting and become a lady stenographer.' Everyone laughed, the conversation moved on, but Rosie hadn't sounded as though she was entirely joking.

Dear me! thought Emily. 'Well, Rosie, before you submit your fate to that, maybe you'd like to help me with an idea I have had about my garden.'

'Your garden? That sounds like a jolly idea,' Rosie replied, instantly thinking of spades and forks and all that surplus energy she seemed to have been given and didn't know what to do with. 'But why me? What I know about gardening could be written on a penny stamp. Tom Hayter would be scandalized if I offered to do anything more than dead-head the flowers – and then only under his supervision.'

Emily smiled, recalling the fearful symmetry of Hayter's borders here at Steadings. 'All gardeners become frightfully proprietary, I'm afraid.'

'Have you decided to stay at Leysmorton then, Lady Fitzallan?' Rosie asked, looking as though the thought pleased her. 'They said you'd only be here for the wedding.'

'Perhaps I'll stay a little longer.'

'Well, of course I'd be glad to help you, though I can't see what use I can be.'

'We all have to learn, and I'm sure you're a young woman with ideas,' Emily said, thinking of the project she had in mind. 'Come over, when all the dust has settled after the wedding – you mustn't spoil your hands for that – and we'll sort something out.'

Rosie met the glance of her grandfather, following all this with amused interest, and realized she was not expected to refuse. Lady F was used to people obeying her. But Rosie liked her, she had nothing else to do, and it might be fun.

Across the hothouse peaches Stella sipped her wine and toyed with a few grapes. Nervy, brittle as glass, thin as a stick in a midnight blue, bias-cut dress against which glowed a modern – and no doubt expensive – jewelled and enamelled dress clip in peacock colours. She had seemed somewhat subdued all evening, very pale, perhaps as exhausted by the wedding preparations as she claimed. Emily's glance had rested from time to time on her and on Dirk, seated next to her and

45

not wearing his glasses, and registered how carefully, excessively polite they were to each other, repeatedly meeting each other's glances and then looking quickly away. So that's the way of it. Another complication. An explanation, perhaps, of Dirk's apparent reluctance to return to live at Leysmorton. Dangerous proximity?

If she did decide to take up permanent residence at Leysmorton again – and Emily had begun to acknowledge that the idea had been getting under her skin ever since she entered its gates; she had found herself lovingly stroking certain pieces of furniture and assessing where refurbishment was needed, and eyeing parts of the garden with speculation – *if* she came back to live here she could see difficulties springing up before her like daisies in a lawn. Unthinkable to ask Dirk and his sister to leave, but it might turn out equally unthinkable to live with either.

Five

'Oh my dear, isn't she simply too lovely for words?'

'One would expect nothing less of Diana – or indeed of Stella.'

The great-aunts, Hugh's sisters, nodded in agreement as the organ music swelled and Dee made the entrance she had planned, walking down the aisle on the arm of her father and receiving the gratifying response she had confidently assumed. A collective gasp of admiration spread through the assembled congregation and handkerchiefs went to eye corners at this vision of virginal loveliness – at the bridesmaids behind her, a shimmering column of gold, at the six-year-old flower girl looking so sweet, and the young page, very manly in his miniature Highland dress.

'*So* like dear Lavinia – such a pity she isn't here to see.'

'Let us not get carried away, Jane, we all have to go sometime. Think of the fortune this Scotchman is heir to,' stage-whispered Aunt Dorothy, Lady Dedington. 'Whisky, of course, but one can't be too particular nowadays—'

'A castle in Inverness! Such a romance!' breathed Aunt Jane, who had once nearly kicked over the traces and married a curate.

'Shhhh!'

The aunts subsided.

The congregation, still war-weary, had embraced this non-austerity wedding with open arms and dressed to the nines. Stella, slender within the cleverly cut folds of heavy, Hindu brown slub silk, with a Reboux hat from Paris swathed in modish veiling, her long blonde summer fur dripping luxuriously over one shoulder, outshone them all. But who could also help noticing the black-haired girl with the Cleopatra fringe in that daring tangerine and black frock, accompanied by the stocky young man who looked as though he wished he wasn't there? As for me, I'm in company with the dowagers now, thought Emily, in her dove grey silk. She could afford the irony: the outfit was, after all, Paquin, and her diamond earrings, though small, were of the first water.

The bridal procession reached Hamish and his best man at the altar and he stepped forward to meet Dee, his ears bright red, nervous but suitably impressive in the Erskine tartan, his black jacket with silver buttons and his war medals, and a skean-dhu stuck into the top of his stocking. Having relinquished Dee's train, Rosie relieved the littlest bridesmaid of the burden of her flower basket and held the two children's hands so that neither would become restless. Emily made a note to tell her how charming she looked, how pretty her red-gold hair, and to find a way of commenting discreetly that two of the other bridesmaids were only slightly less tall than she was. The best man produced the ring on time, Miss Pilgrim managed 'The voice that breathed o'er Eden' very well, considering the organ needed new stops.

A radiant Dee emerged into the sunshine half an hour later as Mrs Hamish Erskine.

It had rained the day before and the weather had turned cooler, but it was bright enough to hold the reception in the immaculate garden at Steadings, where the striking-looking pair whom Emily – and everyone else – had remarked on in church introduced themselves to her. So this was Poppy Drummond and her brother Valentine, the little boy to whom she had sent occasional presents on Paddy's behalf, and who had sent such stiff, polite little letters back. He seemed awkward, perhaps moody, unlike his sister, who smiled and talked a lot and had a tinkling laugh. She is too determined to please, thought Emily, alerted, which I shouldn't think is her usual style. She was rather relieved when, after a while, with a look from under her eyelids at her brother, the girl left them and drifted off to be immediately surrounded by several young men.

Valentine turned out not to be moody at all, simply harassed by the formal wedding clothes which seemed not to fit him too well, and slightly constrained, for some reason, in the presence of his sister. After she left, he smiled at Emily, found her a seat on the terrace, brought her strawberries, and then relaxed and began to talk naturally, encouraged by her interest. She drew him out and learned that he had survived the war, and was not long down from Oxford. Relaxing even more, he confessed when she asked what he was doing now, that he had written a novel, which to tell the truth had been rejected by the Markham

49

Press, then immediately looked annoyed with himself for having said so much.

'Sorry, you don't want to hear about that. I've drunk too much of this stuff,' he said, setting down his champagne glass on the stone balustrade. He looked hot and tugged at his tie. 'What I'd give for a beer!' His eyes followed Rosie as she once more took charge of the page and the little bridesmaid, who were rushing about, hot and overexcited, too full of ice-cream, and changed the subject. 'I say, she's a topping sort of girl, Rosie, isn't she? Oh Lord, look out, here's her father.' He looked wildly around, but Gerald was intercepted by a great-aunt. 'Lucky escape.'

'From Gerald? Why should you want to avoid Gerald?'

'Oh, I don't, not really. Well, yes, of course, my book. I'm a fool, I shouldn't have said anything about that – told you I'd had too much bubbly.'

'Well, I'm sure he won't embarrass you by mentioning it in front of other people.'

'Might be better if he did, perhaps – talk about it, I mean. To me, anyway. I'd like to know where I've gone wrong, and all that. Where I go from here.'

'Why don't you have a word with Dirk?'

'Stronglove?' His glance followed Emily's, to where Dirk was basking in the admiration of two of his lady readers. 'Oh, mine's not his sort of book at all.'

'Nevertheless, he must know a thing or two, to be as successful as he is.'

'Perhaps I will,' he replied uncertainly. His eyes

50

strayed again to Rosie, who caught his eye, smiled, blushed and looked away.

This young man interested Emily. 'Come down and stay with me. I should like to get to know you better – on my own as well as Paddy's behalf. Next week?' she said impulsively, as Poppy rejoined them. And then, in what was fast becoming a constant reminder, she thought: I'm only a guest, I shouldn't be issuing invitations . . .

'Stay with you? Oh, er, thanks, I don't know,' Val murmured in some confusion, but Poppy had overheard and had no such inhibitions, seeing herself included in the invitation.

'Why, how *kind*! We'd love to, Lady Fitzallan!' Her face fell. 'At least, Val can – I'm afraid I shall be too busy. I'm a business girl, you know.' She explained the interior decorating business, which was, however, struggling, she admitted with a deprecatory little laugh. Though to tell the truth, she was getting sick of it, a bit sick of London, too. She thought she wouldn't mind living in the country. Val listened without expression, Emily with amusement at the thought of this little London sophisticate turning into a country mouse.

'All right, *coming*, Archie!' Poppy called to the best man, who was beckoning, holding out a glass he had procured for her. 'Do excuse me.' She flashed a smile and wandered away again.

'Your sister is a very popular young lady. And very pretty.'

He followed her glance. 'Archie Elphinstone certainly thinks so. I wish she'd give him a bit more encouragement, only . . . well, there was somebody else, but . . .' He shrugged. Another

51

one killed in the war, Emily thought sadly. 'You mustn't mind her,' he went on awkwardly. 'She's a good egg, really – works very hard, you know. Only, we're both rather in the soup nowadays . . .'

Emily recollected what had happened to these two young things, and was sorry. Their mother had run away to Italy with someone reprehensible and had never been spoken of again, whilst their father, an inveterate gambler, apparently totally bereft by her desertion, had managed to lose every brass farthing he possessed with a speed that had left even his betting cronies gasping, before shooting himself dead in despair.

'Please, Valentine, I should like it very much if you would come down and see me.'

'Is that the young chap who's written the book about the war that's no good?' asked Rosie, taking the unoccupied seat next to her grandfather, who'd had enough of standing about.

'Rosie, my dear, discretion, discretion!' But no one was near enough at that moment to overhear. 'On the contrary, there's a great deal about the book that's admirable, or so your father tells me. He's an angry young fellow, and there was a lot he needed to get off his chest, but that's not sufficient, you know. Won't do, I'm afraid. As it is, it's just not publishable – or not by us.'

'I thought you had editors to correct spelling and grammar and that sort of thing?'

'Hmph. I believe there's nothing much wrong with his spelling, or his grammar, come to that.'

'Then what?'

'Timing, mostly. The sentiments are there, but

52

. . . well, nobody wants to be reminded of all that suffering, my dear. Besides, whether there's anything else in him is debatable.'

Rosie looked disappointed and once again her eyes strayed to Valentine, and to Poppy, who had been at the same school as Dee and had sometimes spent holidays at Steadings. She had grown so smart, unlike her brother, though Rosie thought him handsome in a dishevelled sort of way, and rather scornful of all this flummery, which made him even more interesting. Perhaps she'd get a chance to speak to him, and wondered what they would talk about if she did.

Hugh, too, was wondering about Val. An idea stirred.

Once, in the hideous time after her brother David had been shot down in flames over Flanders, in one of those cardboard and string contraptions they called aeroplanes, Hugh had thought that Rosie might take his place at the Markham Press – women nowadays baulked at nothing – but although there was a bright intelligence there, he had soon had to admit that her father was right, she was not cut out for work in a publishing firm. Her interests were wide, however, her sympathies equally so. She would find ways of fulfilling herself, very likely in caring for others, in marriage most probably, which Hugh thought a very good thing. He had a good many reservations about these so-called career girls and their unseemly ambitions, which he'd always been afraid would come to the fore once they got the vote. But he rather liked the cut of that young feller's jib.

'Leave it to me, Rosie,' he said, and reflected

that he seemed to be saying that quite a lot lately. He might have a word with Emily first.

Mr and Mrs Hamish Erskine departed in a shower of confetti for a honeymoon in Biarritz. And then it was all over.

Six

'Shall I tell you a sad secret? I come over here to Leysmorton quite often when I want to hide with a book,' Rosie admitted, making a face, guilty, as if confessing to a sin.

Odd, that, Emily thought, in a household whose existence depended on the publishing of books. But Stella was definitely not of a bookish persuasion and probably frowned on too much reading, whilst here Rosie could read undisturbed; Markhams had always been free to take advantage of the Leysmorton House gardens.

'It must always have been like this,' Rosie went on, adding romantically, 'sort of timeless.'

'Somewhat less in need of attention than it is now,' Emily replied drily.

'Then we'd better get started on this mysterious project of yours, Lady Fitzallan.'

'It's not mysterious at all. Come with me and I'll show you what I have in mind.'

They walked towards the end of the garden, Rosie trundling the wheelbarrow she had come equipped with, complete with tools she had commandeered: a pair of tough gloves, fork, spade and a box of matches, all ready to start the bonfire they intended to make, as a start. Emily had resisted the impulse to check Rosie's good intentions by telling her that someone else could be found to do the preliminary hard work. She was young, strong and healthy, and besides, it was quite on the cards that a modern girl like her might be offended if it was suggested something like that was beyond her.

The empty patch of ground was a place no one bothered with, at the farthest extent of the estate, a clearing that came as a surprise after an awkward approach through a dense, dark little copse. They made unsteady progress, Rosie manfully managing to keep the barrow upright along a path which was not much more than a track, where either side, under the beeches, bluebells were a picture in spring, but were now dying their unlovely death in a spread-eagle of decaying leaves. In February there would have been swathes of snowdrops, followed by aconites, and windflowers in great drifts of white. At one spot, overhung by hart's-tongue ferns and mosses, a mysterious little spring bubbled through the rocks, then disappeared. You could find prim-roses, thick as clotted cream, on its banks early in the year.

The clearing into which they emerged, blinking, was separated from the copse by an overgrown hawthorn hedge blanketed by bindweed, through which honeysuckle scrambled upwards in search of the light; bristly stems of sweetbriar held pure, delicately pink blossoms, and white flowering elders grew rampant. The rough grass outside the spreading reach of the great yew tree which stood there, black-green against the sky, was a foot high.

Beyond it the high wall which surrounded the property was in need of attention. Bricks and coping stones had fallen off along its length, and in one place it was down to the lowest course,

56

making an opening large enough for anyone to step through – enlarged, no doubt, by those needing a short cut, across the meadow bright with buttercups at this time of year, then the stepping stones over the river, and thus to the road leading to the village. The loose bricks had been tossed around anyhow, most of them landing on top of the remains of the old tree house, making a large heap stitched tightly together by stinging nettles, brambles, ground ivy and couch grass. The spot had a forlorn and neglected air, and for a moment the scary childhood feelings Emily had always tried to pretend didn't exist – about the tree especially – were almost real again, and goose pimples rose on her arms. For all that, this had been their very own place, above all Clare's, and it was an affront to see it looking so desolate.

'Oh dear, I'm afraid it's going to be a daunting task.'

'Not to worry! Leave it to me,' Rosie said.

Emily had explained her intentions, and Rosie immediately donned her gloves and began to tear out brambles preparatory to clearing away the fallen masonry, anxious to do it alone, while Emily perched on what was left of the wall, watching her cheerful exertions, half wishing she could join her. It was at times like this that one became impatient with one's own physical limitations. What she hoped for should not take long – in fact, she wanted little more than to return this remembered spot back to what it had been: half-wild, wholly mysterious. Perhaps the effort needed would prove to be a waste of time and energy, but that scarcely mattered. The point was

57

to exorcize at least some of the ghosts that were disturbing her peace since she had come home.

No ghosts, however, were hovering on this mild, soft summer morning. The Hecate tree, it seemed, was in its benign mood, the sun filtering through its thickly needled branches onto the loose scales of its purplish brown bark. It was over a hundred feet high now, gnarled and scaly, its fluted trunk formed of several growths from the root bole which had fused together to make one trunk of immense girth. A fissure at the base made a doorway right into the hollow at its dark secret heart, a hidey-hole where Clare hid her treasures: the little heap of small, pearly pebbles, a string of 'magic' blue beads, a place where she would duck in and pull Emily after her, to crouch in the dark and hide from hateful Miss Jennett, their horrid governess, who would never have dreamt of peering into such a nasty place. Emily had never liked being in there, in fact she'd hated it, though she would have died rather than admit it to Clare. It didn't smell nice inside and sometimes, faintly, you could hear the snuf-flings and squeaks of the bats who had made their roost high up. She felt inclined to shudder as she wondered if the bats' descendants were still there.

It was Clare who had prevailed upon Papa to build them a tree house in the yew's branches.

It went up in a day, made by Gifford, who did all the carpentry work around the house and garden, out of planks sawn from a mighty beech which had been torn from the earth in one of the great winter storms, revealing spreading, unbelievably shallow roots to have anchored such a giant to the earth. A tree unlike the Hecate tree. Nothing grew beneath the dense canopy of the yew except its own knotty roots, and though they were visible, pushing up through the dry and dusty earth, they spread like claws to maintain a secure foothold in the ground.

'Last for ever, that will,' Gifford had said, positioning the sturdy ladder he had constructed for them to reach the finished structure, firmly settled in a cup where the branches spread from the trunk. Emily was sure it would. Anything Gifford made was, like him, solid, heavy and everlasting, like the yew itself. She liked the little house better than the tree that supported it – although she did not *really* believe any of those creepy things about the Hecate tree; neither did she share Clare's unaccountable fascination with it.

But Clare had gone too far one day, even for Emily, when she had tried to use its powers to bring a curse down on Miss Jennett . . .

It is a day of heavy, enervating heat, when your fringe sticks to your damp forehead and you feel too hot for anything, when even white broderie-anglaise dresses and straw hats feel too heavy. She and Clare have been quarrelsome with each other all day, and as it becomes even hotter they have made their way to the tree house for coolness, only to find it stifling inside. In the clearing below, Clare throws off her hat, flings herself down under the tree and removes her kid boots and knee socks. The dress and petticoats come next and presently she's stripped down to her drawers. 'Oh, come on, Emily, take your things off. It's much cooler.'

59

Emily is tempted. 'If Miss Jennett comes, there'll be trouble.'

'I don't care. She won't come anyway. Not if we put a spell on her.' Clare has donned the magic blue beads and holds a handful of stiff grass she has twisted and tied up into a roughly human figure.

'Clare! You wouldn't dare!'

'Oh, yes, I would. We can swear on the tree.'

'Not me.'

'Don't be a baby. Swear on it! If you put both your hands on the trunk and say what I tell you, something awful is bound to happen to Jennett.'

'That's wicked. And you don't mean it.'

'Oh, yes, I do. Well, anyway, something to magic her away, to send her off in a puff of evil smoke. Come here and say it with me. Like this.' Clare stretches out her own arms as far round the rough, scaly trunk as they will go and leans her cheek against it. She begins to chant. 'I swear by—' There is an ominous rumble of thunder.

'I don't want to.'

'Then I'll do it myself. I swear by—'

But Emily has had enough. 'No!' she shouts, into the sudden heavy silence that has descended over everything. Even the birds have stopped singing. 'I won't! I hate this old Hecate! There's nothing magic about it – it's just a silly old tree!'

And at that moment lightning splits the sky and the first heavy drops begin to fall. Emily flees, pursued by terror and pelting rain, into the house.

But when Miss Jennett fell down the stairs and twisted her knee, which didn't get better for ages and made her cry a lot, and in the end caused her to leave, she never again questioned Clare's belief in the power of the Hecate tree.

'Last for ever, that will,' Gifford had said of the tree house. Well, it hadn't lasted forever, any more than Gifford himself had. Fifty years later, the yew was still there, but the little house was no longer lodged in its branches. It was now just a heap of timber, collapsed or blown down by the wind, nothing left of it but rotting, piled-up planks that had been dragged onto the rough ground beyond the spread of the tree's swooping branches and its carpet of dried needles, and tossed into a heap along with the fallen masonry.

Rosie, heaving bricks to one side, tearing out nettles, brambles and tenacious trails of ground ivy, was by now breathless, hot and perspiring with her exertions. She stood back, looking at the wood beneath. 'We're going to need some paraffin, or petrol. This isn't going to catch light easily. It's damp and rotten underneath the top layer. Ugh.' She threw a few more stray bricks aside and tugged at a stubborn plank. The wood seemed originally to have been laid in a rough pyramid, as if intended for just such a fire, but the weight of the bricks and other debris tossed on top of the wood had flattened it. The plank finally came loose and Rosie staggered back. Then stood, staring, the blood draining from her face.

'Don't look. Don't look, Lady Fitz—'

But it was too late. A glance had been enough.

There was no mistaking what Rosie was staring at. A human skull was a human skull, even when it was stained and yellow and a dandelion thrust itself obscenely out of one eye socket.

Seven

Rosie was trying to believe what she had been taught – that snap decisions about people were unreliable, that you shouldn't allow pre-conceived ideas to enter into it – however, she was honest enough to admit her instant antipathy to the detective from London probably had a lot to do with men who had deep-set eyes and black hair that grew in a widow's peak, simply because they reminded her too much of the terrifying illustration of an evil demon in a book she'd had as a child. It was hardly fair to blame him for something he couldn't help.

All the same, she found her hackles rising at the judgmental looks she felt this man, Detective Inspector Novak, was casting around the dear, untidy old Leysmorton library, missing nothing of its shabbiness, and not seeing how unchanging, how *reassuring* that always made it. Even more annoying was his frankly incredulous attitude towards their activities in the clearing, before that gruesome discovery. What had she and Lady Fitzallan actually been doing there? Why had *two ladies* found it necessary to disturb that pile of stones and timber? To clear the ground ready for planting? No? Then what was the purpose, what was the clearing to be used for?

The 'purpose', Emily replied, fixing him with a look, very Lady Fitzallan, was for nothing more than to get rid of the unsightly rubbish that had accumulated there. She, too, was having problems with Novak's appearance, though for different reasons. He had brought a reminder of the past: Yerevan, and Stepan Saroyan, the young and handsome Armenian whose life Paddy had saved, and who had thereafter seen it as his mission to educate Paddy into the injustices of Armenian politics, bringing untold trouble and also passing on the tuberculosis which had eventually caused Paddy's death.

Unintimidated, Novak left the subject hanging in the air, almost as if he still thought she was hiding some ulterior motive, some knowledge about that macabre . . . *thing* they had unearthed!

Rosie, who was having dreams about that skull, tried to pull herself together. Stop it! Don't imagine aggressive attitudes where none exist. Detective inspectors from Scotland Yard would naturally have a different approach to Sergeant Chinnery from Kingsworth, who was sitting there beside him, his thick neck red above his uniform collar, trying to appear as reassuringly kind as always. He looked as hot and uncomfortable and out of place as he undoubtedly felt – nasty, this, these sorts of things just didn't happen around here, in the peaceful Netherley community, least of all at Leysmorton House! He couldn't conceal that he was manifestly relieved to have outside support, though he still looked as if he wished himself elsewhere.

That went for Rosie, too. There was nothing new to tell – she'd been through it all before. Several times, in fact. Everyone at Leysmorton and Steadings had been agog for details when the grisly discovery had been made – and then she'd had to repeat it all again to successively higher authorities after Grandfather, who had taken charge of the situation as he always did, had reported it. Firstly, she'd had to tell it to Constable Pickles, Netherley's only representative of the police force, then to his superior, Sergeant Chinnery at Kingsworth, who had bicycled over to question them himself, and now to this detective inspector from Scotland Yard. When really there was nothing more than the simple facts of how she'd begun to clear the heap of debris until . . .

She swallowed as the image of the grinning skull swam before her eyes yet again, despising herself for feeling so squeamish about it. It was horrible, and macabre, but she was mortified to find she couldn't take it in her stride. 'It's a joke, isn't it?' she'd whispered when the thing had come to light, though an icy trickle was running down her spine. 'Someone put it there as a joke.' Skulls were objects of grisly comedy, and some person with a perverted sense of humour must have decided to give whoever found it a shock – always presuming they had known that disgusting pile of rotting timbers was likely to be dug up in the foreseeable future.

'I shouldn't think it's any form of joke, Rosie, dear.' Lady Fitzallan, her voice not quite as steady as usual, had put a supportive arm around her and said they must leave things as they had been found, and not attempt to cover up the grinning obscenity. And of course the skull was no joke, no theatrical prop, either; it was real, and what was more, it

65

was attached to a body – or the skeleton of one. The police had to be informed, and very soon they were swarming all over the place. The situation had evidently been serious enough to warrant the chief constable, a long-standing friend of Hugh's, making a request for the investigation to be taken over by Scotland Yard, although from her grandfather's rather wry comments, Rosie conjectured that their presence might have more to do with the status of Leysmorton House and its owner than any shortage of local resources, as the chief constable had claimed.

Whether that was true or not, this un-English-looking detective inspector – he had given his name as Adam Novak, though he had a London accent – was now in charge and had asked to see them all; those who lived at Steadings as well as those here at Leysmorton. The only one missing was her father, who had already left for Clerkenwell before Novak arrived. So here they were, her mother and her grandfather, as well as herself and Lady Fitzallan, and of course Dirk and Marta – Dirk wearing those bottle-bottomed specs he was supposed to wear all the time, but didn't. Because of course, looking like a goggle-eyed insect wouldn't suit the handsome, romantic Dirk Stronglove image.

He might have been forced to wear them today because he had one of his bad headaches. Marta, sitting on the edge of her seat as though she couldn't wait to get back to her potions and jams, kept throwing anxious glances at him. She did this all the time nowadays, which Rosie thought must be very irritating. But then, most people

66

found poor, well-meaning Marta Heeren irritating. Like now, when she had on a bilious green cardigan that she hugged around herself as though she was cold, on a day so hot even the breeze coming through the open French windows hardly made a stir of difference to the room's stuffiness.

'Thank you for agreeing to come here all together,' Novak had begun. 'It will save time initially, though I may want to see you individually afterwards. I won't keep you long.'

And indeed, his questions were brisk and to the point. Perhaps he wanted to get it over with as much as they did. Firstly, Leysmorton House and its occupancy over the last few years. 'I understand there have been quite a few changes, one way and another. You are the house's owner, Lady Fitzallan?'

'Yes, although I've lived abroad for many years.'

'But as I understand it, the house hasn't been left empty – it was always occupied during that time?'

'More or less.'

'We shall need details of anyone who has lived here.'

'Which means me and my sister – for most of that time,' Dirk put in impatiently. 'We were brought up here, and my cousin – Lady Fitzallan – allowed us to stay on until we moved to London.'

'It was then leased to a Mr and Mrs Beresford for a short time,' Emily said, 'while they looked around for a permanent home of their own, or so I believe. I can't tell you anything more about them, I'm afraid.'

'I got to know them a little while they lived

here,' Hugh offered. 'Mrs Beresford had been recommended country air because she'd been very ill, with lung trouble. They weren't here long, six months or so. Rupert – her husband – was a captain in the volunteer reserve and was called up. Tried to get exemption, because of his wife's illness, but it didn't wash. He was one of the first casualties, poor fellow. His wife gave up the lease immediately afterwards and left, and I'm afraid she too died shortly after.'

'You didn't decide to come back here to live when they left, Mr Heeren?'

'Since I'd moved to London in the first place for convenience, there would have been no reason to return,' Stronglove answered shortly. 'In any case, by then I was in the army, too, and my sister was driving an ambulance.' The spectacles he constantly fiddled with went on again. A nervous tic, or when the conversation became difficult? 'By the way, I prefer to be known by the name I gave you, my professional name, Stronglove.'

'As you wish – Mr Stronglove,' Novak replied, after a slight pause. His own mixed Middle European and French ancestry, though by now far back enough to have been almost forgotten, made him well aware of this sensitivity about foreign names. It was not one he had much patience with. 'So – after the departure of Mrs – er—' He consulted his notes. '—of Mrs Beresford, the house was left unoccupied?'

'No. It became a convalescent home. The number of casualties was making the need for hospital accommodation urgent and the army moved in immediately,' Emily said. 'I suppose I could find the exact dates, if you need them.'

Novak waved a hand. 'No need to trouble yourself. There'll be official records.' He paused. 'Before we go any further, I think you should know the results of the initial examination the experts have carried out on the body. He appears to have been there for some time – we can't be certain yet how long, but for the moment we're going along with the probability of eight years or less.'

'He?' repeated Hugh.

'Yes, Mr Markham. It was the body of a man.' He turned to look at Lady Fitzallan as a small, almost imperceptible sound escaped her.

Emily closed her eyes for a moment as the room swam. *Well,* said Clare's voice mockingly in her head, *you didn't really think that skeleton was mine, did you?*

No, of course she hadn't thought it was Clare. Or rather, she hadn't allowed herself to think at all since that moment when Rosie had unearthed the skull. Her mind had been blank with shock and dread. Otherwise, she might indeed have had to admit the unthinkable . . . that the skeleton lying there might be Clare's. And if so, that she had not suffered a natural death. Because what other reason could there have been for concealing a body under a pile of debris, and weighting it with bricks from the wall?

But now . . .

Now it seemed that dreadful thing had happened to some other person, some as yet unidentified man. Somewhere there would be a brother or sister, mother or father, someone who had loved him and would have to cope with the horror. But despite her pity for the suffering of this unknown person or persons, the knot of fear that had twisted itself up inside Emily ever since that macabre revelation began to unravel. Grief was still there, that raw pain which had never completely healed. But it was pain she had learned to live with for most of her life, alongside the unanswered question of how Clare could possibly have been so cruel as to condemn her family to a lifetime of wondering what had happened to cause her to disappear without trace.

She raised her eyes and saw Hugh watching her. He gave her a small, reassuring nod. He alone knew what she had been afraid of, as none of the others could have known – unless Dirk and his sister, too, had heard and remembered that old family mystery. She thought this unlikely. No one spoke of Clare's unhappy story, by now just another legend in Leysmorton's long history.

'Eight years, Inspector?' Hugh said at last, breaking the silence that had fallen on them. 'That seems surprisingly specific, especially in the circumstances.'

'Takes us back to 1914. The beginning of the war,' Novak added, in case anyone should be in any doubt about that. 'Eight years – or less – was suggested as a working hypothesis because of the condition of the skeleton, but also because the victim seems to have been a soldier. Though of course there's always the chance he was a regular, a peacetime soldier, and that he was there even before the war.'

'A soldier?' Marta repeated on a high note.

'There are still traces of his uniform, and his army issue boots.'

The little dog Mrs Markham was clutching under one arm gave a sharp yelp as, slipping her hand into her pocket, she squeezed him too hard. She brought out an enamelled cigarette case, which she fingered nervously but didn't attempt to open, and Novak saw her glance resting on Stronglove. He sensed her resentment at being summoned here. She had so far said not a word.

He watched the others. The girl, Rosie, was looking miserably at her feet, and her grandfather reached out and gently took her hand. Lady Fitzallan, who had lost colour for a moment or two after that little gasp, had regained it and was now sitting with her hands folded quietly on her lap. After the one exclamation, Marta Heeren had resumed the dull, dogged expression typical of a repressed spinster, he thought, surprised by a stab of pity.

Novak had taken an instant dislike to Stronglove, sitting at ease in his chair, for no other reason than his arrogant profile and patronizing manner. And maybe the artlessly careless cravat tucked into the open shirt neck, the flannel bags, the knitted Fair Isle slipover. It was difficult to interpret what he might be thinking behind those magnifying lenses, but Novak suspected he was the only one who had immediately taken in the precise import of the word 'traces', who had realized the improbability of either the leather boots or the skeleton being entirely complete, as over time the insects, beetles and maggots had done their work, and hungry foxes, rats and other

71

predators had found their way to the corpse, leaving only what bones they had not been able to drag away, the heavy debris piled above it having protected the remains of the skeleton.

At last Stronglove said, 'He must have been one of the patients here. The hospital was a convalescent unit – mostly for nervous cases, men suffering from shell shock, that sort of thing, though I believe a few had physical injuries as well. Probably one of them wandered off and met with an accident.'

'If that's so, the hospital records and reports will tell. But I'll say right away it's unlikely. For one thing, if a patient went missing there would have been a thorough search; for another, the traces of uniform were khaki, not hospital blue, which doesn't suggest he was a patient.' He paused again, watching his audience for reactions. 'Moreover, it was no accident. The pathologist reports that the back of his skull was caved in.'

The Peke gave another spoiled little whimper as Stella Markham clutched him too hard. Into the silence that followed this remark she said sharply, 'But it could still have been an accident, surely? Maybe he just fell onto those stones and hit his head—'

'And then someone obligingly covered him up? No, Mrs Markham. He was covered up deliberately. Someone had good reason to hide the body.'

She raised her eyebrows at the rebuke, cuddled Chu closer to her. She looked again at Stronglove and this time their eyes held, but after the merest nod he avoided her glance. 'So, stating the obvious, someone killed him,' he said. His jawline was tense. He massaged what seemed to be a knot of pain between his brows. 'Then who was he? What was he doing here?'

'A visitor for one of you who didn't know you'd left Leysmorton House, maybe?'

Marta, who had flushed to a dull, unbecoming red, spoke up sharply. 'Are you suggesting that I or my brother had anything to do with killing this unknown soldier?'

'Now why should I think anything of the sort, Miss Heeren? But the body being found in the garden of this house does indicate that he came here of his own accord, and was therefore unlikely to have been a stranger, so we have to ask why he was here. It's not feasible to believe he could have been killed elsewhere and then brought here. There'd be a problem with that, wouldn't there?'

Novak's men had had difficulty getting to the spot, the photographers with their cumbrous equipment – tripod cameras, magnesium flashes and whatever else they'd needed – trundling it across the garden, along that awkward little path through the copse and into the clearing. And when the body, although now nothing more than a heap of bones, had been loaded into a coffin shell and then onto a stretcher, a hefty constable had been needed at either end to manoeuvre it back to the waiting transport. The possibility of approaching the clearing from the other direction – via the lane from the village and then the stepping stones across the river, and next the meadow before you reached the breach in the wall – had been discounted from the start.

'You're right, of course,' Hugh said thoughtfully, 'there's no easy access to that spot.'

Lady Fitzallan asked, 'Is there any way of finding out who he is – or was, this man?'

'We hope to get an identification from regimental buttons and so on. We haven't found his cap, though, or any badges.' He gathered his papers. 'I don't think there's much more I need to ask you at the moment, until we do get an identification. There will be an inquest, of course.'

Stronglove said suddenly, 'You're wrong. About the body being here before the war, I mean. I can tell you it wasn't there before I left. One of the last things I did before leaving was to go down to the village shop for cigarettes. You can save a good ten minutes if you go to Netherley across the field and the stepping stones. It cuts a big corner off – and that was the way I always went. The rubble from the wall was still scattered all over the place. I was in a hurry, didn't look where I was going and damn near broke my ankle.'

'And when you came back to live here?'

'Well, it was easier underfoot, the bricks were no longer such a hazard, and that old tree house that used to be in the big yew had blown down by then. Everything was chucked into a pile, ready for a bonfire, I supposed.'

'Thank you, Mr Stronglove, that's helpful. It should help to establish that the date the body *was* put there was in 1914 or after. Eight years – or less.'

'It will help *if* that's the case, *if* he is telling the truth – about the state that clearing was in before the

74

war,' Novak remarked as he climbed into the back seat of the waiting motor, while the ponderous Sergeant Chinnery wedged his bulk in beside him. He gave the constable at the wheel the signal to drive off. 'But how reliable is he, our Mr Stronglove? *Stronglove*!' he repeated with a grimace. 'Must remember to get that right.'

'He writes these adventure yarns, doesn't he, sir? You know, ones with a bit of crime and mystery.' Chinnery would never let it be known to this cocky young spark from London – young to Chinnery, anyway – who he felt regarded him as a back-woods yokel, that each new Dirk Stronglove book was something he looked forward to with pleasure. 'He'll know the advantage of getting the facts straight in a case like this.'

'And the value of prevarication. A seemingly truthful lie.'

'He wouldn't do that,' Chinnery answered, faintly reproving.

'No?' Novak's eyebrows rose. Perhaps not, but there had been an atmosphere in that room, a distinct impression that one person at least was not being entirely open. And the equal certainty that nobody was going to tell him who it was. They would all stick together, as people like them always did. He felt again the sense of hostility he had experienced as he entered the house, as he looked around that library, redolent of money and privilege, faded and shabby as it was, furniture so old the Salvation Army might have thought twice about accepting it as a gift. And those ratty old chair covers – even his thrifty mother, who had been known to put patches on patches, would have given up on them years ago.

'No,' Chinnery repeated more firmly. 'I've known them all my life, and none of them would lie about a thing like that.'

Novak had not chosen to work on this case, but his was not to reason why. Wheels had turned. Strings had been pulled. Pressure had been brought to bear. And here he was, where he'd been sent, far from his usual haunts, the patch he worked and the lawless and unstructured lives lived within it, a seething immigrant population, of the foreign and home-grown variety, every man for himself, nothing to lose. Events moved fast there and that was pretty much how Novak liked it. It was like wine in the veins. He found this country air enervating, and this place at the back of nowhere even more so, where even the police seemed to think they had all day to do the simplest task – and needed help from outside when it extended any further than that. He wasn't optimistic about his power to achieve a quick result in this case, but failure on his part wouldn't do his reputation any good, so he didn't have much choice.

Nor did he like dealing with folks like Strong-love. He, Adam Novak, had fought in the war, risen through the ranks to captain and rubbed shoulders with men like him. Most of them had been good sorts, but that had been in a different situation, when they'd all been in it together. Now they were back in Civvy Street and some had forgotten that the war had supposedly levelled out distinctions.

He looked at his watch again. There was an arrest he hoped to make that night. If that fellow who was driving the motor stirred his stumps, he could get to the Blue Anchor in time. Unless the tip passed on to him had been an attempt to make a monkey out of him, his latest quarry should be drinking there, unsuspecting.

Emily dreamt vividly that night, of things she had not dreamt of for many years. The dramatic discovery beneath the Hecate tree had in a strange way brought back a past she had tried resolutely not to dwell on for most of her life, so painful had the comparison been with what her life had turned out to be.

But dreams are of a different order to one's waking, sentient life. Perhaps she had dreamed of the past because that day, for the first time, she had asked herself why she had never really attempted to confront it properly.

Eight

Then, 1875

Mama – Leila – was not a beauty, though she had piles of shining black hair, a clear, pale complexion, soft dark eyes and a mouth designed for smiling. Emily never remembered her losing her temper. She was gay and loved company and things happening, quite the opposite of Papa, that big, often taciturn man who smelt of pipe tobacco and had horny hands with dirt so ingrained under the fingernails it was impossible to remove entirely, making Mama say she was ashamed to be escorted out to dinner by someone who looked like the undergardener. But she laughed when she said it, and straightened his tie and tried to smooth his hair and said he was still the handsomest man this side of Mount Olympus, and who minded a little grime when he brought her armfuls of roses he had grown himself?

'Roses for my girls, my three roses,' said Anthony once, memorably, and then reddened to the roots of his hair, having astonished himself as much as them.

He said he hated London, and for the most part steadfastly refused to accompany Mama when she made her periodic visits there, to stay with her sister, Mrs Arbuthnot. Why waste his time there, where Uncle Laurence, a dull stockbroker, could talk of nothing but making money and his stamp collection, when he, Anthony, could have been pruning, grafting, planting? As for Aunt Lottie, her kind of life was beyond his comprehension; she never came home before two a.m., conducted her correspondence from her bed until noon the next day, and then filled the rest of the time with as many social events as she could fit in.

Unlike Clare, Emily loved the occasional times when they were allowed to accompany their mama to stay with the Arbuthnots, in the house from where you could hear Big Ben, two years older than Emily, booming the time across London. On the notably rare occasions Anthony could be persuaded to join them, both parents would come and say goodnight before they went out to dine, or to the theatre, Mama smelling delicious in a whispering frou-frou of taffeta skirts, and Papa miraculously transformed into a smooth and well-brushed stranger in a stiff shirt with a gardenia on his lapel.

But mostly, Leila made her visits alone, while Leysmorton counted the days before her return. The girls played with their friends, the Markham girls, and Anthony let them roam the countryside on their ponies, galloping along the rides through the great beech woods and up to the high chalk escarpment on the Downs, from where you could see over three counties. Sometimes they rode through the village and bought ginger beer in bottles with a glass marble stopper from the pop-bottling factory, or they might go by way of the gaunt red-brick convent. Back home, there was the little house in the Hecate tree, their special place where no one else was ever invited, not even the Markham girls; Dorothy would have taken charge and wanted things done her way, and Jane would have been too timid to climb the ladder.

When Leila returned, the house came alive again: presents for everyone, tissue paper everywhere as she unpacked the new hats, shoes and gloves she had bought, her hair worn in a new style, her eyes sparkling as she told them of the amusing plays she'd seen, the opera, dances, suppers she'd attended.

Emily lapped it up eagerly. It was what she herself longed for – wasn't it? To be grown up, to put one's hair up, be presented at court, become the beautiful Miss Vavasour and eventually marry a handsome man, possibly a young lord. Yes, of course it was. Except that sometimes, as they grew older, she began to wonder if Clare had a point when she continually asked, would a life of such undiluted pleasure be enough?

Her daughters were in danger of becoming little savages, running wild and with dirt beneath their fingernails from grubbing in the earth like their father, Mama suddenly decided. Moreover, the teaching they received from the genteel but ineffectual spinster who had followed Miss Jennett amounted to little more than the three Rs, and though too much education was unnecessary for girls, it was time lessons were supplemented with a few accomplishments and social skills designed to help them grow into young ladies.

The solution was a young art student named

Christian Gautier, half French, who was engaged during his vacation from his London art college to tutor them in drawing and painting, and to improve their French. A good-natured, gangling young fellow with a shock of untidy hair, he was something of a clown and made them laugh, though his efforts to teach them did not make too many obvious inroads into their ignorance. Yet he had an ability to capture with a few pencil strokes everything Emily laboured to do and never remotely succeeded in achieving. Clare, on the other hand, lost interest in the garden, her pony grew fat with too little exercise, and her hands became grubby with oil paint and charcoal, rather than earth. Her sketches and watercolours earned her praise and much attention from their young tutor, which seemed to overwhelm her and sent her into furious blushes. The French of both girls remained of the schoolgirl variety, Christian being more interested in improving his own English.

He was with them for only two or three months, after which he returned to obscurity as far as they were concerned, but he had sowed the seeds of ambition in Clare. She had always sucked up knowledge of any kind as if she were drinking it through a straw, and from then on, she persisted in the notion that she wanted nothing more than to devote her life to becoming an artist.

Ambition and everything else, though, receded into the background when their world collapsed without warning. One day Mama was there, chatting and smiling, telling them stories and letting Emily adorn herself with her jewellery and totter

81

around in her shoes, pretending to be grown up, with Clare looking on with disapproval – she was fifteen by then, beyond such childish activities, if ever she had been interested in them – and the next, Mama was gone.

Emily hadn't known there was to be a baby. She was young for her years, though very much aware that there were things connected with being married that she mustn't ask about. Clare said she had known about the baby. How? Emily desperately wanted to know, but she wouldn't say.

In the desolate time that followed Leila's death, Anthony was unreachable, and the girls were left to their old nurse, Nanny Kate, now upgraded to the post of housekeeper. Kate Bunting was a woman who covered a soft heart and an all-embracing love for children with a matter-of-fact exterior and a refusal to accept any silly nonsense about Hecate trees.

Perhaps it was her firmness which in the end finally brought about Clare's silence on that subject. Even she had been shaken by Miss Jennett's abrupt departure after that curse – it *was* a curse, Emily knew, not just a spell as Clare had called it at the time, maybe because a spell didn't sound so evil – and perhaps she still felt guilty and was afraid the dark magic really was potent, and dangerous, and that was why Mama had died. At any rate, she dropped any mention of the Hecate tree and its arcane attractions as completely as she had given up messing about in the garden, and from then on any spare time she had was concentrated wholly on her painting and drawing, with the fierce absorption and intensity she had previously given to magic lore and dark secrets.

Inevitably, when the time was approaching for her eldest niece to come out, to be presented at court, Aunt Lottie arrived, eager with plans and intentions. Clare listened and then politely said no thank you, she would rather attend one of the art schools in London, preferably the Slade, scandalizing Mrs Arbuthnot who, childless herself, had been looking forward to supervising both girls' coming out, that most important rite of passage, and had constantly badgered Anthony about it ever since her sister's death.

'Art school? Painting? *Models?*'

'Female students are not allowed to draw or paint them undraped, Aunt Lottie.'

Her aunt paused, silver teapot in hand, and stared at Clare, trying to believe she was not being impertinent. 'So I should hope, miss.'

Lottie had a mental list of young men whose mothers she knew, who were of the right age, had been born into the required station in life and with sufficient wealth, whom she had already earmarked for one or other of the girls. Now she turned her attention to this, more important than any mere girlish whim of the moment. Clare stiffened when, regardless of what had just been said, their aunt began to outline her plans.

'Not just now, Lottie,' Anthony pleaded, as little anxious to hear this as Clare. Though he had at last roused himself somewhat from the dazed disbelief which had followed Leila's death, he had grown increasingly grey and stooped, and more than ever wished for nothing to disturb his quiet life.

'Yes, *now*. The child cannot possibly know what's best for her. This is one thing you cannot close your eyes to, Anthony. Your girls won't stop growing up – and I'm quite prepared to give up my time and see them both through their first season. It's what Leila would have wanted,' she finished, incontrovertibly.

When this conversation had taken place, Victoria had still been on the throne. Women had magnificent bosoms and wasp waists, due to the corsets they wore, and Mrs Arbuthnot was no exception, though her whaleboning was not allowed to creak like Nanny Kate's did when she moved, or a roll of fat to appear across her shoulders where the stays ended. She stood in front of Anthony, adamant, as upright as if she had a ruler down her back, as indeed she might have had as a child, to improve her posture.

Anthony said evasively, 'Lottie, don't you think it might be more of a question of what Clare really wants?'

'Nonsense! Clare is barely eighteen years old, she cannot possibly know what she wants. I'm afraid you are spoiling your girls, Anthony – don't you wish them to make the most of their chances? Do you want to see them condemned to become *spinsters*? Even you must allow that one is simply nothing without a husband!' If she had had a fan with her, she would have rapped his knuckles smartly.

'Well, of course, everyone knows that's what it's all about,' Clare observed. 'Why else would parents spend so much money on a mere girl, if not to get them married off?'

84

She looked particularly angelic as she spoke, almost childlike, with her pale, soft skin and the fall of her flax-blonde hair. It was impossible to believe the remark had come from her, until you saw the expression in those green-gold eyes. Mrs Arbuthnot, for once, was rendered speechless.

'My dear,' said Anthony, looking helpless, or as helpless as a big, shambling bear could look, bewildered at these signs of defiance in this child who was perhaps his favourite, but whom he had never really understood. 'My dear Clare.' But he was wavering, and after a week of Clare's determination not to give in, he put up no more opposition. He had always been a man easy to persuade, and easily defeated. And paradoxically, like many such people, he could be stubborn once he had made his mind up. Clare was, as all her family knew, already a talented artist, and she mattered more to him than Aunt Lottie. Foiled of her role of chaperone and matchmaker, Mrs Arbuthnot washed her hands of the whole business and departed in a huff to take the cure in Marienbad.

Clare, then, had not been forced into enduring the ritual of coming out. No presentation at court in a white silk dress with Prince of Wales feathers in her hair, no hours spent learning to curtsey and walk backwards from the royal presence without tripping over one's long train, no parties and dancing with perspiring, eligible young men whose duty it was to find a presentable young woman to marry and give them heirs. Instead she was enrolled at the Slade, as she had wished. There was, however, no question of her being allowed to live alone and unchaperoned. She must go home each night to stay with Aunt Lottie, who was to some extent mollified by the assurance of being able to keep an eye on any flighty tendencies her niece might show while away from the parental home.

For consolation, Anthony, as always, lost himself in his beloved garden. Life continued to be tolerable only because of his garden, especially his roses.

By the time it was Emily's turn to be launched into society, she too had grown less enamoured of the prospect. For one thing, she had been impressed to see how Clare had blossomed in her exciting new life, in the freedom she'd found amongst those unconventional Bohemian young people, her fellow art students, whom she now called her friends. For another, Emily was appalled by the willy-nilly shunting of the Markham girls into the marriage market; horrified at seeing Dorothy wedded to a rich but incredibly dull young peer with an impeccable family history – though Dorothy herself made no objection, and indeed preened her feathers at being so fortunate – she did her best to comfort the wretched Jane when her tentative romance with the curate from Lower Kingsworth was nipped well and truly in the bud and she too was hustled into marriage with a rich man thirteen years older than herself.

And in any case, by then Emily was basking in the warm certainty that the man who wanted to marry her was already present in her life. He had not asked her yet, but she was under no delusions that he would, soon.

* * *

She had always been there, somewhere in the background of Hugh Markham's life, Emily, the youngest Vavasour sister, an impulsive and happy child with bouncy dark curls, quite unlike her elder sister, Clare, that odd, secretive and somewhat fey girl, who made him uneasy.

As a student at Oxford, like most of the other undergraduates revelling in their first taste of freedom, Hugh had drunk too much and taken part in certain youthful, reprehensible escapades they had thought amusing at the time. He rowed for his college, played a good deal of rugby, joined several clubs and societies, and with all this, regrettably neglected his books to the extent that he received warnings about being sent down. But since he was basically a conventional young man, in his second year he pulled his socks up, and by the time he left he was reckoned by his tutors to have turned out promising enough, all things considered, and a rattling good fellow by his friends. He had had one or two skirmishes with girls from the town, and nearly been caught by the daughter of one of the history dons, but when he came home and rediscovered Emily, now blossoming with the quick warmth, gaiety and generosity she had inherited from her mother, he fell headlong in love with her and knew that here was the girl he must marry.

He was astonished, and delighted, when he dared to hope she might feel the same. He knew, however, that he would have to wait for the right time to ask for her, until she had come out and had her London season. Her immediate future was inescapably mapped out for her, just as his own was.

Hugh had always known he would go into the family publishing business with his father, and eventually take over. What many of his friends looked down on as a rather mundane prospect did not dismay him. He loved books, and the thought of producing them gave him pleasure. In the event, he found himself head of the Peregrine Press sooner than he had expected. His father, ailing for some time, died suddenly within a few months of Hugh joining the firm, in the summer Paddy Fitzallan arrived at Leysmorton. And with the winding up of his father's affairs, and implementing the changes he hoped would put the business back on a firmer footing than it had been of late, Hugh did not see what was going on under his nose until it was too late.

Clare had been at the Slade for almost two years, and when she came home that Easter the announcement that she was not going to return dropped like a stone thrown into a still pool.

'It's better to leave now rather than waste any more of my own time, and everyone else's,' she said flatly, as if no further explanation was needed, as adamant about abandoning her training as she had been about starting it. Her disappointed family weren't content with that. They wanted to know what had gone wrong.

'It's no use,' was all she would say. 'I'm not going back and that's all there is to it. It doesn't really matter, you know.'

'That's not all there is, and it does matter.' Emily, closer to Clare than anyone else, felt that there had to be more to it, that this arbitrary

88

decision must conceal a bitter disillusionment, and maybe something more that she couldn't put a name to. 'What else is wrong?'

'Nothing, why would there be?'

'Because I know something is, for you to give up like this.' Clare had grown very thin, and was even paler than usual. She didn't care what she wore and scraped her hair back unbecomingly. That elusive attraction of hers had been quenched.

'I've done the best I can,' Emily got her to admit at last, 'and it's not enough. I've done no work fit to be seen, according to the tutors—'

'But might that not be just to spur you on? They're not there just to praise.'

'—*and* according to myself. I can see it now. Compared with most of the others, I shall never be anything more than a talented amateur, so why try to be anything else?'

Emily felt there was some flaw to this logic, but she couldn't see what it was. After all, perhaps it was true, perhaps Clare was exceptional only in the eyes of her admiring family. What was certain was that Clare would never be able to bear being thought second-rate.

'Leave her alone,' Nanny Kate said sensibly, 'she'll find something else. She always has. She needs something to knock the nonsense out of her.'

'This, Anthony, is what comes of letting her have her own way!' declared Aunt Lottie. 'If we had found a husband for her, none of this would have happened – and please don't tell me again, Clare, that you'll never want to marry, because that is something I refuse to believe of any young woman.'

'Even if it should happen to be true?'

Lottie pursed her lips, but Emily believed Clare had meant it when she'd said, 'I'll try anything once – anything except being married. Once you've done that, there's no going back.' She had never cared for boys, except perhaps that young tutor, once, and did not like any man except Anthony.

'She'll change her mind,' he said hopefully, 'won't you, Clare, when the new term starts?'

But when that time came, she was still at Leysmorton and Anthony, baffled, retreated into a hurt silence. Clare retreated too, to the room she had called her studio, where she spent a great deal of time alone, and where Emily was very much afraid she was destroying much of her work. When she emerged she was preoccupied and spoke sharply to anyone who tried to talk seriously to her. At that, Nanny Kate took matters in hand and berated her soundly for what she called the sulks, and at last this had some effect. She began to make the effort at least to put up a front of normality. But it was a miserable time for everyone.

Until Paddy Fitzallan breezed into their lives, and everything changed.

Nine

He was something of a protégé of their aunt's, Paddy Fitzallan, whose father, Daniel, son of an impoverished Anglo-Irish family, had been an old friend of Lottie's – perhaps an old flame, judging from her reminiscent smile when she spoke of him. A slight young man whose eyes were a blaze of blue beneath unruly dark hair, with mobile features and engaging manners, Paddy came with her recommendation. He had pretensions to journalism and was, he said, writing a series of articles on gardens, and eager, with Anthony's permission, to write about Leysmorton.

'A newspaper?' Anthony seemed bemused at the idea of his garden being of such general interest.

'Well, no, possibly some magazine or other,' he replied airily after a moment. 'If they'll have it.' He ran a hand through his curls, dishevelling them even more, and laughed. 'Perhaps you'll spare me some of your time, sir, and share your knowledge with me?'

'How long is all this likely to take?'

'Oh, some time, I should think,' Paddy said, waving a vague hand. 'One mustn't rush these things.'

'Then you must stay with us until you've finished.'

'I say, that's awfully good of you. Are you sure?' He looked suitably astonished, but pleased, and Anthony smiled.

People liked this delightful young man on sight.

He took very little, including himself, seriously. This was fun, and lightened the atmosphere of Leysmorton House considerably. Much of his youth had been spent with his footloose father, who had abandoned his sickly wife in Ireland while he roamed the Continent as it pleased him. Paddy, after leaving school, had roamed it with him until, two years ago, when Daniel on a whim had taken himself off to India and the Far East. Since then, Paddy had chosen to go his own route.

Emily liked him, and especially the way he made her laugh. Conversation with him was refreshingly different from that with most other young men she'd met. Even Anthony smiled more as Paddy went about the garden with him, taking notes.

'But words are poor things to convey all this,' the young man confessed to Emily as they wandered the paths through the sweetly scented herb garden. He bent and plucked a stem of lad's love, sniffed at it then reached for her hand and tucked the aromatic sprig into the bracelet on her wrist. 'I wish I were an artist, and then I could sketch it.' Struck with an idea, he paused, still holding her hand. 'Would your sister happen to have any sketches I might perhaps use?'

Emily did not think she – or Paddy – should ask Clare. It was evident that she was the only one who was not prepared to be charmed by him, having met him at their aunt's and not been impressed. She had trained that clear, sharp gaze of hers onto him when he arrived, and remarked acidly, 'Well, I never expected to see you here, Mr Fitzallan. Out of your milieu, are you not?'

'You never mentioned you lived in a house with such a beautiful garden, Miss Vavasour – but when Mrs Arbuthnot spoke of it in such glowing terms, I knew I had to write about it.'

Clare pressed her lips together and made no further comment until she and Emily were alone. 'Don't trust him, Emily. I've seen quite a lot of him one way or another at Aunt Lottie's, but I only needed to speak ten words to him before I knew he was bad. Dangerous, too, I shouldn't wonder.'

Emily wanted to laugh. 'Dangerous? Bad? Are you sure you don't mean mad as well?'

There was nothing brooding and Byronic about this slight young man, except perhaps his good looks and artless curls. Something different, exciting, yes . . . but dangerous? Holding her hand and talking nonsense might be thought a little flirtatious perhaps, but hardly dangerous.

Despite his work on the garden, Paddy managed to be able to spend a good deal of his time with Emily. One day, they had ridden out to the Downs, to the very edge of the high chalk bluff overlooking the wide expanse of the flat lands below. Reaching the summit, they had reigned in their mounts, thrown themselves down on the turf, with the wide landscape below stretching out towards Netherley, the huddle of its roofs, the church spire and Our Lady's convent, square, red-brick and alien. 'What would Clare say if she knew I was riding her horse?'

'She can't object. He's been eating his head off for too long. She seems to have lost interest, and he needs exercise.' Emily often rode Jupiter, a spirited two-year-old, herself, for just this reason.

'I'm not so sure.' He paused. 'She doesn't like me, I'm afraid.'

This was so patently true it would have been ridiculous to deny it. And though it didn't take a clairvoyant to see that he wasn't much enamoured of her either, that was obviously not the point.

'I wonder why?' he went on plaintively, and added with a self-deprecatory little smile, 'Most people do, you know – like me, I mean.'

Emily smiled in return – one couldn't help it, this childlike desire to be liked was disarming – but she had no idea why Clare had taken against him. She was generally very clear-sighted about most things, but also given to making snap judgments about people, and although Paddy attempted to make himself agreeable to her, she responded only with cool politeness. With a jolt Emily heard him continue, 'Well, at any rate, she – none of you, if it comes to that – will be bothered with me much longer. I'm ready to leave Leysmorton.'

'But – what about your article? You haven't finished it yet, have you?'

He waved aside the last few weeks' work as if it had been of no consequence. 'True, but it's not coming up to scratch, I'm afraid. It isn't as if it was commissioned, though, so it doesn't matter in the least. I don't actually think I'm cut out for doing that kind of hack work.' He pulled a stem of grass and began chewing it. 'It isn't really what I want to do, anyway. I'm off to India.'

'India?' She tried to keep the dismay from her voice, though in a way it was no great surprise: he made no attempt to hide his insatiable wander-lust from anyone.

94

'Yes, I'm going to join my father. Something different,' he went on animatedly, 'that's it. I want—' He stopped.

'You want what, Paddy?'

'Who knows? The whole world, I shouldn't wonder.' He was joking, but looking at him it did not seem too high an ambition. It made you feel Paddy could have anything he chose: his eyes shining, the light crisping his hair, his mouth curling in a confident smile as he looked at his future, the world at his feet, surely.

'But why India?'

'My father's taken up tea planting there.'

'You want to be a *tea planter*?'

'I could do worse, I suppose. But there are other things, too . . . there's a great deal that's wrong out there, you know,' he went on, 'injustices that people here are totally ignorant about. Trouble's always brewing in India, has been ever since the Mutiny—' She must have looked as blank as she felt. 'You have *heard* of the Mutiny? It's recent history, after all.'

It might have been in the Dark Ages for all Emily could recollect – if it had featured at all in her education, which she doubted.

The Mutiny had happened not twenty years before, he reminded her, though before she was born, of course. The hitherto loyal sepoys employed by the army of the British East India Company – until then the virtual governors of India, he further enlightened her – had turned their guns on their officers. Terrible massacres had occurred, which in the end had resulted in the government of India being taken over by the

95

British Crown. The company's legacy was still there: there were injustices, there was fighting. The Indians needed help.

'Paddy! You're not thinking of going out there as some sort of – mercenary – are you?'

'A mercenary? Where do you get these ideas from, Emily?' He laughed. 'No. I'm not a fighter, not in that sense, but if I was out there, I could write about what's happening and let the world know the truth. Somebody should do it, and I know I can,' he said, his face alight.

A flicker of doubt momentarily ran through her, but this was an astonishing and much better side to him than she had seen before, and her recognition of it was reflected in the eager face she turned to him. He looked, as if seeing her for the first time, and at once became very still. And then he said an amazing thing: 'Come with me. Marry me and come with me, Emily.'

She was almost literally knocked breathless with the suddenness, the daring of it, and at the same time filled with a wild excitement and delight. The breeze fanned her blazing cheeks. She dared not look at him. Her heart fluttered madly with the impossibility of it . . . she would *never* be allowed to marry him, she thought, as she followed the flight of a large bird sailing into the valley below, free and graceful. Although he liked Paddy well enough, her father would never agree to it.

Below, in that wide, flat landscape, a farm cart lumbered along the winding road towards Kingsworth. The slow river wound alongside. In the distance the sails of a windmill stirred lazily.

And from then on, his eyes were only for her. There were secret kisses, notes under her door, poems, sweet glances exchanged over the candlelit table in the evenings . . . and slipping out to meet him in the summer-scented darkness.

Ten

Try as she would to forget it, for the last two
months a ghoulish picture of that wretched skull
had kept reappearing, dancing before Rosie's eyes,
just when she least expected it. But now, at last,
the image seemed to have gone, or at least slid
away to lie curled up at the edges of her mind.

This morning's post had brought a letter from
Dee, inviting her to stay for a week or two with
her in her new house in London. Rosie reread it
doubtfully. She didn't know whether she was
awfully keen on the idea – and if it had been her,
just returned from honeymooning with her new
husband in Italy, a gawky younger sister butting
in was the last thing she would have wanted. *It
must be frightfully dull for you down there, too
dreary all on your ownio, my poor lamb*, Dee
had finished, *and the wretched firm takes up so
much of Hamish's time—*

Was this brilliant marriage of Dee's beginning
to drag already?

It wasn't that Rosie objected to what would be
included in the visit: buying new clothes – as
long as Dee didn't try to force her into primrose
yellow – getting one's hair waved, learning to
smoke and use make-up, the latest dance steps,
jazz music. As Dee said, it would be fun. To be

modern, that was the thing, but – to be like Dee and her friends! Rosie made a face. That meant she'd also have to stay awake until dawn, drinking dubious-tasting cocktails and – oh horrors! – making the sort of bright, silly conversation Dee's set used all the time, and which she was jolly sure she wouldn't be much good at – or even like. And anyway, she suspected the invitation had been prompted by Mother, mainly as an introduction to finding some young chap who'd be willing to take on such unpromising material as Rosie for life. As always, Rosie's mouth set when she thought about Stella.

She put the letter aside to be answered later, when she'd had more time to get used to the idea. First, there was her morning ride, without which the day always seemed more pointless than usual, and with the rest of it empty before her, she might wander over to Leysmorton to see if Lady Fitzallan needed any help in the garden. That is, if Emily wasn't absorbed in the brisk plans she was making for the house itself, in particular what must be done to give back to the library what she called its sense of self-respect.

Rosie was spending quite a lot of time over at the big house with Emily. She wasn't at all the person Rosie had grown up hearing stories about: the wild young woman who had married in haste and run off to India with an unsuitable man called Paddy Fitzallan and led a wicked life. These stories had mostly come from Aunt Dorothy, Lady Dedington, that pillar of rectitude, and Rosie had begun to wonder whether they might not have been coloured by exaggeration, if not downright jealousy . . . Paddy Fitzallan must have been a great deal more fun than old Uncle Dedington, who never spoke a word that wasn't necessary. Although she was no longer young, Lady F was friendly and approachable – and she didn't seem to mind Rosie's company, despite the difference in their ages. Rosie sort of thought of her as the grandmother she had never known, though she was not at all grandmotherly, and she liked the hint of mystery about her past, and the exotic life she'd led. It was a pity she couldn't be persuaded to talk about it much, though Rosie had tried questioning her in a casual sort of way, in between being shown how to cut and prune, dead-head and plant. She was learning a lot in that direction, and was keen to learn more. That was of course why she went over to Leysmorton so often. It had nothing to do with the fact that Valentine Drummond had been working with Dirk Stronglove for two or three weeks now, and that there was always the chance that he might see her out there in the garden, and when he did, take time off from his duties and come out to speak to her.

Some time later that same morning, after visiting a small house on the edge of Netherley village, making the duty call which every police officer dreads, Inspector Novak was dropped off at Steadings, while the motor went on to Leysmorton. Within a few moments he was speaking to Hugh Markham, informing him there had been a breakthrough in the case of the murdered soldier found on their neighbouring property.

100

'Glad to hear it. Taken enough time, hasn't it?'

'That's the army for you, sir.' Novak didn't offer any further information, but added that he thought Hugh might like to come over to Leysmorton with him and hear what he had to say – 'and maybe your granddaughter, too, if you can both spare the time.'

'Rosie?'

'She found the body, Mr Markham.'

'Hmm, so she did. I'll get them to find her. I think she's in the stables.'

He went into the house, and returned after a minute or two, soon followed by Rosie, dressed in a blue Aertex shirt and breeches, her skin glowing and her red-gold hair curled damply on her forehead. Although she caught her breath when she saw the inspector and heard the purpose of his call, she made no objection to accompanying them, and the three of them walked across to Leysmorton, not speaking much, avoiding the subject of his visit. He saw Rosie cast several nervous glances at him, but not being the sort of policeman who wasted time on small talk, he let the silence continue until they arrived at the big house. The police motor was now parked on the gravel outside the front door, and waiting beside it stood his sergeant, Willard, who'd driven them down. No Sergeant Chinnery today. Large, middle-aged and bowler-hatted, Willard nodded and accompanied them to the terrace at the back of the house that overlooked the gardens, where a few canvas chairs and a table stood.

Dirk Stronglove was lounging in one of the chairs, not doing anything obvious, but a notebook and pencil nearby suggested he might be deep in thought over his latest book. He proposed they went indoors, where there were more comfortable seats, but Novak politely declined, recalling how the interior of Leysmorton House had discomfited him previously. He liked it better out here on the terrace. Though he was indifferent to gardens as a rule, he could see why this was said to be exceptional – and even he could appreciate the scent of flowers rising to the terrace. Gardens like this were not much in evidence in Stoke Newington, though plenty of small back plots were lovingly tended. Not theirs. Hannah kept their small terrace house neat as a pin, but the garden at the back was a mess. He was always promising her, and himself, that he would find time to sort it out, but he never did.

They waited in silence while Marta Heeren and Lady Fitzallan were sent for. Marta arrived last, pulling on the same hideous green cardigan she had worn previously, breathlessly apologetic: she had been in the far reaches of the garden, gathering berries from the elder bushes that were allowed to grow there.

When they were all assembled, Willard licked his pencil, adjusted the elastic band around his notebook and prepared to take notes. For such a large man, he was adept at making himself unobtrusive. He sat a little to one side, four-square on a stone bench set just outside the window, his stout legs planted firmly on the flagstones, the pencil between his thick fingers poised to fly across the pages. He could do a hundred and eighty words a minute and never had difficulty in transcribing his notes. He was a bachelor, and a dahlia-fancier in what spare time he had, and when they were at their best, there was always a fresh, eye-dazzling bunch of plate-size blooms for Novak to take home to Hannah. Presents for Novak's children at birthdays and Christmas as well.

Novak got straight down to business and told them that enquiries had revealed that the dead man was, or had been, a private soldier in the Bedfordshire Regiment, that his name was Peter Sholto, and that his father had been informed.

The stunned silence from everyone but Lady Fitzallan made it clear she was the only one to whom the name meant nothing. 'Peter Sholto?' she enquired. 'Who was he?'

'A young chap from the village, who worked for me for a time,' Stronglove answered after a moment. His face had blanched, and he fished about on the table for his spectacles. Presumably those thick lenses magnified or brought the people and objects around him into better focus, but when he chose to put them on, they also obscured his expression.

'But Peter Sholto's dead!' Rosie protested. 'I mean, killed in the war, just before it ended.'

'Not so, I'm afraid. It appears he came right through the fighting.'

'That needs a bit of explaining,' Hugh said.

'He was in fact waiting for his discharge when he disappeared, just a couple of days before he was due to be given his demobilization papers. It was still desertion, technically speaking, though the war had been over for five months. Some men

103

still hadn't got their release. Bureaucracy, disorganized chaos, whatever you might choose to call it. Everybody was fed up – I can vouch for that, I was one of them, we were all desperate to get back to Civvy Street – and refusal to stick to the rules wasn't as uncommon as you might think.'

He spoke as if he knew what he was talking about, and Hugh wondered what sort of soldier he had been. Something about him suggested a resistance to obeying orders, an independence that wouldn't go down well with authority; slightly careless of his appearance, without the spit and polish of an ex-soldier, or even a policeman, come to that. Or perhaps it was simply that he was wearing plain clothes, the lack of a uniform, which gave that impression.

'Didn't the army go after him?' he asked.

'The usual enquiries were made but in the end nothing came of it, seems he slipped through the net.'

'But why did his father tell everyone he had been killed?' Rosie was still disbelieving.

'When the military police came looking for his son, and Mr Sholto learnt what had happened, he says he'd rather people thought his son dead than a deserter, so he put it about that he'd been wounded and died in the last days of the war.'

A silence fell.

In these tight communities – and Netherley was a very small village – people would have every sympathy and do all they could for a man whose son had died fighting for his country, that much Novak knew. But if that son was branded a deserter, whatever the circumstances – no. Not when a dozen or more other young fellows from the village had given their lives during those terrible years and would never return. If Peter had deserted, his father had counted on him having more sense than to return to the village. Now the man, poor devil, must be feeling as though he'd made a self-fulfilling prophecy.

Novak was glad to see that one person here at least understood the father's attitude. 'Sholto will be damned cut up,' Hugh Markham murmured. 'He thought a great deal of the boy. Hard to imagine how this came about . . . must go and see him.'

'He's saying he doesn't want to see anyone,' Novak warned.

'Edmund Sholto's a very reserved man. He doesn't have many close friends in the village, but I potter down there once or twice a week. We play chess and talk. I think he'll see me,' Hugh said quietly, although it seemed to Novak he did not relish the prospect of the visit. He did in fact look quite upset.

'You realize what this means?' Novak went on, addressing them as a group. 'It moves forward the date he was killed – to some time *after* his desertion. After the hospital ceased operating.'

'But it must have been before Marta and I returned to live here,' Stronglove said quickly.

'Possibly, but not necessarily. The spot where he was found is a long way from the house, Mr Stronglove, and not often visited, as we've established. He could have been killed there – and buried – at any time after he left his unit in March 1919, without anyone being the wiser.' He paused. 'He wasn't killed too recently, though, our experts judge.'

'The body being a skeleton, of course.'

Novak ignored the sarcasm. Beneath it, he sensed tension in the man; indeed, he felt it running between all these people, just as he had when he'd first talked to them. He hadn't yet got the measure of any of them, though he found the youngest, Rosie Markham, easy enough to read. Instinct told him he ought to heed his feelings, the suspicion that something was being held back, but no one was going to give anything away. His glance eventually came to rest on Marta Heeren, blocky and plain, staring mutely across the garden, fingering the glass beads round her neck as if disassociating herself with what was going on. Her fingers were stained purple-red with juice from the elderberries she'd been picking. As if suddenly aware of his attention on her, she scraped back her chair and without a word lumbered through the French windows and into the house, her hand to her mouth. A door banged and silence fell.

'She was fond of Peter,' Dirk said after a moment.

Lady Fitzallan made as if to follow, but hesitated and sat back down as he shook his head.

Now why should the news that the skeleton was that of young Sholto have upset Marta Heeren, of all these people here, so much?

His former army commander had described Peter Sholto as having a fair but not outstanding record when he had fought with the regiment on the Western Front, a young man of intelligence, educated, but he'd remained a private – not officer material. No calibre. No leadership qualities, he'd said stiffly. (Not really a gent, Novak had supplied to himself.) The CO added that as far as he knew,

Sholto had not been unpopular, though he couldn't say if he had made a friend of anyone in particular in the unit.

It was Lady Fitzallan who broke the silence, remarking quietly, 'The house was empty. I suppose it's possible he came here to hide, after his desertion?'

He gave her a quick nod. 'It's possible. And if he did, that the person who killed him knew that's what he intended, and followed or met him here.'

'Look here,' Stronglove began. 'If Peter came back to Netherley at all, surely he would have gone home, to his father, not come here. How sure are you it *was* Peter?'

'I think we can be reasonably confident about his identity, sir. And whether he intended to go and see his father or not, he came to Leysmorton first. Mr Sholto hasn't seen his son for over four years, since his last leave.'

'One of his army pals who followed him then, wanting to settle old scores maybe?'

'Maybe. But it's just as likely to be an old enemy chancing on him when he got back to Netherley and following him for the same reason, a quarrel that suddenly erupted – or half a dozen other off-the-cuff reasons, if it comes to that. The question is, *why* did he leave his unit? Was he deserting, or did he intend to return? It's not unknown for men to disappear in response to some family emergency or something of that sort. But speculation's pointless until we have more to go on.'

The identification was good, they no longer had a nameless victim on their hands, but Novak's instinct was telling him this might be as far as they were going to get. Everything was against them. Very likely it would remain one of those unsolved wartime mysteries, of which there were more than was generally known. Three years had elapsed since the young soldier's disappearance, at a time when the nation was still getting back on its feet, pulling itself together after the disruption of four years of bloody warfare; when many people were still displaced from their pre-war lives, homes, habits and routines, and the disappearance of one man after the annihilation of millions was of relatively little importance.

He frowned. No. You had to believe it was important, that it mattered, even amongst the criminal fraternity in which Novak normally worked, where life was cheap. Any man's death mattered. And this one mattered very much to that man in the village whom Novak had just met and had to inform that his son had been murdered – and evidently to Miss Heeren as well. He could not even begin to imagine receiving such news about young Oliver or little Evie, his own two; nor could he imagine ever recovering from such a blow to the heart.

He was beginning to realize that this had ceased to be just another job, to be wrapped up as quickly as possible. Certainly, he was going to have to pace himself, adjust to a different way of working. But he *would* find the killer, he resolved, not just to chalk up one more case solved, but to bring to justice the person who had deprived this young fellow of the right to the life before him, left him in such an ignominious grave and his father's heart breaking with grief.

'We need to know more about the victim. His death may well be concerned with something that happened during his time in the army, though his having been killed here indicates possible connections with his life before that, so if any of you can think of any reason why this might have happened – his habits, anyone who disliked him, anything at all – I'd be grateful if you'd let me know.' Flipping open the cover of his pocket watch, he gave it a quick glance. 'I'm going to have to leave you, but I shall need at some point to speak to those of you who were close to him.'

'I wasn't particularly close to him,' Dirk said shortly. 'He only worked for me.'

Hugh said slowly, 'For myself, I scarcely knew the boy – generations apart, you know – but I can tell you now that his father was concerned about Peter. He was restless and not showing any signs of settling down to anything. Edmund was naturally upset when the boy volunteered for the army, but at the same time, he thought it might be the making of him. Maybe he got involved with the wrong sort while he was away?'

'As someone more his age, you would presumably have known him better, Miss Markham?'

'Rosie was just a child.'

'Yes,' Rosie said, looking up from contemplation of her polished riding boots. 'I was only eleven when the war started, and he was grown up.'

Marta Heeren's alleged fondness for the boy wasn't referred to. Novak knew he would have to speak to her, but she clearly wasn't in any fit state to be questioned at the moment. He stood up, nodded to Willard who closed his notebook

109

with a smart snap, and thanked them all. 'I think that's as far as we can go for now. We shall be continuing with our investigations, of course, and we'll let you know if anything else transpires.'

After leaving them all outside on the terrace, Marta had blundered through the library and into the hall, where she came to a halt and gazed wildly around as if she didn't know where she was, uncertain where to go. Today was the morning when one of the village women turned out her bedroom, lunch was being prepared in the kitchen, and trying to find privacy in one of the secluded corners of the library, with everyone still on the terrace, wasn't possible. There were a dozen other places in the house where she could have hidden herself, so many in fact that the choice seemed an impossible one in her confused state, and in the end she simply sat down on the big oak settle, where for only the second time in her adult life she burst into tears. Peter! Oh, Peter! Why did you have to come back here?

Peter, slim and lithe, with smooth olive skin, eyes like black obsidian and thick eyelashes any girl would have given her soul for . . . He had reminded her, when she had first seen him, so much of Dirk when he was the same age.

As a little girl, Marta had not taken to her new stepmother, Florence Vavasour, who had married her widowed father, a big, stolid Dutchman. Florence was a tight-lipped woman who did not believe in spoiling children, but it was not for taking her mother's place that Marta resented her: she did not even remember her mother, who

110

had died when she was a baby. She had felt excluded, no one now noticed her or wanted her affection, and she tried to gain attention by naughtiness: getting her pristine clothes dirty, savagely destroying and defacing the few toys and picture books her new stepmother allowed, baffling her father. That changed when Marta first saw her little stepbrother in his mother's arms, a newborn baby with an angry red face, tiny starfish hands and unbelievably delicate, pearly fingernails. Where jealousy might have been expected, from precisely that moment on she had loved him with a fierce protectiveness that had lasted all their lives.

Was it only this memory of caring for Dirk that had made her love Peter, or the fact that Dirk, a grown man, no longer needed her quite so much?

How long she sat there, she didn't know, but presently she managed to pull herself together and dry her eyes. Her heavy face fell back into its usual stoic expression, and after a moment or two she thought she might be ready to go into the kitchen and get on with her wine-making.

But just as she prepared to go, Dirk and the two policemen came into the hall as Dirk escorted them to the front door. Novak and his sergeant hadn't noticed her in the shadows at the far end, but Dirk had seen her and now came towards her. He sat down beside her and put his arm around her shoulders. 'Maartje, Maartje.'

The sound of her real name, now only ever used by him, nearly upset her again. It had always been she, the big sister, who had looked after, comforted and protected him, but Dirk for his

111

part was more tender with her, more under-standing, than he was with anyone else. They had always supported one another, and always would. She would never let him down. It would be all right.

She let his hand stay where it was for a moment, then drew away. She didn't like to be touched by anyone, sometimes not even by Dirk. She took a breath. 'Run along now,' she said, standing up. 'I expect you have your work to attend to.' Like a small boy, he obeyed. It was his instinctive reac-tion to his older sister.

Nellie Dobson, who came in daily from the village to cook, had brought one of her grand-children with her – it was little Violet today – and Marta could hear her prattling in the kitchen. She pushed open the kitchen door and went to the table, where she sat with Violet on her knee and felt the warmth of her small body, and smelled the baby smell of her hair while she showed her how to pick over the elderberries with her fat little fingers.

'I suppose I can go and change now,' Rosie said, after the police and Dirk had disappeared. Hugh, too, rose from his chair.

Emily said, 'Please, Hugh, stay a moment, if you will.'

Rosie left them and they sat for a while without speaking. The August garden, at the end of a long, hot summer, was beginning to look exhausted, the trees heavy with leaf, some already yellowing, the first steps towards the year's gentle slide into autumn. Only the Hecate tree stood far off, dark and unchanging, its black-green shape silhouetted against the sky.

Hugh looked expectant as Emily turned to him. Perhaps he was hoping for the talk she had promised when she first arrived, and which he had, with admirable patience, not pressed her for.

'There's something on your mind, Hugh.'

He grunted but didn't say anything for a while. 'You noticed. Yes. In a way, I feel responsible for all this.'

'You? How?'

'Responsible in that I brought them to Netherley, Edmund and his son.'

'Which doesn't mean,' she replied after a moment, 'that you should blame yourself for the boy's death. Who is Edmund Sholto?'

'He lives in one of those two cottages belonging to Steadings – you remember them, just outside the gates, where old Mrs Cantor used to live. When she died and her cottage became vacant, I offered it to him. He had bought a bookshop, specializing in antiquarian books, in St Albans, that's how I came to know him.'

'Of course.' Emily knew Hugh's interest in books had always extended beyond the actual publishing of them. He possessed a fine collection of old and rare volumes, and some valuable first editions. Bookshops drew him like a magnet.

Sholto had come to the area after his wife had died following a long illness, which had been a particularly harrowing time for both him and their young son. Peter was about ten when they left Cornwall, and Edmund wanted to get right away from it all, for both their sakes, make a new start.

113

He decided to settle in St Albans, where he found good schools for Peter and a bookshop for sale, with accommodation attached. But, added Hugh drily, having a passion for books doesn't necessarily bring in a living. Edmund had been a schoolmaster and was in no way a man of business. The bookshop did not make money and he was lucky enough to sell it before it collapsed completely. It was then Hugh had offered him the vacant cottage.

'That was an act of kindness.'

'Kindness?' He raised an eyebrow. 'Self-preservation, more likely. There's no one else in Netherley I can talk to with the same degree of compatibility.' He rose to go.

She knew he hadn't told her everything. If she pressed him, he might tell her what he was holding back, but she felt she had no right. There were many things she hadn't told even Hugh, dearer to her than anyone else, and never would.

Eleven

When the prospect of working for Dirk Stronglove
had first been mooted at Dee's wedding, Val had
scornfully dismissed the idea. He told Poppy he
would have to be desperate to take on that sort
of job. 'And I don't believe I'm that far gone,
not quite, not yet.'

'Since when have you been able to afford to
be so high-minded? Lots of men would simply
jump at such an offer. It's only a temporary thing,
anyway, isn't it?'

That had certainly been made quite clear in that
first brief chat he'd had with Stronglove. 'True.
Until he finishes his current book, while he makes
up his mind whether to have his eyes operated
on or not. Poor devil, what a decision to have to
make! He's quite keen to have someone working
with him who might have an understanding of
what he's about – actually, he's quite impressed
by Oxford, me reading English and all that.'

'There you are, then.'

'Haven't you been listening to a word I've said?
I can't take it.'

But his protests had been token, because Poppy
had been quite right. He wasn't in a position to
reject any reasonable job, especially one which
offered a decent remuneration, as this one did.
And despite what he had said, here he was, living
in at Leysmorton because Emily had suggested

that was the only thing for him to do, Netherley being miles from any main line station, and Val not having any transport. Yesterday, Dirk had suddenly announced he needed a day off to give himself a break, and Val was free to do the same. So he had taken the opportunity to come up to London to collect more of his belongings – and to see a man he knew about the purchase of a second-hand motorcycle. On a borrowed bicycle, he'd ridden over to Kingsworth Halt to catch a train which eventually brought him to London.

He had been thankful, when he'd come to see Poppy in her smart little London shop, to find Xanthe Tripp absent. Waiting while she left him in order to accept delivery of several large parcels that had arrived at the same time as he did, he looked around, feeling he was in Aladdin's cave – though one for initiates. One had to admit, Poppy really had flair, even if the ornaments, fabrics and furnishings bore no resemblance to anything anyone looking for comfort would wish to have in their home – apart from some rather nice cream leather sofas. He knew that Mrs Tripp's interest was less in the artistic side of the business and more in finding clients who wanted to keep in the swim and leave the stuffy old pre-war ideas behind. There were apparently plenty of those, but regrettably few who could afford to implement this and follow the fashions of the moment.

'How is work at Leysmorton, then?' Poppy asked as the door closed behind the delivery man. 'I trust you're managing to survive without prostituting your art?'

'No sarcasm, Pops, please.' He paused. 'It was old Emily who recommended me to Stronglove, I'm sure of it.'

'Indirectly perhaps. She and Hugh.'

'She's obviously decided we both need looking after – this job for me, and I hear she's commissioning you to redo her library. Can that be true?'

'Yes, what fun.'

There was a slight pause. 'I'd be very sorry to see the Leysmorton library looking anything like – this,' he observed cautiously, casting another glance around at strange, angular lamps and sleek, streamlined furniture, fabrics in violent colours, 'and sorry if you're asking too much. It's jolly decent of her to try and help us, after all.'

'It's not entirely up to me. I *do* have a partner, you know.'

'I do know,' he said, his tone sharpening.

'Don't be tiresome, Val. Give me a little *credit*. There won't be any drastic changes to the library, and I'll see to it that we certainly won't overcharge. She's – actually, she's really rather an old dear, isn't she?'

'Lady F?' Val raised an eyebrow at this very different tune Poppy was now singing.

'All right,' she admitted, flushing as she bent to retrieve a stray piece of thread from some newly made, wavy-striped black and white curtains, presumably meant to resemble zebra skin. 'Maybe I was wrong, perhaps one shouldn't judge a person before you've met them properly. And she *has* wangled you that job and everything . . .'

Val let it pass. 'What's your opinion of Stronglove?' he asked abruptly.

'I don't know him well enough to have one. I used to see him occasionally when I stayed with Dee in the school hols and that's about it.'

'He calls me his amanuensis.' He laughed shortly. 'Better than dogsbody, I suppose, which is what I really am.'

'Does it matter *what* he calls you, ducky, when he's paying you so well?'

'Not if you look at it like that, I suppose . . .' He wished they didn't both have to be so aware of money, but it was difficult not to be when you'd been as hard up as they had for so long. He shrugged. 'Oh, it's not so bad, really.'

In fact, in many ways he felt sympathetic to Dirk, struggling to finish a book while coping with the problem of his failing eyesight. So far Val had been able to work with him better than he had thought possible, although Stronglove had a high opinion of himself, a result of the acclaim brought to him by his books, which in Val's lofty view did not rate highly in the literature scale. But since working on the new book with Dirk, he had to admit to a grudging admiration and respect for the craftsmanship and hard work which made them so successful.

'I'm no good at dictation,' Dirk had said right at the beginning, 'too many second thoughts and the need for alterations and crossings out. You'll have to do what the young chap who worked for me before the war did – decipher the scrawl my handwriting's become and get it all into reasonably good shape. Anyway, I don't suppose you do this shorthand malarkey – but I hope you do know how to use a typewriter?'

Val had replied diffidently that he had taught himself to type. He didn't feel it necessary to explain that he'd tackled this during the writing of his own novel. Stronglove hadn't mentioned that he knew about his attempt at authorship – though Val was sure he must have been told about it – and Val himself certainly wasn't ready to discuss it, not at this stage anyway.

Although his new employer was touchy about his work, and often in a strange mood, as if he had something on his mind, almost certainly due to the operation hanging over him, Val had decided that, all in all, the job wasn't turning out so badly. Apart from bringing in some money, there was an added bonus in the shape of Rosie Markham. So far, he'd managed to exchange little more than pleasantries with her because she and Lady Fitzallan, working in the garden together, had always looked too busy and absorbed to be interrupted for long. It was a state of affairs he intended to remedy.

'What did you want to see me about, Val, coming so far out of your way? You came over here specially and you must have had a reason for that.' Poppy looked pointedly at a black ceramic disc without numbers, only white hands, and flicking back a wing of black hair regarded him narrowly. She looked as glossy and enamelled as the clock. 'Come on, I haven't got much time.'

'I came to see you, Poppy, because I thought you might want to know that the police have a name for that skeleton that was found at Leysmorton.'

'Me? Why should I want to know that?' Her groomed eyebrows rose in mild surprise.

'You might want to sit down before I tell you who he was.'

Earlier that day, while Val was pushing the pedals towards Kingsworth Halt, the middle-aged chauffeur who drove the Daimler for both Hugh and Gerald was waiting on the neat gravel sweep that led to the front door of Steadings, ready to drive Gerald to the publishing house at Clerkenwell as he did each day. He repolished the already pristine wing mirrors as eight resonant strokes of the clock above the stables at Leysmorton floated clearly across to him. Slow, again. That clock hadn't kept good time since the old man, Anthony Vavasour, had died, but Deegan checked his pocket watch again. Ten past eight, and Gerald, who invariably came out on the dot of eight, was nowhere to be seen.

He was in fact looking for his wife to say goodbye before he left. He had expected to find her sitting up in bed as usual, scarcely awake, sipping tea and flicking through her post, but her maid informed him that Madam had been up for an hour and had gone out for a walk. What? Stella, usually inaccessible until eleven, after her bath and a leisurely dressing routine, out at this time of the morning? For a walk? Gerald, momentarily confused, looked around the house but found no sign of anyone – breakfast already cleared away, Rosie out riding, and his father shut into the snug little room the children called his den (as if he were a lion! grumbled Hugh) that was now his own private sitting room, where he always spent the hour after breakfast with

120

The Times and everyone knew not to disturb him. After a moment's consideration, shrugging his shoulders, Gerald went out to the motor car and told Deegan to drive off. It was just another of the things he didn't understand about Stella lately. Or more truthfully, he admitted, clenching his jaw, one he understood only too damned well.

Dirk and Stella met in their usual trysting place, as it amused Dirk to call the old pavilion, a sort of folly built in a distant part of the Leysmorton garden by an eighteenth-century Vavasour who had been fond of the view across the undulating fields and woods to the chalk hills in the distance. It was set on a little rise and offered views of anyone approaching and a door at the back for a discreet exit, a useful back-up should anyone take it into their heads to come here, unlikely as that was. The pavilion, falling into disrepair, its furniture decrepit, had of recent years almost been forgotten.

Although it was barely eight o'clock, at a time when Stella was normally being wakened by her maid with a cup of Earl Grey and a water biscuit, this morning she was dressed, immaculately as ever, in lime green linen, and made up with care. She had put Chu down on one of the old cushioned rattan chairs, where he sneezed and looked offended at the dust raised by his body weight. She bent over the little dog, murmuring endearments, then straightened. She appeared cool and collected, though her hand shook a little as she accepted a light for her cigarette from Dirk.

'Darling, you mustn't worry.'

121

She gave him her thin, closed smile and drew deeply on her cigarette.

When the identity of the skeleton found under that rubbish had been revealed, Dirk's first, primitive emotion had been one of anger. How dare he? How dare Peter Sholto come back like this, from the safely dead, to haunt them? More than that, to threaten? Then, last night had been spent wrestling with nightmares, waking in the darkness at three o'clock in the morning in a cold sweat. The terror had receded with returning consciousness, seeming like nothing compared with the ever-present despair about his failing sight, shadowing him like a grey ghost. Yet now, in the light of day, the sense of outrage about Peter Sholto was no less, and the feeling of imminent danger was resurfacing, bubbling like the lava just beneath the surface of a sleeping volcano. Danger for himself, yes, but for Stella also. As if they didn't have enough problems.

He took the cigarette from between her fingers, pinched it out and threw it to the ground. Chu gave the sharp, yapping sound that was his impression of an outraged bark as the cigarette flew past his ear. Stella let Dirk take her in his arms, for once ignoring the little dog. Dirk felt her bird-like bones, and looked with concern into her white face and the curious flecked hazel of her eyes under the thinly arched brows, with the small crease between them that was fast becoming permanent. Close up like this, he could see without the spectacles he was coming to regard as both his cross and his salvation. He constantly worried about what would happen to these secret meetings

122

when his eyesight grew so bad he could no longer stumble about, even with the assistance of the stick he now needed to help him get around outdoors with any degree of dignity.

'I always told you,' Stella said, 'that little – that creature – would bring trouble.'

'He was useful. But he's dead, we've nothing to fear, my love, nothing.' He wished he could be as certain as he had attempted to sound.

'Well. Well, you know, this must be the last time we meet.'

Dirk stared. 'The last? God dammit, no!' he said violently.

'Darling, for the time being, *yes*, I'm afraid. Big-footed policemen all over the place and all that, we have to be careful.'

He stared at her again. Stella, with her thin, sideways smile, bitter, discontented and, he suddenly saw, bored. Oh God, was that all it had been, all this time? A little dalliance, to alleviate the ennui? But after a moment he saw the sense in what she had said and reluctantly nodded in agreement. He looked wretched, but she did not offer to comfort him.

Marta, an inveterate early riser, was finding it utterly impossible to look on what had happened with her usual stoicism. She too had slept badly, and forced herself to sit down and face the situation with the help of the third cup of coffee of the morning. She made good coffee, strong and bracing.

She would have felt better if she could have talked to Dirk, but he was not around. She had heard him moving about early that morning, although he hadn't joined her for breakfast. She went into the study and, finding it empty, she remembered he had given that nice young Valentine the day off.

She knew where he would be, in that place they thought so secret. Her lips twisted at the thought of that woman. She did not go and seek him out; it was better that they kept up a pretence of secrecy. She was used to keeping her own counsel about his affairs anyway, and Dirk was no longer the little brother he had once been, who had confided his woes to her and allowed her to comfort and kiss him better. In her heart she knew she had not been supplanted – look how kind he had been to her when they had heard that terrible news about Peter being found. She thought she might make him one of her sweet puddings for supper, the Dutch ginger butter cake he so loved. Peter had liked that, too, in fact he'd liked most of the things Marta made. Tears began to roll down her cheeks again.

Emily was dreaming as she had not done for years, and last night had been no exception.

In her dreams she travelled continents. Egypt . . . sand, dust. Feluccas crossing the Nile against ineffable sunsets. Ancient monuments and the awesome silence of the Valley of the Kings. Cairo and its din, dead donkeys in the canals, natives in dazzling white, with smiles to match. Egyptian nationalism.

South Africa . . . Mafeking, the Place of Stones, on the veldt. Haunting singing from the native kraals in the evening. The war against the Boers. The Seige. Baden-Powell, the hero of the hour. Natives dying of starvation. The more-favoured rest surviving on horse meat and mealie porridge.

Armenia . . . a parched, stony land where wild flowers in the mountains grew stiffly, conditioned by the thin soil. Almond blossom in the spring and fountains everywhere in the dust-bowl of Yerevan, a city old as Babylon. Tall-hatted priests. Mount Ararat across the Turkish border, its snow-capped peak rosy against the blue sky. Turkish oppression and genocide – nowhere had fascinated Paddy more. Nowhere had contributed more to his downfall.

But above all, she dreamt of India . . .

Twelve

Then

She had long ago pushed India and what it meant into a closed drawer at the back of her mind, along with all the other memories she did not care to revisit. But who knew what alchemy brought memory to the surface? Occasionally unexpected things, a stray word, the scent of sandalwood or jasmine, the hint of certain spices in food would unlock the drawer and there she was, rummaging among the sights, smells and sounds that had once been so familiar.

India overwhelmed her, her first sight of it and ever thereafter. Nothing about it was moderate. Everything went to extremes: beauty and ugliness, wealth and squalor, famine and plenty, drought and flood, pitiless sunshine and relentless rain.

Perhaps she had looked forward too eagerly to a new, strange and exciting life, an exotic paradise, but when she and Paddy arrived, the immediate reality was so contrary to her expectations that her spirits sank into her shoes. Where was the brilliant sun, the deep blue sky? Instead, nothing but towering banks of grey cloud, heavy humidity and a thick, oppressive heat. Wearing her lightest clothing, the moment she stepped unsteadily onto the quay from the steam launch which had

126

brought them across the choppy waters of the harbour, perspiration prickled under her arms and ran down between her shoulder blades and her breasts. You could almost taste the air, soupy, steamy and metallic. They said that despite the recent rain which had left puddles already drying to dust on the quay, the monsoon season had hardly got into its stride; the rainfall was still intermittent, just squally showers that merely heralded the succession of torrential downpours that would inevitably come later.

At least the tea plantation (the tea *garden*, she had learnt) was in the hills. Where it will be cooler, she thought with relief, not so humid, where we might make another sort of garden, English style, Paddy and I . . . and Paddy's father.

Where *was* Daniel Fitzallan? He was supposed to have met them, but he had not been waiting at the disembarkation point as he had promised, and Emily was forced to wait in the clamouring chaos on the quayside while Paddy went to enquire for him. Most of the ship's other passengers soon departed, including Mrs Maybury, a kindly young matron whose husband worked as an administrator in the Indian Civil Service, and who had taken Emily under her wing on board ship. She was returning from Home, where she had been compelled to leave her two boys at school, and had been glad of company to take her mind off it. She promised to keep in touch. 'Don't expect too much at first, my dear, India's like nothing you've ever been used to – it will take time for you to adjust, and to make friends.' Kind advice, from the wisdom of experience, that sounded ominously like a warning. 'Before you leave Bombay, we must meet again, make sure you have a chance to enjoy yourself. The Prince of Wales is to visit soon and there's sure to be a vastly entertaining time ahead.'

Emily doubted there would be the opportunity to join in any such frivolities before she and Paddy departed for Assam, but she smiled and thanked Veronica Maybury, who kissed her warmly and departed in the carriage that had been waiting for her, leaving Emily by the sheds that flanked the quay, alone with their luggage, her ears assaulted by the din surrounding her on every side.

Workmen, barefoot and wearing nothing but a dhoti tucked up between their legs, scuttled about carrying the trunks, bags and baskets belonging to disembarking passengers, while others unloaded cargoes onto bullock carts, trotting along, bent almost double with tea-chests – sometimes two – roped onto their backs, or balancing immense bundles on their heads. People jostled and pushed past her, jabbering incessantly in an unintelligible language. Unavoidably, she breathed in the malodorous fusion of smells: the cloying scents that did not mask human body odours; a breath of something that brought to mind Aunt Lottie's High Church in London – incense perhaps; an acrid tang like bonfires; the stench of rotten meat, and worse.

By the time Paddy returned, after a fruitless search for his father, there were no horse-drawn tongas to be had to take them to their hotel – Watson's, *the* place to stay, for Europeans – and they were compelled to hire a rickshaw for themselves and their luggage, pulled by a single

128

man, a demeaning circumstance which shocked Emily but seemed of no great import to the man himself, who cheerfully picked up the shafts and set off on naked feet at a great pace.

'If this isn't just like my father!' Paddy's lips twitched, amused rather than annoyed by the situation. 'Most likely he's forgotten what day we're arriving. At least I hope that's what it is,' he added obscurely, but just kept smiling when she asked for an explanation.

Emily forced herself not to press him for one. There was a strong element of hero-worship in the way Paddy regarded his father, glossing over minor peccadilloes, and she was beginning to find her new husband was very good at answering questions he did not like with only a smile. Which was . . . not exactly annoying, but a tiny blip in the perfection of their so far blissfully happy time as man and wife.

It had not happened without opposition, her marriage to Paddy. Aunt Lottie, predictably, had not been slow to have her say. First Clare, and now *Emily*! Emily, hitherto the one who never gave any trouble, throwing herself away, getting ridiculous notions about marrying Paddy Fitzallan, charming as he was. Her father must rouse himself and put his foot firmly down, talk some sense into her. Even Anthony could not countenance this.

Any doubts Anthony might have had when Paddy asked for the hand of his daughter in marriage, he appeared to have smothered, however. As usual, he let events dictate their own course, retreating from

129

the upheaval that would have ensued if he had forbidden her – and in any case, why should she *not* marry the boy, he had answered, silencing every objection Mrs Arbuthnot put forward. Paddy Fitzallan was a likeable fellow, of good family – his father was a baronet, he would inherit the title. An impoverished baronet, that was true, but that didn't trouble Anthony overmuch. It mattered little to him whether the man his daughter had chosen to marry was a prince or a pauper – there was the money left in trust by her mother for when she married, as well as his own marriage settlement. And there would eventually be the not inconsiderable sum of what he had to leave. 'If that's how you feel, child, I won't go against you,' he had said finally.

Shortage of money was not a circumstance that ever needed to be considered in the Vavasour family; it was always there, and it had never crossed Emily's mind to discuss such mundane matters as her inheritance when she and Paddy had talked about their wonderful future together. And neither did Paddy mention it.

The dreaded hurdle of her father's acceptance having been surmounted without much pain, Clare's fierce opposition came all the harder.

'It's too ridiculous – you don't know the first thing about him!' she declared, appalled, not to say incredulous, that Emily could be so naïve.

'Enough to know that I love him and he loves me. And if Papa has no objections, why should you?'

'Oh, Emily, you're such a *child*! Papa will do anything to avoid confrontation. Haven't you found that out yet?'

Stung as she was by these aspersions on her youth and general imperceptiveness – and with a mere two years' difference in their age! – Emily knew there was some truth in this final point, though nothing would have made her admit that was the reason Anthony had given his consent so easily.

She looked at her sister imploringly, 'Please be happy for me.'

'How can I possibly be, if you insist on throwing your life away – and that's just what you will be doing, with someone like Paddy Fitzallan. He's nowhere near good enough for you.'

But then, no man would ever be good enough, in Clare's opinion, Emily thought sadly. For Emily, though even more for Clare herself. Since it was an argument she would never win, she did not pursue it. 'Paddy is leaving for India in less than a month. And he wishes me to go with him, as his wife. Which I shall do, Clare. Nothing you can say will stop me.'

Clare made one last attempt. 'Well, on your own head be it, if you insist on ruining your life. But at least think of Hugh. Don't do this to him, Emily. You'll break his heart. As well as your own, when you've come to your senses. He's the best man you'll ever know.'

Telling Hugh was what Emily had been dreading most. She shrank from it, though she knew it had to be done, and quickly; she couldn't leave him to hear it from someone else, though absolutely the last thing she wanted to do was to hurt him.

When she did tell him, on a heavenly night of June and roses, sitting in one of the 'sentry boxes' below the terrace, with the little fountain tinkling away, she was for a moment frightened when she saw his face. Yet Hugh, who could be counted on always to do the correct thing, merely asked, after several long moments, 'Are you sure, Emily, absolutely certain?', and when she replied yes, she could not be more so, he said stiffly that in that case he had to hope she would be very happy. Though somehow it didn't sound like Hugh, his voice as distant as if it came from another planet.

Rather unconvincingly, she tried to believe that he could not have loved her, not as Paddy loved her, otherwise he would have made more objections. She had forgotten the joy, the quiet certainty she'd had that he really cared for her, that the quite proper kisses he had given her once or twice had meant as much to him as they had to her – then.

Because all that had been before Paddy. She hadn't known then that the kisses of a handsome Irishman could make stars explode in your head, or light up your mind with dreams.

Progress along the road to Watson's Hotel was surprisingly steady, considering the number of times the rickshaw man, trotting on at a tremendous speed, had to dodge nimbly between lumbering bullock carts, swaying cows, other rickshaws and the noisy press of barefoot humanity that surged out onto the road: women wearing saris in rainbow hues, their kohl-rimmed eyes downcast, or shielding their faces, men clad in dhotis and turbans of all colours, children darting everywhere, half-naked, black-eyed, while between them sellers of water sold tea and sweetmeats

132

from trays suspended around their necks. Smoke thickened the air from burning braziers cooking strange-smelling food at the thronged roadside, among stalls that appeared to sell everything.

Emily could see few white people, other than those she suspected were Englishmen, in light-weight shantung suits and solar topees, their ladies in wide, shady hats, but they were riding in horse-drawn carriages which cleared a path by driving smartly along in the centre of the road, kicking up dust. Behind the road, to one side, stretched a great huddle of lanes and alleys of broken-roofed shacks. And right there on the sidewalks, amongst the discarded rubbish and the feet of the crowd, crouched unidentifiable sleeping bundles of rags, sharing the space with maimed and limbless beggars, holding out supplicating hands. Many of them were children.

The crowds lessened somewhat as their rickshaw neared the city centre, the road grew wider and was lined with shady trees; more and more conspicuously splendid buildings appeared, magnificently embracing Eastern and Western architectural styles, no doubt meant for purposes of colonial administration or where the nawabs and other rich Indians lived. There were sounds of tinkling water and hints of quiet gardens behind walls which shielded them from the teeming street-life and the poverty outside their gates.

Watson's, when they reached it, had its own grandeur – its soaring atrium and the way it discreetly and expensively catered for the comfort and well-being of its solely white clientele. Indian servants stepped forward immediately to relieve them of every article of baggage, others stood by ready to anticipate any further wish. Paddy, approached by the manager, was obviously relieved to be told Sir Daniel was here at the hotel, though he was in his room, confined to bed. He had unfortunately been indisposed for some time, and was still far from well.

'I see.' Paddy nodded, his smile disappearing. 'In that case, we must go to him at once.'

Emily hung back. 'You should see him alone, Paddy.'

'No, come with me. He'll want to meet you.'

The fever that had taken hold of him had abated but had left Daniel weak as a kitten and still not altogether back in his head from the places he had inhabited for – how long? Days, weeks? No telling, but he was lucid enough now to know that he must have been ranting aloud, and God knows what he'd been telling the world. If a drowning man sees his life before him, he had been drowning, that was for sure, and the tatters of his life, the footloose, wandering years had come back through his delirium, sometimes to torment him, though he seemed to recall hearing himself laughing aloud at times. And why not? It hadn't all been bad. Not at first. Moving across continental Europe, doing anything he could to scratch a living: teaching music to spoilt little girls in Italy; copying scores in Vienna when he was at rock-bottom, acting as accompanist to a lieder baritone who travelled the Continent; Paris for a time, where he had been the lover of an operatic diva . . .

134

He dozed, and dreamt again of himself, frittering about on the edges of the music world, suddenly sick of it. Meeting this man home from India, a tea-planter, and becoming fired with the notion of doing something different, a man's job, amongst other men, giving him a purpose, and perhaps another chance, if it wasn't too late.

It hadn't turned out like that. Did things ever turn out as one wished? he was asking himself as he woke, fretful, needing to remember something elusive, on the edges of his consciousness. He struggled to sit up. It was too hot. He let himself fall back on the pillows.

What in the name of God had he been thinking about, coming to India? From the first, he had hated it: the flies, the dust, the heat, and most of all the relentless bloody rain – although the climate of Assam was better than here in Bombay. He could not understand the customs, the language or the people. The food made him ill. The only white men he met were the military and government officers, who were not to his taste at all, nor he to theirs, their wives and daughters off-limits to him.

It came to him as he struggled to remember. Paddy, whom he had sent away, was coming back! This time with a new bride. Good for him! The boy needed someone to look after him. He, Daniel, had never been good at that. Loved the boy, yes – oh God, yes – but that wasn't always enough. He had needed a mother, but Daniel hadn't needed a wife – and sickly, demanding Philomena would have been a feeble wife or mother for anyone. Being with his father had been a more attractive proposition, not only for the boy, but for Daniel as well. At least Paddy had had the good sense to marry somebody with money . . .

Daniel began to think that he might, after all, get better.

The wide, sweeping staircase took them up to Daniel's room, where they found him propped up in bed. Paddy's face went rigid with shock. It did not take much for Emily, too, to see that his father was not merely indisposed; here was a very sick man indeed. Against the pillows was a ghost of the handsome, gay and dashing fellow Aunt Lottie had remembered, a grey and gaunt wreck of a man, thin to the point of emaciation. 'Good to see you, my boy,' he whispered.

'And you, too, Father. What have you been up to this time?'

'Bad bout of jungle fever, that's all. Over now.'

Paddy stood stiffly by the bed, then bent and dropped a kiss on the haggard forehead. As he straightened, his eyes went to the bottles on the bedside table. Daniel managed a smile – or perhaps rictus might have been a more apt description. 'Won't find anything there but medicine.'

After a moment, Paddy murmured, 'Glad to hear it.'

The sick man turned his head. 'So this is Emily. Come here, Emily,' he croaked.

Ashamed of her reluctance, Emily slowly approached the death's head on the pillows. With astonishing strength, he caught her hand and held it so tight she thought her fingers might break. 'Think I'm going to like you, Emily. Young, but promising. You've nice, steady eyes. You'll be good to my boy, won't you? Better than I've been, eh?'

What sort of answer could one give to a question like that? 'I – I hope so.' With an effort, she was able to smile and not wrench her hand from that ghastly, fleshless clutch of dry bones. But he could not sustain the effort of holding on and presently let it drop.

Emily slept the heavy sleep of exhaustion that night, the supplicating hands of the beggar-children peopling her dreams, and when she opened her eyes she found Paddy was already awake, lying on his back, staring into the darkness that was lit by the dawn light coming faintly into the room, and further dimmed by the swathes of mosquito netting suspended above their bed.

She reached out and he let her take his hand, but there was no warm, answering pressure. Last night, after their talk with Doctor McLellan, he had not seemed able to accept the comfort she offered. She hoped for better things this morning, but he seemed as far away as ever.

It must be so hard for him. In England, the prospect of being with his father again had filled Paddy with a scarcely contained joy that had sustained him halfway across the world – only to be met with a situation like this.

'Doctor McLellan said the quinine he's been administering is doing its work,' she reminded him. 'Your father's going to get better.'

A mosquito zinged outside the netting that shrouded the bed. From somewhere beyond, in this never silent city, there came sounds – shouts, the distant, spine-chilling howl of a hyena, a temple bell tolling. Emily thought she caught, faintly, the strains of plaintive, twanging music. A bird woke to the day with a shriek.

Paddy said, 'Oh, he'll recover from the malaria, I have no doubt. For now.'

To Emily's inexperienced eye it had looked as though Daniel Fitzallan was not long for this world, but McLellan had briefed them on the illness that held Sir Daniel in its grip, its prognostications, its treatment. Malaria could, and regularly did, kill countless thousands here in India. This bout of Daniel's had been very serious, and although it would probably recur, he was on the way to recovery. *This* time, he had qualified, eyeing Paddy thoughtfully.

He said now, 'My father's dying, Emily. Not only of the malaria. He's dying of years of too much drink and there's no recovery from where he is. The doctor knows it, he knows it himself, and he knows that I know. He's tried to stop from time to time, but it never lasts. That was why we . . . why he sent me away, I think, why he came to India alone. He was ashamed to let me see.'

Day after day, cooped up in the steamy heat of the hotel, where Daniel, although slowly gaining strength, still kept largely to his room, Emily had looked anxiously for news from home. The letters she longed for should have followed them and been here by now – mail came regularly by the steamers which plied across the seas – but there was nothing. Her own letters had not been answered. It seemed to her she might well have sailed across the ocean and dropped off the edge of the world, for all anyone seemed to care at home. It didn't surprise her overmuch that Anthony hadn't written. He was no hand at letter writing, but why had Clare not done so? She had not troubled to hide the fact that she was angry and upset over this marriage, but she had in the end put her own feelings to one side and embraced Emily when they parted, saying that she prayed she would be happy, truly, and promising to write.

Emily was finding homesickness unexpectedly hard to bear, and she was made more unhappy by Paddy's lack of understanding, so absorbed in his own unhappiness. 'Oh, there'll be letters soon enough, plenty of time yet,' he said dismissively.

'It's not like them. They must know I'm longing to hear from them. They're my family, after all.'

'Your family,' he repeated, looking at her oddly. 'No, Emily, we're your family now, my father and I, aren't we? You'd better get used to that idea.'

'Well, of course you are, but so are they, still. I can't help worrying.'

He shrugged and looked sulky. 'What about me? My father's been so ill and all you care about is news from your precious family.'

'Paddy!'

'They don't always come first,' he went on petulantly, but then, seeing the hurt on her face, he pulled her into his arms, said he was sorry. He covered her face with kisses, patted her hair and then, since his father was sleeping, took himself off to the British Club where he had been accepted as a temporary member and where he could play polo to work off his frustrations. Emily was left alone so much that she thought about contacting Mrs Maybury, but when she had mentioned this Paddy had not been pleased, reminding her they would not be here long enough to form friendships.

There was no mention of any proposed move to the tea plantation – though of course there was no question of moving out of the hotel until Daniel was much better. The fever kept returning, intermittently, while outside, the rains which had begun in earnest, crashed down, making rivers of the roads and flooding great areas of the city. The humidity pressed down unbearably, like a lid. Emily had a headache that threatened to become permanent.

Day after day she sat in the hotel, rereading the books she had brought with her, writing her diary and yet more letters home, wondering how long they, too, would remain unanswered. And as she listened to the rain drumming on the roof, she tried to tell herself that it was worry over his father that was causing the change in Paddy.

When the longed-for letter eventually came, it wasn't from Clare, nor from Anthony. It was addressed to her in Hugh Markham's firm, clear handwriting. For a moment, she stared at it and then put it into her pocket, unopened. It was nearing sunset, when the world would be blotted out in an instant, but there was still light and a temporary respite in the rain. She took the letter out to read alone in a tiny, shady courtyard at the back of the hotel, where she would not be interrupted.

140

She turned the thick envelope over. *Hugh?* She slid her thumb under the flap and opened it.

The blood drained from her face as her eyes jumped from one phrase to another. Then she read it again, forcing herself to read more slowly. She knew now why it was Hugh who had written this.

The rapid darkness descended and still she sat on the edge of the pool in the centre of the courtyard. A bat, black and silent, swooped before her face, followed by another, huge by comparison with the pipistrelles that used to make their home in the Hecate tree, yet she didn't flinch. Night time had brought no amelioration of the steamy heat, and the little courtyard felt like the inside of a cauldron. The ceaseless noise of India went on around her. A sweeper somewhere outside the hotel cleared the paths with a scratchy broom, scritch, scritch. A Hecate tree so laden with purple blossoms that you could not see its leaves shaded the courtyard. Hecate? Of course not, how foolish. It was a jacaranda, so overwhelmingly laden with purple blossom that it looked artificial, unreal. It was not the Hecate tree. The garden out here wasn't Leysmorton. There were red and white lotus blossoms and water lilies, richly fragrant and with waxy petals and wide green leaves almost covering the surface of the little pool, but here in this hotel courtyard there were no roses.

Clare, Hugh wrote, had disappeared from Leysmorton, simply disappeared into thin air. She had left the house, saying only that she was going for a walk, and hadn't been seen since. Emily was grateful that Hugh had not attempted to hide anything, but had simply stated the facts. Clare

141

had gone, two days after Emily and Paddy sailed, without a word, taking nothing with her and leaving no clue as to when she would be back, if ever. There had been no quarrel, nothing to indicate that she had ever intended to do this. The police had been informed. A search had been made, the river dragged. There one moment, gone the next, as if someone had cast a spell over her and magicked her away, just as Miss Jennett had been magicked away.

Aunt Lottie had insisted Emily should not be worried with this temporary aberration of Clare's, for after all, she would have to come home sooner or later, or at least let them know where she was. But as time went by, when it became evident she was not going to come back, or not very soon, Anthony had asked Hugh to write. He was too upset to put pen to paper himself, too distraught; it would have been an impossible letter for him to write.

'I must go home.'

Paddy stared at her disbelievingly.

'*What?* Are you mad? All those weeks at sea? By which time your thoughtless sister will most probably have returned. Even supposing you could do anything to find her if she hasn't.'

She ignored that 'thoughtless', but her spirit did indeed quail at the thought of another journey like the last, all those endless weeks – which hadn't seemed endless then, but fascinating and coloured with new experiences, exhilarating perhaps because she and Paddy were together, and in love? – only to find, when she reached

142

England, that Clare had returned, with some simple explanation . . . That at least made sense, even though this situation didn't seem to have much to do with common sense.

She felt torn between two loyalties. She was a newly married woman in love with a husband who had already frightened her by showing himself capable of petty jealousies and sulks when it came to her family. On the other hand, her beloved father was coping with this situation alone.

'I *must* go, Paddy! Don't you understand? My father – he's alone, he needs me—'

'But *I* shall be alone if you go – and I am your husband, may I remind you. And *my* father needs me. Needs us both. You have other duties now, Emily, in case it has escaped your notice.'

The coldness in his voice was something she had never heard before and hoped not to hear again. I have been married barely a month and already I am quarrelling with my husband, she thought desolately.

'I *must* go home, for a while at least. I *will*.'

'And how do you propose to do this?'

A silence thick as dust lay on the room.

She stared, not understanding what he meant at first. Then she did. She could not travel without money, and when she married she had given up all rights to any money of her own. That was what the law said. It had been one of the reasons Clare had cited for never getting married. Emily was virtually penniless.

Wild thoughts raced through her mind. She would find the money for her fare home from somewhere. Borrow it – but from whom?

'What kind of wife wants to leave her husband after a few weeks?' Paddy demanded, grasping her wrist so that she winced and pulled away. Then just as suddenly as his rage had come on, it left him as he saw he had really hurt her. 'Oh, God, I'm sorry, I didn't mean to hurt you. It's just that things seem so bad here, and without you . . .' His eyes suddenly filled with tears, a lake of blue. 'Don't leave me, Emily! I don't deserve you, but I don't know what I'd do if you ever left me. I'll make it up to you for everything!'

She stayed silent for a long time. This was the man to whom she had made her vows before God. The man she was still determined to love. At last she said evenly, 'No, I shall never leave you, Paddy. Forget I ever spoke about going home. Things will be better when we get to the hills, to the plantation, where it's cooler.'

He looked at her for a moment without saying anything, and then he said, 'There is no tea plantation. My father lost it months ago.'

He had grasped her wrist so hard she had the bruises for weeks. He never touched her so roughly again, but ever afterwards, when the same sort of situation occurred – as it did, throughout their marriage – she looked at her wrist and remembered the livid bruises and knew that had been the time when she had put Emily Vavasour behind her forever.

Life with Paddy was not all sunshine, but you could not live with someone for nearly forty years without making the best of it.

144

Thirteen

Now

Not for the first time, Poppy and Xanthe Tripp were crossing swords over Poppy's proposals for the refurbishment of the library at Leysmorton. Mrs Tripp had ideas for a quick makeover that would bring everything up to the minute, banish the dreary, ponderous furniture of previous decades – too yesterday, my dear! – and replace it with contemporary pieces with sleek, uncluttered lines.

But even Poppy, modern as her own inclinations were, could see what a huge mistake that would be. She could appreciate that replicating the library's original, very expensive fabrics and wallpapers would mean going far beyond their usual reach, and that employing traditional craftsmen would be costly also, but the results would not jar the sense of what was right for a venerable old house, and for this Poppy was prepared to dig in her heels. Such schemes as Mrs Tripp envisaged were not even to be contemplated. More to the point, Emily was their customer, she pointed out, and would never agree. They would lose the order altogether – and the possibility of further recommendations – if they were not careful. She picked up the proposals, so scornfully dismissed by Mrs Tripp, which she had put together following her first visit to Leysmorton. 'Just take another *peep*, Xanthe . . .'

'We've already discussed ideas for these new chair covers, Marta and I,' Emily had said, generously including Marta in the decisions. 'But we can't make up our minds. We don't want to make the rest of the room look sorry for itself.'

'That can happen,' Poppy smiled. Quickly taking advantage, she added, 'So why not do it all, then? We – my partner and I – could see to it for you.'

The other two exchanged a look of alarm, obviously recalling reports they'd heard of the mirrors, lacquer and chrome in the London house Poppy and Xanthe had furnished for the newly-weds, Dee and Hamish. Poppy caught the look and smiled. 'Nothing drastic. I know you only wanted new covers – but maybe some fresh paint, and wallpaper?'

Emily was taken with the idea. 'You're right. Perhaps a little reupholstery, too.' The whole house was scuffed and fraying at the edges and, to be fair, that wasn't entirely due to its wartime occupation – probably hardly at all, in fact. Leysmorton had never been a grand house, just a family home, where familiarity had rendered its increasing wear and tear invisible to the inhabitants. It was obviously time to address the overdue problem. 'What do you think, Marta?'

'It will mean an upheaval. Dirk brings his work in here.' That was true. He came to work sometimes on the table by one of the big, low windows that overlooked the terrace and let in floods of light. 'He likes to look out over the garden.'

Emily sat on the edge of the sofa, her spine straight and her silver-streaked dark hair nicely cut, her country clothes impeccable, her feet shod in expensive leather. Poppy thought that if the reports of her rackety life had been true, it had left no traces on her composed face, or in her manner. 'But Dirk has a perfectly adequate study,' she was reminding Marta gently.

Marta lowered her eyes. 'Well of course, it's up to you.'

Poppy wondered why Emily didn't shake this irritating woman. But that was none of her business, so she jumped up to make a quick, darting tour of the room, assessing its potential. Fine old furniture, thankfully none of it the impossibly ponderous and overelaborate pieces of some earlier decades. Nothing here that a repolish wouldn't put new life into. She came to a halt at the portrait over the mantel that dominated the room: a woman, Lady Fitzallan's mother, without doubt – the same intelligent brown eyes, the thick dark hair, the curve of the lips – wearing something rose-coloured, and a rope of pearls. Her eyes narrowed as she looked from it to the lovely old Aubusson carpet. 'Nothing too feminine, not in this room, but not too masculine either. Some dark green, and some light, and maybe ruby or crimson. Light paint. How does that strike you?'

After a few moments' thought, Emily had smiled and said, 'Oh, yes, I think so. When can you start?'

And at that, Poppy, acknowledging that she might actually enjoy the prospect of planning something so different from their usual commissions, had allowed herself to think about commissioning the whole house.

She had said nothing of that idea to Xanthe on her return to London. Not yet . . .

'"This shop exists to promote modernism",' Xanthe reminded her sharply now, quoting from the advertising brochure they had put out when they started. 'Everyone has had enough of living in the past—'

'Not everyone. You and I, perhaps,' Poppy said, trying to be kind to Xanthe, who was forty-two if she was a day. 'But we do need clients of an older generation as well, if we're to keep going.' She flicked through the pages of her notebook to hide her irritation. Increasingly, she faced the sad truth that their small business venture was in crisis, and their relationship was not standing up to it. They were pulling in different directions.

She tried again. 'You haven't seen Leysmorton. It's a *centuries*' old house and the library is simply *beautiful*. It's ludicrous to think of—' She stopped herself, then added, making it worse, 'It's a question of taste.'

Her partner's pale, powdered cheeks took on a spot of colour. Her thin red mouth set into an even thinner line. The shop bell tinkled. She took a deep breath, smoothed down her skirt and her frown, pinned on a smile and went forward.

As the customer approached, Mrs Tripp's smile slipped. It wasn't unusual in these straitened times for men to be wearing clothes that had seen better days: pre-war Savile Row suits and Lobb hand-made boots that still said quality in every stitch, however well worn they were. But this man's navy blue serge suit had never seen Savile Row and said nothing except travelling salesman, or even – her heart plunged – debt-collector, a dun, one of those who had plagued her ex-husband throughout the exhausting, debt-ridden existence she had shared with him.

She gave him a frosty good morning and was not reassured when he showed her his warrant card and asked for her partner. Dripping icicles, she spoke over her shoulder. 'Miss Drummond. You have a visitor.'

A look of dismay, quickly veiled, crossed Poppy's face when he told her he was from Scotland Yard, and that his name was Novak, Detective Inspector Novak.

'I'm sure,' said Mrs Tripp, with a quick glance towards the window where a young couple appeared to be hesitating over the only exhibit, a rather beautiful, elongated ceramic black cat on a white tripod, standing on scrunched emerald velvet, 'your conversation would be more private in the office.'

As the shop bell went again and the couple entered, Poppy took Novak into a room at the rear of the premises, where a small desk, stacks of cardboard boxes and a drop-leaf shelf bearing a gas ring and the wherewithal for making tea didn't leave much room for anything but a couple of stools. The kettle was on a low light and she asked him if he would like a cup of tea.

'I wouldn't say no, Miss Drummond.'

He waited, perched on one of the stools, while she busied herself with the tea-making, her movements quick and impatient.

149

'I know why you're here, though not who sent you,' she said abruptly, turning and handing him his tea in a wide black and eau-de-nil patterned cup with sharply sloping sides and a large saucer. 'It's about Peter Sholto, isn't it?'

'So you've heard about that?'

'Yes – my brother told me. Valentine. He's working for Mr Stronglove at the moment.'

Ah, yes, the untidy young man at a desk in the corner of Stronglove's study, who had been waved a dismissal when Novak was shown in.

Smooth, affable, urbane, Stronglove had apparently decided to cooperate. 'Anything I can do to help, Inspector. Though I've told you, Peter Sholto and I only came into contact when he was working here. I'm a busy man and it didn't leave room for chat about his personal life. I believe he was friendly with the young Markhams, but you'll have to ask them about that.'

'You said before that your sister was fond of him? Maybe she could help.'

'Marta? Well, yes, she did take a shine to him, you might say. Poor, motherless boy and all that – but then, she wasn't alone. Most women seemed to find him attractive. Cigarette, Inspector? No?' He crossed the room, took one himself from a box on a low table and lit it. Turkish smoke filled the room. He performed each action smoothly and without hesitation. Close up, he could evidently see well enough, and in a room that was familiar he moved around easily.

'And Peter? Did he reciprocate?'

'Who can say? He didn't give much away. Agreeable enough young chap, but hard to get

150

beneath the surface.' He paused. 'A bit deep some-times, actually.'

'How long did he work for you?'

'Not long. Twelve months or so, I suppose, just before the war – until I moved to London, in fact. Nothing of a job for a young fellow like him, really.' He tapped ash into an onyx ashtray and added, 'To be honest, I felt it was time for us to part company, anyway.'

'He wasn't good at his job?'

'When he kept his mind on it, I found him useful.' He hesitated again. 'Good secretaries are hard to come by. It's not as easy as you might think, finding the right man.'

Novak had recently interviewed a businessman who had a *woman* secretary, but they were every-where now, women. They'd even infiltrated the police.

Stronglove said unexpectedly, 'These spectacles – I don't wear them as a decoration, you know. They say I'm going to need an operation, sooner or later. Not a pleasant prospect and I have to confess I'm funking it.'

'As anyone might, sir. I'm very sorry. The war?'

'No, not at all. My eyes weren't so good even before then, so being able to speak several languages, they made me a translator. Cushy number.'

This self-deprecation was not how Novak saw Stronglove. Working as a translator had been valuable and much-respected work in wartime, and he was in no doubt that this man would be well aware of his worth.

'I only mention the eye problem because I expect you're wondering why I need a secretary at all.

151

My manuscripts are a mess, I have to confess, so at the moment I need a man who can deal with the business of getting them ready to send out to my publisher – as well as proof-read and so on.'

'So why *did* you want to get rid of Sholto?'

'As I say, he was – satisfactory, shall we say – when he didn't have his mind on other things.'

'Such as?'

'Oh, nothing specific.' He hesitated. 'Apart from what I felt was a slightly unhealthy interest in the contents of this house.'

'You mean you thought him dishonest?'

'Pilfering the spoons? Lord, no. It was the old furniture that interested him, the craftsmanship and so on – or so he said – but frankly, I thought it a little sad that a young chap of his age should have nothing better to do. Interest is all very well, but he took it too far. I reckon he drew and made notes on every piece of furniture in the house.' Scorn underlined his words.

An unusual interest, Novak acknowledged, but – unhealthy? A budding connoisseur, perhaps. People who had a passion for things often began early; they said Mozart was composing piano concertos aged seven. Novak suspected a smoke screen: there were other, more cogent reasons for wanting to get rid of the boy.

'As it turned out, the decision was made for me when I decided to move to London,' Stronglove went on. 'When war broke out, I heard that Peter had volunteered for the army.' He paused. 'Well, I suppose everybody was a patriot then.'

It was at that point that the new secretary – young Drummond – had returned and Novak, sensing that was as far as he should go with Stronglove at that time, had left.

'It wasn't Val who sent you here, was it?' his sister said now.

'It was Mrs Erskine who told me where I would find you.'

'Mrs—?' She frowned, then gave a little laugh. 'Oh, yes, of course, you mean *Dee*. You've seen her.'

Indeed he had. Smart, blonde little Mrs Hamish Erskine in her modern bijou house just off Sloane Square, with her pretty pursed-up button of a mouth. A smiling, sugar-coated sweetie with a hard centre. She had been in a hurry to go out, all dressed up in summer silks and a daring little hat, fragrant and made up, a diamond on her finger the size of a walnut, taking meaningful looks at the diamanté watch on her wrist. He'd known straight away he'd get nothing from her, but she'd been on his list of those young people who had known Sholto – and she lived conveniently in London.

'Why did Dee send you to *me*?'

'She told me you knew Peter Sholto.'

She turned her head rather sharply. '*Did* she indeed? Well, she knew him better than I did, they lived in the same village, after all. I only met him when I spent school holidays at Steadings, with Dee and her family, when he made up a four for tennis.' She bent her head to take a sip of tea, but not before he had seen something resembling a sharp flicker of pain in her eyes. They were her best feature, her eyes, luminously grey-green with dark pupils, beautifully shaped,

153

thickly lashed and slanting slightly upwards under winged brows.

'The other three – that would be Mrs Erskine and yourself – and Mrs Erskine's sister?'

'No, not Rosie, she was only a little girl. It was me, Dee and her brother David, who was in the Royal Flying Corps in the war. He . . . wasn't one of those who came back.' Her bent head, as she took another sip of her tea, hid her expression. 'I'm very sorry Peter's dead. Especially like that. It's too shocking.'

'But not altogether surprising, Miss Drummond?'

She flushed. 'Did I make that so obvious? Well, to be *absolutely* truthful, I suppose I'm not entirely surprised he got into trouble – though not to that extent. He would *meddle* with things and . . . and I'm afraid he could be rather beastly at times, you know.'

'In what way?'

'Would you like some more tea, Inspector?'

He shook his head. 'No, thank you.' He'd had enough trouble holding the fashionably designed cup by the little triangular lump that was the handle to risk another, and besides, he had not been offered milk, and the lemon in the tea had made the inside of his mouth shrivel up.

'Perhaps I've said too much.'

'This isn't a time for discretion, Miss Drummond.'

'All the same, I shouldn't have spoken like that. Peter could be awfully charming, when he wanted to be. Most people liked him. He talked a frightful lot of rot sometimes, and he didn't like it if you didn't go along with what he wanted. But it was nothing really, nothing that really *meant* anything

154

. . . not now that he's dead, anyway.' There was a shine of tears in her eyes as she added, 'He didn't deserve to be killed.'

'Why do you think he deserted and came back to Leysmorton, Miss Drummond?'

'How should I know that? And as I said, Dee knew him better than I did.'

But Dee Erskine had said just the opposite. She had implied that Poppy Drummond knew Peter Sholto very well. And what might that have meant – *not now that he's dead*?

Fourteen

Jogging home peacefully along the village street, Rosie's morning ride was interrupted when from the direction of Kingsworth came the distant sound of a motor car. After the closure of the hospital at Leysmorton, a motor was once again an event in peaceful Netherley, interesting enough to cause two little boys to abandon their game of marbles and run to watch. A woman washing her windows turned to stare, and Rosie prudently reined Dandy in and turned him aside into Cat Lane.

She held him still as the open-topped motor approached the village at a great rate, but although the driver, whom Rosie recognized as Archie Elphinstone, the best man at Dee's wedding, slowed down considerably, he didn't stop. Poppy was in the passenger seat, a long voile scarf wound around her head and streaming out behind her, and when she saw Rosie, she leant out and waved. 'Sorry, can't stop, darling!' she called, and blew a kiss. 'On our way to Leysmorton.'

Rosie decided she wouldn't go over there then, not this morning. Lady F would be too absorbed in other matters to want her around – and besides, Rosie, who had once adored Poppy, wasn't sure that she liked the smart, brittle person she had become.

It was after the horrible death of her father that Poppy had been invited to spend holidays at

156

Steadings. Rosie, who had never before met this distant relative, who happened to be at the same school as Dee, had been afraid on that first visit that she would turn out to be a miserable creature, constantly in tears about her father and putting a damper on everything, but she turned out to be fun. She was very obliging and would even help Stella with her diary and correspondence, something no one else would do – Stella was lazy about answering letters and hopeless at fixing and remembering dates. Everyone liked Poppy. It had been a wonderful summer, until everything fell apart – until the Awful Thing with her mother had happened, and then the war, and dearest David going away to fight for his country and being killed. And though nowadays Poppy was very bright and amusing when you met her, she wasn't fun any more.

'What beautiful pearls!'

'Yes, lovely, aren't they?'

'I expect they're yours now,' Poppy went on speculatively.

Emily lifted her eyes from an inspection of the samples Poppy had brought and spoke to the men who were positioning stepladders to lift down her mother's portrait in its heavy gilt frame. 'You can take it down now. But please go carefully.'

She sank onto the old sofa, happy enough to just watch. There had been a lot to do in preparation for the redecoration of the library, even with these two men Hugh had insisted on sending round from Steadings to help with the heavy work: shifting weighty furniture, rolling the carpet, taking

157

down the moth-eaten tapestry curtains that weighed a ton-and-a-half and had descended to the floor releasing clouds of decades-old dust. The books, thank goodness, could be left as they were, in their glass-fronted cases, while the decorating went on.

There were hundreds of books – enough for the room to be called a library, covering two walls floor to ceiling as they did – and huge sagging chairs where you could curl up to read in front of the enormous stone fireplace, but it had never been just a library. It was more of a general living room, the place where people naturally gravitated – for teatime, or just to chat, for playing cards in the evenings, for gathering round the old walnut piano with its brass candle-sconces, where the girls had practised their scales and listened to Mama playing Chopin or the latest songs.

It must never be changed too much. It smelt of happiness still, of Mama's lily-of-the-valley scent, the resinous fragrance of Christmas fir needles, toast, Papa's roses in the summer, their scent floating in from the Rose Walk, or from where they were massed in big silver bowls on the tables. Of the lost days and years.

While Poppy darted about, leaving written instructions for the painters and making notes for herself, Emily kept her eye on the portrait as the men cautiously manoeuvred the frame down from where it had hung ever since it had been commissioned. It was said to be an act of courage to have oneself painted by G. H. Watts, who was not interested in surface prettiness or even beauty, was not merciful and would only paint people he liked – for a very large fee. Still, it was an acceptable, if not flattering, depiction of Leila. She wore no jewels, apart from the rope of pearls, their milky lustre glowing against the rose-coloured silk of the gown she wore. Emily found herself unable to take her eyes off them. *The pearls, yes*!

Marta stood by the doorway as the men manoeuvred through with their bulky burden. She looked flustered, not liking her routine to be disturbed. She had thought Hugh's offer to send men to help was unnecessary and her cooperation had been grudging. Now she began to follow Poppy around the room, adjusting dust covers, moving this and that.

Emily watched with half her mind still on the pearls. What had happened to them? It was suddenly an urgent question. They were a family heirloom, passed on to Clare as the eldest daughter when she became eighteen, but she had never had occasion – and certainly no wish – to wear them. The only jewellery Clare ever consented to wear was the tiny gold crucifix round her neck. Anthony had kept the pearls safe in a secret drawer in his desk. Yet there had been no mention of them in his will. Emily herself had forgotten their existence completely until Poppy's remarks a few minutes ago had forced them to her attention.

How could she not have remembered something so important? And what had become of them?

It was warm enough for an informal lunch on the terrace, the company including Val, as well as Poppy and Archie Elphinstone, the large, agreeable young man with a shock of blond hair and a rugby player's shoulders who had driven her down from London and then cheerfully pitched in to help. As it was Nellie Dobson's day off, Marta had seen to the lunch herself. Cold cuts of yesterday's mutton joint, boiled potatoes and beetroot were a disheartening experience, Marta's cooking skills stopping short at her jam and cordial-making, or a few cakes, but the meal was saved by a crisp fruit tart made the previous day by Mrs Dobson from redcurrants grown by Marta, which elicited approval from Archie, who availed himself of three slices.

He was an easy and amusing chap, and the conversation flowed. Poppy, though bright and animated, seemed a trifle less so than usual. When the subject of the murdered man found in the grounds was casually mentioned, she shuddered and said 'Please!' and the subject was dropped by mutual consent. A darkness had come into the lives of all of them with the death of Peter Sholto. It had touched them, whether they liked it or not. Everyone in Britain had grown familiar with death – the obscenity that had resulted in the eclipse of a whole generation of young men – but this was different, and no one wanted to think what it might mean.

Novak still couldn't think why he had been put on to this case. It was a double-edged sword: a feather in his cap if he solved it; a black mark if he didn't. It would have been nice to think somebody had their eye on him for promotion, but he thought it was more likely that no one else had been available. Though there could be no particular urgency associated with a case that

160

had lain undetected for so long, and he had other miscreants in plenty to occupy him, he had been left in no doubt that this investigation must not be allowed to stagnate through lack of drive and initiative on his part, which did much to stiffen his resolve to figure it out as fast as he could. Today, he had left Willard behind in London to follow up enquiries into anyone with whom Peter Sholto might have had connections in his army days, while he drove himself down to Netherley with the intention of speaking to Marta Heeren.

He wasn't looking forward to the meeting. His brief encounter with her had made him sure it would not be easy. So when he had found himself walking along the village street and passing the house belonging to Nellie Dobson, the woman who worked in the kitchen at Leysmorton, he'd decided to put her off a little while longer. In any case, he always preferred to employ the methods he usually found enlightening, going the back way first, getting impressions about the situation, in the long run as important as facts, from those who worked below stairs. As often as not, they knew more than their employers ever dreamt about what went on above.

He'd been given a mug of strong, sweet tea and a slice of fruit cake, and they were now sitting in the sun on a bench outside the door of one of the black-and-white timbered cottages with their cheerfully jumbled gardens clustered along the winding road that ran through Netherley – cottages which outsiders found so picturesque, while those who lived in them suffered from rheumatics, smoking chimneys and the necessity of sharing an outdoor convenience.

161

'Oh, she's all right, Miss Heeren is,' Mrs Dobson was saying. 'A bit touchy sometimes. Why do you ask?'

'Touchy about what?'

She stretched out her arm to push to and fro along the brick path a huge, ungainly perambulator containing the angry-faced, restless baby she was minding. 'You never know,' she said, leaning forward to adjust the child's rumpled covers. 'Like treading on eggs, sometimes. Fussy. She enjoyed being mistress at Leysmorton before the war, or as good as. Still does.'

'Was the house empty for long after the hospital closed?'

'Nigh on a couple of months. We had to see everything put back just as it was before she'd consent to move herself and her brother back, me and half a dozen more from the village. You know what some folks are like.'

She settled down for a gossip, a comfortably built, nice-looking woman with hair that might once have been red but was now an indeterminate sandy-grey.

'You don't like Miss Heeren?'

'Oh, I wouldn't say that! You speak as you find, and she's very good to me. Fond of kiddies, she is, doesn't mind if I take any of the little ones with me when I go to work along there. It's one way I can help my daughter out . . . that's my Ivy, worn out with four under six, God help her, *and* working half-time at Sankey's, poor duck.' She nodded in the direction of the sprawling shed further along the road, the only village industry, once a place where straw had been split before

162

being sent in bundles to the hat factories in Luton, Novak had learnt, now a pop-bottling factory. 'Not that *he'd* care.'

Sensing that a delinquent husband featured largely in this tale of woe, and that Mrs Dobson might be prepared to go on in the same vein for some time, Novak nodded sympathetically and quickly remarked, 'I expect things have changed at the house, now Lady Fitzallan's back?'

'Miss Emily? Well, I expect she'll be going back to that place of hers abroad – Madeira, isn't it? Leysmorton has unhappy memories for her. Seems to me she's never got over that business of her sister.'

'What business was that?'

'Oh, donkey's years back. I'd just left school and I was only an underhousemaid there, so I never knew much about it. Servants only know what they're told – or what they pick up. Miss Emily got married very young, not much more than a girl. It happened all of a nonce, the house was in an uproar, preparing for a wedding at such short notice – and not two days after, when we were looking to get over it, her older sister, Clare, disappeared. Neither hide nor hair of her ever seen after that! We reckoned she must have been kidnapped and murdered, but they never found out. It upset the master, Mr Vavasour, I can tell you. Never the same after that, both daughters gone, and Miss Emily living abroad and never coming back till now. I reckon it was a good thing his sister and her children came to live with him. It's not good for a man to be on his own.'

'Those children would be Mr Stronglove and Miss Heeren?'

'That's right.'

'I'm told Peter Sholto was a favourite of Miss Heeren.'

A guarded expression crossed her face. She rocked the pram harder. 'Like I said, she likes children.'

'He was hardly a child.'

'He was when she first knew him, when he and his dad came from St Albans – and I reckon he always seemed like one to her, as they do. Fairly doted on him, in fact.' She added reflectively, 'I'm sorry about Peter – that it had to end that way. He was a lovely kiddie, a real charmer.' The baby, waving angry fists, suddenly began to howl. 'There then, lovey, there there,' she soothed, plugging its mouth with a dummy. 'Well, he still was, when he grew up – when he wanted to be. He could say he was sorry with a smile that could whistle the birds off the trees.' She smiled herself. Marta Heeren hadn't been the only one who'd been charmed.

'And what did Peter think of Miss Heeren?'

She considered that for a moment. 'You know, I don't reckon anybody ever really knew what Peter was thinking.' Which pretty much confirmed what Poppy Drummond had said of him, and Stronglove, too. 'But he was nice to her, I'll give him that.'

'And Mr Stronglove? He's never married?'

'Not he! I reckon his sister looks after him too well.'

'Hardly the same as a wife – but maybe he's not interested in marriage?'

Her face averted, she stared out across the

164

cabbages and dahlias, the bean sticks and the hollyhocks. A bee from one of the hives at the end of the garden droned past. She either did not know what might be implied by that, or didn't want to acknowledge that she did. Novak in fact knew by now that Stronglove had been a colourful and sought-after figure on the pre-war social scene in London, something of a literary lion, with his name linked to several women in the more salacious gossip columns.

'Well, maybe he isn't interested, maybe he is,' she said at last. 'But we can't all have what we want, can we?'

'They went to live in London before the war because it was more convenient for his literary connections. Why do you think he came back afterwards?'

She looked sideways at him. For a moment he thought she might be going to tell him something he wanted to hear. Then she shrugged. 'Well, you can't have missed noticing that he's having trouble with his eyesight.' He didn't think that was what she had intended to say. He also thought she didn't like Stronglove much.

'It's pretty bad, I gather.'

'She wants him to go into hospital for an operation, his sister does. I don't blame him for not wanting to. You never know whether you'll come out of them places or not.'

'My sentiments entirely.'

The baby had spit out its dummy and its cries for attention were fast becoming a roar. 'I reckon he needs changing, don't you, lovey? Come to your nan, then.' She plucked the squalling child,

165

hot and red, from the nest of tangled blankets and rocked him. 'If you want to carry on talking, Inspector, you'll have to come inside with me while I see to him.'

'That won't be necessary,' Novak said hastily. 'You've been very helpful, thank you, Mrs Dobson.'

She gave him a long look. 'If I've said too much, I'm sorry for it. We were always told in no uncertain terms when we went to work for the gentry that you kept your mouth shut about what you saw, whatever they did – and believe me, what they got up to, some of 'em, it'd make your hair curl! – or you could say goodbye to your job, without a reference . . . but I can't get over that poor boy.'

He waited for what else she might be about to say, but she put the baby to her shoulder and went indoors.

He walked down the village street, thinking over the conversation. Nellie Dobson knew more about Stronglove than she had been willing to divulge, and he had to wonder why. Did she know why he had been unwilling to dismiss Peter? Sholto had apparently not been the ideal secretary, yet Novak did not think Stronglove at all the man to have baulked at dismissing him. In fact, he had openly said he had toyed with the idea. But he had kept him on.

It also seemed there was a question hanging over Stronglove's decision to return to Leysmorton to live. It was true that his failing sight could have provided a good reason – or excuse – for quitting the London scene and burying himself out here, but intuition told Novak that was unlikely to be the case.

Fifteen

At Steadings, they had finished lunch on the terrace. Poppy, finally satisfied that she had left instructions that could not possibly be misinterpreted by the decorators, looked at her watch and gave a little scream. 'Heavens, the time! Darlings, I must *scoot*.'

'Always rushing about, nowadays,' Hugh grumbled, but he smiled at her. He'd always had a soft spot for Poppy, had once hoped she might become a granddaughter-in-law. He would have liked her even better had she allowed herself to be still for a minute. Her youth and energy made him feel like an old buffer, but he admired the way she was trying to make something of her life – she and that brother of hers, whom Rosie seemed so taken with. He looked across the table at Val and saw something he'd learned to recognize with the years: honesty, and a steadfastness of purpose that time would prove. Rosie could do worse. But his glance as it passed on to his granddaughter was worried. Had her mother not noticed anything amiss with her lately? Nothing outward – she looked just as blooming with health as ever – but to Hugh, it was obvious something was troubling her. She was listless and seemed far away. He told himself it was merely being in love for the first time that had taken hold of her; something that could afflict anyone, no matter what one's age, he reflected with a grim humour. But he hoped she was not still having nightmares about finding the remains of Peter Sholto.

At last Emily, who had been on tenterhooks all through lunch, was free to escape upstairs.

Reaching the landing, she turned in the opposite direction to her own room and carried on beyond the turn of the corridor, then several steps down, until she stood outside the small room tucked in halfway between flights.

Since her arrival back at Leysmorton, she hadn't been able to bring herself to set foot across the threshold of this place that Clare had insisted on calling her studio, feeling an almost superstitious aversion to opening the door and stepping back into the past. What sleeping devils might she disturb? But now she didn't hesitate for a second before pushing open the door.

It seemed the studio had rarely been entered since Clare had last closed the door behind her. It held the musty closeness of an unaired room, one which faced north so that it never got much sun, though a sizeable oriel window provided the reflected light Clare had claimed was necessary for her work.

Her painting things still stood in the bay formed by the oriel – the empty easel, a trestle table holding a jumble of boxes of paints and jars of brushes, a pile of cleaning rags – otherwise the room was tidy. It must have been cleaned from time to time, though not recently. Emily could detect a thin layer of dust on the floorboards and, when she approached it, on the cleared surface of the low oak chest of drawers – an *objet trouvé* reclaimed as a sort of desk by Clare from amongst that jumble of despised pieces despatched to the attics. She pulled up the only chair in the room and at once began to open the large drawers, still stuffed with work Clare had left behind. Two drawers held a dozen or so of her art school books filled with thumbnail sketches and anatomical drawings in charcoal, pen-and-ink or pencil, and there were more on mere scraps of paper, plus a few watercolours and small oils on canvas. Clearly that orgy of destruction Clare had embarked on when she abandoned the Slade had been halted before she had destroyed her entire output of work.

Someone, at sometime, had removed all Clare's personal belongings from the drawers and cupboards of the room she and Emily had once shared, and where Emily now slept, and it was in the bottom drawer that she came across what she had hoped, but scarcely dared to believe she might find. From amongst more assorted drawings she lifted the cream morocco leather jewel case, velvet-lined in scarlet, twin to the one she herself still owned. Presents from Aunt Lottie. On the lid were Clare's initials, elaborately stamped in gold. Inside were the bits of jewellery she had owned as a child, achingly familiar . . . the little turquoise ring, the corals, the carved ivory bracelet and her silver christening locket.

The pearls were not there. Emily had not expected they would be.

Wild theories had been put forward at the time of Clare's disappearance: she had been taken by force, kidnapped, and would be held to ransom; she had met with an accident, or even been murdered. But no demand for money for her release had been received, neither she nor her body had ever been found, and the theories had been gradually abandoned. Difficult as it was to accept, it had become all too apparent that Clare had left of her own accord – though reason still demanded to know why, or how.

Why had she not taken anything with her, only the clothes she stood up in? How had she left the village without any obvious means of getting away, other than her own two feet? Presumably she had walked the seven miles to Kingsworth – a distance that wouldn't have presented any insuperable difficulty to a fit young woman like Clare – but after that, what would she have done without the means to support herself? She had never had any money of her own except her monthly dress allowance from their father, which quite often, uninterested as she was in clothes, she had left untouched. The money left in trust by their mother, for when she married or reached the age of twenty-one, had never been claimed.

What had been so dreadful about her life – her family, and everything else that implied – that she had felt compelled to renounce it so completely?

The bitter, unanswered questions, as unresolved now as they were then, tumbled about in Emily's mind, but the missing pearls went some way at least to providing the answer to the question of money, and why they had never been passed on to Emily when Anthony died, as might have been expected. Was it possible he had never noticed they were missing – or even forgotten their existence?

Well, she herself had forgotten them, hadn't she? And it was quite possible that Anthony had never had cause to open that hidden drawer, especially if nothing else was kept in there.

Clare, then, must have taken them when she left. Not fabulously expensive, the pearls were still valuable enough to have supported her for an appreciable time. The mechanism for opening the 'secret' drawer was no secret within the family – and they were, after all, her own property, to sell for money to start her in the new life she had chosen for herself.

Chosen.

She had not been kidnapped, murdered or met with an accident. Emily had come to know that – and not only by inner conviction. She had known for certain that somewhere, Clare was alive.

The birthday cards had arrived every year: shiny, deckle-edged postcards, elaborately bordered, a picture of the romantically dark, velvety red roses of the kind Emily had loved, inserted into an envelope and sent to wherever she had been in the world.

Apart from the printed greetings on the front, there had never been any message. The backs of the cards were always blank, but Emily knew without any shadow of doubt they had come from Clare. Posted in London, that great city where anyone could become anonymous if they so wished, the envelopes had been typewritten. Emily had never known whether they filled her with hope, because Clare must certainly be alive, and still cared enough to remember her birthday, or with despair and frustration because they were

171

no help in leading her to where she was. She had known Clare had to be dead when they ceased.

'I must write and tell Father!' she had cried, running to Paddy, when the first card arrived.

'How do you know it's from Clare? More likely you have some secret admirer.'

She ignored his attempt to turn it into a cheap joke, another dismissal of anything to do with her family as of little interest. Even something as shattering as this. The tactic was not new, she had grown used to it, but it still hurt. 'I know it's from Clare. He should be told, Paddy, told that she isn't dead.'

He was annoyed with her persistence. 'If she isn't, she patently doesn't want anyone to find her.'

This at least was undeniably true – the anonymity of the envelopes, the lack of any message proved that – but at least Clare had wanted her to know that she was still alive. Ignoring Paddy's disapproval, Emily *had* written to her father.

He, too, had seemed curiously unmoved by her excitement, and she was bewildered by his cold reply. 'If Clare chooses to cut herself off from her family, then that is her loss.' Clare had always been his favourite, but he would never let anyone see how much her continuing silence had hurt him.

How had Clare known where to send the cards? It was certainly not Anthony who had kept her abreast of Emily's moves. She had always suspected it must have been their aunt who had done so, although right up to her own death she had refused to admit to any such thing, or even to discuss the matter – and why, indeed, should

172

Lottie have helped Clare, the niece of whom she had always disapproved?

In the end, Emily had been forced to accept the heartbreaking fact that she was powerless to do anything to unravel the old mystery. And when the birthday cards ceased, and she knew Clare must be dead, and really lost to her forever, she realized that even that was easier to bear than believing her still alive but cruelly not wanting to have anything to do with her grieving family, and with the mystery of her disappearance left unexplained.

Now, with an effort of will she put those thoughts behind her and addressed herself to the contents of the drawers. She braced herself and began a half-hearted attempt at the task of sorting methodically, at the same time searching for something she liked and could keep. She found a few watercolours that she thought she would have framed.

At last she was left with only one pile, and after staring at it for a while, she pushed back her chair and walked to the window-seat, knelt on it and pushed at the window to open it. It was stuck, but eventually it moved and she leaned out, taking calming breaths.

This was the view which had been so familiar to Clare, across to Netherley and its Norman church, the bottling factory and the red-brick convent on the outskirts, with the beech woods and the rising line of the chalk hills in the distance. Oddly enough, it was perhaps one of the only windows in the house from which one could not see the old yew.

She refused to believe anyone could become

possessed by a tree. Yet the stack of drawings on the desk behind her disputed this. Dozens, maybe scores of depictions of the Hecate tree, in one form or another: twisted or writhing, deformed or upright, sinister in aspect or benign and beautiful. And one disturbing drawing, finely drawn in pen-and-ink, of the goddess Hecate herself, standing at a crossroads, tall and grave, holding her two hounds on a leash with one hand, the other holding aloft the torch that would light the way of travellers through the Otherworld.

Eventually, Emily forced herself back to the desk and shuffled the drawings together, ready to stuff them out of sight. One had floated to the floor. Bending to pick it up, she saw it was a single sheet folded into four, not another drawing at all, but a letter written on onionskin paper that crackled when she opened it to reveal a spiky foreign handwriting in faded ink. Written in French, the only address was *Grenoble*. It began, simply: *Ma chère Clare*, and it was signed, *Amicalement, Christian*.

Christian. There had only ever been one Christian – that young French tutor who had been with them for a short while that long ago summer, the one who had inspired Clare to take up art. Emily could not, after all this time, clearly put a face to the name, but she remembered he had left to continue his studies and they had never heard from him again.

She had never heard from him again.

It was, however, apparent that Clare at least had been writing to him: Emily's French was not at all good, but the beginning of the letter made it clear it was part of a continuing dialogue. It

174

was dated after she had left the Slade, before Emily's marriage, not more than a week or two before Clare had done her disappearing act. For a moment, Emily sat, stunned, before attempting to read on, only to find it was making no immediate sense. She needed pen and paper to sort it out. There was no pen, and the ink in the inkwell that stood on the desk had dried up decades ago, but she rummaged in the top drawer and found a pencil and an India rubber. It didn't take her long to realize she was going to need more than pencil and eraser. She needed a dictionary – more probably, a translator.

Novak left the official motor in the yard of the Drum and Monkey while he went to make his call on Marta Heeren. After his talk with Mrs Dobson, it seemed to him that for all the awkwardness he envisaged, a visit to her would not be wasted. In fact, it seemed possible she might be more enlightening on the subject of Peter Sholto than anyone else he had yet spoken to, and that included Peter's own father.

That last thought, when he found himself passing the place where Edmund Sholto lived, one of two small, identical cottages just outside the gates of Steadings, made him hesitate, then change his plan again. He hadn't seen Sholto since the day he'd had to inform him that his son had been murdered. The man had not then been in a state to be subjected to rigorous questioning, and in any case in his experience parents were often the least likely to know what their offspring were up to.

175

Sholto himself opened the door. Not yet fifty, maybe younger, with prematurely white hair and a scholarly stoop to his shoulders. There was a touch of frailty about him, too, and the elderly-before-his-time impression was accentuated by the baggy cardigan and leather slippers he wore. The eyes that regarded Novak as he greeted him, however, were bright and intelligent. 'Inspector Novak. Please come in.'

He seemed to have recovered somewhat from the baffled incomprehension with which he'd received the news of his son's murder. 'You have some news?' he asked at once.

Novak shook his head, and saw the expectation leave Sholto's face as he turned away in resignation. It would have been better to wait and see the man when he had something to report. Then he remembered Sholto had promised to look for photographs of his son. 'Did you find any photos, Mr Sholto?'

'A few snaps, though I doubt if they'll be any use. Faded by now.' It had been a routine request, and Novak wasn't sure that photographs, faded or not, would help, but Sholto offered to get them. He seemed glad of something to do. 'They're upstairs. Make yourself comfortable meanwhile.' He indicated a chair.

It was a dark cottage, and this room was very small. The furniture was nondescript, apart from a small walnut table and a low chest, both of them beautifully and elaborately inlaid, but the old leather armchairs were deep and comfortable, as Novak found when he sat down, the stuffing escaping from cracks on the arms. In pride of place

176

on the mantelpiece was a sepia photograph of a pretty dark-haired woman in a light dress, a long rope of pearl beads round her neck. There were several pictures displayed, but most of the wall space was occupied with books – so many, it seemed as though Sholto must have brought his entire stock here when he sold up.

Sholto came back as he was examining the paintings. 'They remind me of home.'

Home had evidently been by the sea. Novak wondered if Sholto himself had painted them, a pleasant group of oils, almost certainly amateur efforts. His interested gaze rested on harbour views and fishing boats, angry seas and sunsets; there was one of a lifeboat being hauled in and another of fishermen mending their nets, one of women waiting, shielding their eyes and looking out to the horizon.

'Cornwall,' Sholto said. 'I like looking at them, though I suspect no one would place a high value on any of them. I know a good deal less about painting than I know about books.' He handed Novak several blurred snapshots and a framed charcoal drawing. 'These are all I have of Peter, I'm afraid.'

He crossed to the sideboard and held up a bottle. 'Scotch?' Novak waved a declining hand. He had work to do and it was three o'clock in the afternoon. Sholto looked at the bottle as if he'd surprised himself, and put it back. 'I used to be a schoolmaster,' he said, settling into his chair as Novak examined first the photos, then the drawing, 'teaching young children, which I found very rewarding. I had a notion that in their tenth year,

177

children are more receptive and eager to learn than at any other time. This is Peter at that same age. An old artist friend did it, the same chap who did those paintings.' He waved a hand towards the walls and smiled slightly. 'He was better with human subjects. This might give you more idea than the snaps. They won't be any use, will they?'

Nor will this, Novak thought, as he accepted the portrait from Sholto, appealing as it was, a head and shoulders of the child Peter. He had been a beautiful boy, certainly, with close dark curls, high cheekbones and a winning smile. The artist, however amateur, had captured an eager look of bright anticipation. Someone should have told him to stick to portraits.

'We really need something later. I'll keep the snaps for the moment, though. If you come across anything else I'd be glad to have it.' He handed the portrait back. 'You're a long way from home, Mr Sholto. What brought you to these parts?'

Sholto contemplated the empty grate. 'My wife died and the place where we'd been so happy was suddenly too much. Too many memories . . . I wanted a complete change and I became a bookseller. I'd collected books for years, old books, though nothing terribly valuable, as and when I could afford them. I heard that a man I'd bought from was selling his business and I scraped up the cash and bought it.'

'St Albans, wasn't it?'

'Not my best move.'

'We all make mistakes.'

'A disastrous one in my case,' he said ruefully. 'It put me in Queer Street, no doubt about it. If it hadn't been for Hugh Markham, we'd have been left with nowhere to live, Peter and I. Hugh often came into the shop to buy books, and we struck up a friendship. He offered me this cottage, and occasional work for the Markham Press, as a publisher's reader. Which means I've just about enough to exist on, if I'm careful.' After a moment he added, 'I'm not an entirely well man – poor heart, you know – and I've been advised to take things easy. So the pace of life here has suited me.'

Novak said, 'I'm afraid I have to ask you some questions that might be painful, about Peter. We're going to have to dig into his personal life as deeply as we can.'

Sholto didn't reply at once. 'Your sergeant searched his room and found nothing,' he said at last.

'That's true.' Novak had glanced round the small bedroom that Peter had occupied before leaving Willard to it. Nothing would have escaped the sergeant, and the search had indeed been unproductive, though as Novak recalled, it had hardly been an onerous task. A bed, a chair and a small chest of drawers was all the furniture the room contained. An alcove with a curtain suspended from a high shelf across it had formed his wardrobe: two suits and an overcoat, and in the drawers just the usual – shirts, socks and underwear.

No tennis racquets, cricket bats, school trophies or photographs, other boyhood paraphernalia. No books – though there were enough of them downstairs. Neat, tidy and anonymous, not the usual room of a boy or a young man. A room where he slept, and no more, revealing nothing of himself.

'Tell me about his friends, Mr Sholto.'

179

'Friends? Well, there were boys he'd been at school with and so on, but no one special, apart from the Markham boy, David. They were on very good terms. In fact Peter was somewhat lost when the war came and David joined the RFC. It was hardly a surprise when Peter himself volunteered.' He patted his pockets, looking for a pipe, which he brought out but didn't attempt to light. He sat with the bowl in his hand, looking at it for some time without speaking. 'They were hardly more than boys, didn't know what they were letting themselves in for,' he said sadly. 'But then, did anyone? And I suppose it came at the right time for Peter, he was at a loose end after Dirk Stronglove had gone off to live in London and left him without a position.'

'Had Mr Stronglove dismissed him?'

Sholto reddened. 'Not in so many words. But I think the London move was a good excuse. I somehow think they were not actually getting on very well.'

'Why was that?'

'I'm not sure. He used to shrug and say it was a job, and I couldn't get much more out of him than that.' After a moment he added, 'To be truthful, Peter couldn't settle on what he wanted to do with his life. He'd tried his hand at various things but nothing seemed to work. Nothing I suggested filled him with any enthusiasm and that caused a few father and son arguments, as you might expect – unresolved, I'm afraid, as they usually are.' He smiled slightly, but Novak thought that despite his diffident manner, Edmund Sholto might have been a formidable opponent

180

in an argument. 'Then Marta Heeren persuaded him to work for her brother. She . . . always took a kindly interest in Peter.'

Novak wondered if her interest had lain only in Peter's direction. A widower like Edmund Sholto might well present an attractive prospect to an unmarried woman like Marta Heeren. But he saw his mistake as Sholto went on quickly, his mouth turned down, 'Too much maybe, she encouraged the wrong ideas in him.' He didn't say what these were.

'Working for Stronglove – was Peter himself interested in writing?'

'Good heavens, no – that sort of thing wasn't Peter!' He paused. 'Although you know, I did once wonder . . . He had some old notebooks he was always scribbling in, he was very secretive about them, wouldn't show them to me and said they were nothing but doodles when I asked. I haven't found them anywhere so I expect he destroyed them when he joined up.' All at once he came to a decision and stood up. 'Come with me, Inspector.'

Novak followed him out of the back door and down a brick path, through a surprisingly spruce garden. As in other Netherley gardens, sunflowers and pinks flourished among the cabbages and bean sticks, but the rows of vegetables were neat, and there was an arch with a Dorothy Perkins clambering over it. Beside the door a huge patch of rhubarb grew rampant.

He followed the older man to a large shed. Garden implements were stacked just inside the door, but this was no potting shed. Most of the space was occupied with woodworking equipment: a sawbench and saws, chisels and other tools neatly lined up in a rack, a small lathe, and stacks of new wood leaning against the walls. 'This was my son's main interest. I'm not handy – gardening, yes, nothing else. But Peter – this was his forte. The little table and chest you maybe noticed in the house—'

'They're very professional – and you say they were Peter's work?'

'Give him a piece of wood and he could do anything with it. That was the talent he'd been given, that he should have been using, but I'm afraid he regarded the idea of making a living using his hands as rather infra dig.' He shook his head. 'Such a waste. The boy had so much to offer. If only . . .'

The saddest two words in the English language, it often seemed to Novak, hung on the air. Fleetingly, the thought of his own two children passed through his mind, little Evie, and Oliver, whose highest ambition at the moment was to be an inventor or, God help him, a detective like his father. How would he feel if they grew up to disappoint him, didn't take the chances life offered?

'Perhaps he'd have come round to it,' Sholto said. 'His interest came from my father – it was his hobby, too, and Peter had his tools.' He frowned. 'Actually, I don't know what's happened to them. I'll have to scout around. I wouldn't want to lose sight of them.'

'He took a great interest in the old furniture at Leysmorton House, I'm told.'

'Did he? I didn't know that – but he would, wouldn't he?' He considered for a moment. 'I never thought to show your sergeant this shed

182

when he looked at Peter's things. He might have found this if he had.' He turned to one side and extracted something wrapped in sacking from behind a leaning stack of wood and placed it on the bench. 'Go ahead!' Pushing his hands into the pockets of his woolly cardigan, he stood back to let Novak unwrap the covering.

The box underneath was about twelve by six, five or six inches deep, with a small, ornate brass keyhole. It was handsomely polished, its lid inlaid with 'oysters' of richly whorled, blond-edged, chocolate-brown wood. 'It's laburnum,' Sholto said, reaching out to smooth its soft patina. 'The dark is the heartwood and that yellow round the outside is the sapwood. It took him weeks to make.'

'It's quite remarkable.' It was more than that, Novak thought, a thing of beauty, like the little table and chest.

'Yes.' Sholto stood looking down at it. 'I rarely went into Peter's room. I'd no reason to, and no one else does. I look after the house myself, there's not much to it, and Mrs Baxter next door takes pity on me and does my washing, cooks the occasional meal. It was only after you told me that the body you'd found was Peter's that I went into his room, and that was when I noticed this box was missing from the chest of drawers where it usually stood. Unless the house had been broken into and the box stolen when I was not here – which I'd never had any reason to suspect – only one person could have removed it and that was Peter himself. So I came out here to look for it – the only other place I could think of where it might be – and found it hidden behind that timber. I think,' he said slowly, 'you should take a look inside. It's open – I forced the lock.' Novak gave him a sharp glance as he raised the lid and stood back.

Inside, the box was crammed with fat brown paper envelopes, unsealed but encircled with rubber bands, and in each was a bundle of crisp white five-pound banknotes, printed in black. Novak made a quick calculation. At a rough estimate, the lot probably amounted to something not all that far off his own annual salary, he thought, stunned. He closed the lid and saw Sholto's eyes on him. 'Any ideas about where all this might have come from?'

'I've done nothing but ask myself that since I found it. It has me baffled.' His eyes looked tormented.

When you turned up stones, ugly things crawled from beneath. And blackmail was an ugly word. This man was intelligent enough to know that his son's murder had not been a motiveless, random affair – and that this amount of money, one way or another, represented as good a reason for it as any. How else could a young man like Peter have obtained such an amount? Novak looked again at the notes in their separate envelopes. Regular payments. Realistically, it was the only answer – and Edmund Sholto had known this, too, and must have realized how it would reflect discreditably upon Peter. He could have kept his mouth shut about finding it, yet he had not. Novak wondered how many other fathers would have done the same.

'I think this might have been what he came back for that night,' Sholto said.

184

Novak thought so too. But in that case, why had he gone to Leysmorton, rather than here?

'I never saw him after the war ended, you know. He was expecting his release any day, and I was actually writing my weekly letter to him when I heard footsteps on the path. I jumped up, thinking it was him, home at last, but it was the Redcaps looking for him.' He bowed his head, then raised it and looked Novak in the eye. 'Find his killer, Inspector. It might be a long haul, I realize that. I don't expect miracles – but whatever Peter did that he was killed for, find who did it.'

Novak clasped his shoulder. It wasn't the first time he'd been asked that and he'd always found it impossible to answer.

As a motive, it was as good as any. But who was being blackmailed?

Novak thought of the edginess Stronglove had shown about Peter, and his mind flew back to that first meeting in the library at Leysmorton. He saw again a slim hand fingering an expensive enamelled cigarette case, looks exchanged. Was he correct in assuming a guilty connection between Dirk Stronglove and Stella Markham, and that Peter had made use of it? His instinct told him yes. But would Stronglove – or Stronglove and Stella together – have been willing, or indeed able, to part with such an amount of cash to keep it secret? That might depend on what damage Peter could have done with such knowledge.

Stronglove was a known ladies' man, so would another affair with a married woman bother him too much? It was more likely Stella Markham

185

who would have borne the brunt of such a disclosure. She was in a comfortable niche here, she obviously liked the good things in life, like her daughter – not Rosie, the other one – and he'd be prepared to bet she wouldn't be in a hurry to give any of it up. But would Stronglove have been honourable enough to stump up to protect her, to avoid their affair becoming public knowledge? In fact, how far would she – would either of them – go to save her marriage? To the point of actual murder?

Yes, he thought immediately and unfairly. Stronglove would, if something stood in his way. He knew he was not being objective enough, but his antennae quivered whenever the man's name came up.

But . . . and here he stumbled on the physical aspects of it. Stronglove was a half-blind man – and in any case had not been living at Leysmorton at the time Peter deserted. And a woman built like Stella Markham? Another aspect occurred to him: Stronglove was published by the Peregrine Press. It would hardly have done his standing as one of their authors much good if there were suspicions of him being involved with the wife of Gerald Markham, whom Novak hadn't yet met.

Sixteen

It was one of those melancholic, end of summer days, cool and grey, very still, the sky flat and colourless, when everything seemed sharply etched and defined, hard-edged against the light. From where she sat, in Hugh's room at Steadings, Emily could see along the length of the smoothly manicured lawn, a swathe of velvet down to where a maple at the end glowed as if on fire, its leaves already turned a deep, rich red. Fallen leaves scattered the lawn too, and in the regimented flower-beds nearer the house a gardener worked, tossing into a barrow the summer bedding that had gone over.

She sat to one side of Hugh's desk, sipping coffee while he put aside the letters he'd been writing and began to leaf through the drawings she had brought over. 'Take a look at these, will you, Hugh?' she'd asked as she handed him the large envelope. 'See what you think.'

While he gave them his usual careful consideration, she picked up her cup and walked to the window. Beyond the limits of the garden, far off in the Leysmorton grounds, a figure could just about be discerned: Marta, in her green cardigan, stomping purposefully down a path, busy with her own concerns. Absently she watched the gardener at his task, and was suddenly transported to another garden, fifteen hundred miles away.

187

'Well,' said Hugh at last.

'Mm, yes,' she mused as she went back to her seat by the desk. 'The agapanthus will still be out.'

'The what?'

'Sorry, Hugh.' She was embarrassed to realize she'd spoken aloud. 'The African lilies. In Madeira. I was thinking about them. They grow wild, by the side of the road, an absolute sea of blue and white. Hydrangeas as well. But anything grows in Madeira.'

Madeira, that small, temperate island of volcanic lava rising from the sea, where her home, the Quinta Miranda, stood, reached only by the road that curled upwards in a succession of hairpin bends, twisting at what appeared to be an almost vertical gradient, with dizzy-making drops to the crashing sea on one side, on the other a series of thickly forested peaks, split with deeply cut ravines. A church with an odd, onion-shaped dome and, clinging to the slope, occasional houses and villas, Portuguese style, softly colour-washed with red-tiled roofs and stepped gardens. Every kind of creeper spilling over walls, roofs and terraces in almost indecent profusion, a rainbow spectrum of scarlet, purple and yellow. Her own garden ablaze with purple bougainvillea, morning glory, feathery palms and a bright stream of falling water above a pool. There, at last, she had found a garden other than Leysmorton that she could love.

Hugh was looking at her with an expression she couldn't fathom. 'Is that the answer I've been waiting for? You've decided to go back then?'

'No . . . well, I'm not sure, Hugh.' And really,

188

she wasn't sure, not at all. For a moment back there, experiencing an astonishing pang of something like homesickness for her island home, she had felt an alien here, a stranger in her own land. More than half a lifetime she had spent longing to be back at Leysmorton, and now that she was, she felt out of place, on edge. The idea upset her . . . she did not want to think she could have become infected by Paddy's wanderlust. She knew, though, that it was far more than that which was unsettling her.

'If – if I did go back . . . would you . . .' She took a breath. 'Would you consider going back with me, Hugh?'

'Ah.' A huge warmth spread through him, as if he'd been offered brandy and had drunk it unwisely, all in one gulp. But he pulled himself up, and as he looked at her troubled face, he added gently, 'The world is a wonderful place, Emily, but there is only one home.'

'It was only a suggestion,' she said, looking down at her hands.

'Yes, my dear, I know that.' He folded his spectacles. 'But it's something that needs thinking about – for both of us.'

'Of course. I don't see there's any rush,' she replied, too quickly, because she had expected a different response. 'And you're right. I do need to think about it myself. Meanwhile, what about these drawings of Clare's? I have to confess, they confuse me.' She smiled faintly. 'Actually, it's rather more than that. I'm not easily bothered by this sort of thing, but as Rosie would say, they give me the creeps.' An apt enough expression.

189

Gooseflesh crept on her arms whenever she looked at them. Maybe horror.

He shuffled the sketches together, squared them up neatly in his thin, elegant fingers and put them back in the envelope, precise as always in his movements. If he was disappointed that she had changed the subject, he gave no sign. 'You're thinking they might have something to do with her state of mind before she left?'

'Don't you think so?'

'I don't know, but I don't believe one should imbue them with too much significance.'

She had not included that strangely disturbing drawing of the dark goddess Hecate, and was reminded that after all he knew nothing of Clare's obsession with the myth and magic surrounding the ancient tree. 'That sort of thing's hardly unusual with artists,' he went on. 'Look at the Monets we saw in Paris—' The pause was so brief that she might have imagined it, imagined the taut wire of shared memory that twanged between them, though she hadn't imagined at all the lurch of her insides that always came whenever Paris was mentioned. He went on, in the same reasonable tone, 'How many times has Monet painted water lilies, after all? Or the Houses of Parliament, come to that? And he isn't the only one to paint the same thing repeatedly. Who knows how the artistic mind works? A constant search for something that has significance for them but always eludes being captured in paint . . . some idea or truth behind it? One can only speculate.'

'I don't know, either.' She was pretty sure

though, that this compulsive repetition had little, if anything, to do with Clare's artistic aspirations. Emily herself could not for one moment attribute any supernatural powers, evil or otherwise, to the Hecate tree, but Clare, at one time at least, had been utterly convinced of it, which might amount to the same thing: that she had been pursued and haunted by that childish curse and could not forget.

Although he'd been so cautious in giving an opinion, she knew Hugh would continue to think about it – and about that suggestion she had prematurely and perhaps unwisely mentioned. As he refilled her cup, she said, 'There's something else I'd value your opinion on.'

He raised an amused eyebrow. 'Not more artistic endeavours, I trust?'

She took the letter from her bag. 'When I was looking through her things I came across this as well. You may be able to read more into it than I've been able to.'

He put his glasses on again. The thin paper crackled as he unfolded it. 'French, hmm?' After studying it for a moment or two he said, 'If you want an exact translation, you've drawn a blank here, too, I'm afraid. My French isn't really up to that standard. I can give you the general gist of it, but the language seems rather – convoluted, not to say the handwriting.'

'I've got the gist of it: Clare had some sort of problem – she was asking for his help in something or other . . . that much at least I could gather.'

'So it would seem. Let's have another look.' There was silence again as he carefully reread

191

the letter. 'Yes. It does appear as though she was asking his advice – should she or shouldn't she? Over what? Well, presumably whether or not she should leave art school. If so, he wasn't helping much, was he? Do you know who this man is?'

'Yes.' Hugh wouldn't remember the tutor they'd had that summer, she said, he'd been away at school, but Christian Gautier had been engaged to teach Clare and herself drawing and speak French with them. 'Though Mama was not too pleased with his efforts to improve our French. But it was through him that Clare began to be interested in painting. He left and I never heard of him after that.'

Reading between the lines of this letter, however, it seemed that he and Clare had not only been in the habit of writing to each other, they had also been meeting, in London. And it was clear that Clare had been most anxious – desperate, even – to see him again, and that she had written purposely to ask if he would come to London once more. She had to see him, she must talk to him. If necessary, she would go over to Grenoble.

His reply – this letter – was definitely off-putting, almost smacking of panic. They had already talked, had they not? He was about to be married, he reminded her, to Marie-Laure, his fiancée of two years. The last time they had met, he had advised Clare what steps she should take, though being a man, it was difficult for him to say what would be the right thing. There was no possibility at all that he could come to London and she must certainly not travel to Grenoble. It would be advisable that she did not write to him again, either. *Amicalement. Christian.*

In friendship? 'He doesn't sound much of a friend to me,' Emily said.

'Perhaps not, but look at it this way – young chap, about to be married, another young woman turning up from London with – a problem . . . the attitude's understandable, if not to his credit. Your sister was a dark horse, Emily.'

There was a silence. The words flew through her mind with the speed of a bird skimming across the window. Clare? *Clare?*

'If you're thinking what I'm thinking, Hugh, it's no,' she returned coldly at last. 'No. Not Clare, not ever.'

He stared at her thoughtfully, then shrugged. 'Probably not.'

But in a moment, the nothing she had known about Clare had become even less. True enough, she had been agitated about what she considered her failure at the Slade, must have desperately needed advice, and yet . . . surely there had been someone other than this young Frenchman, charming as he had been, to give it? Why was it so important that she had been prepared to cross the Channel and follow him across France in order to talk to him? Why him especially?

Maybe she had ignored his reply and gone anyway; maybe that was where she had disappeared to. Only Christian himself would know the answer. Crazy notions of going to Grenoble herself to find him came to her, until her usual common sense reasserted itself. This letter was decades old, there was no address on it. She had

193

nothing but a name – Christian Gautier. There might be a dozen men of that name in the city. It was by no means certain that he still lived there, or that he was even still alive.

Hugh said steadily, 'Let it go, Emily. Let it go.'

Putting the letter back in her bag, along with the sketches, she said, 'Before I came back to England, I believed I'd come to terms with what happened to Clare, or at least come to accept that I would never know. I almost thought I was better off remaining in ignorance. But it's different, being here, now I do want to know. I've always wondered, just how hard did they try to find her?'

'My dear, the police tried everything they could, and when they came up with nothing, your father employed that private detective for three months. He found nothing, either, as you know.'

'He gave up too soon then. People don't just disappear like that, unless they're dead. And I know she wasn't dead.'

He regarded her sadly. 'If somebody is determined not to be found, Emily—'

'Did they try the convent? She used to visit there, you know, to talk with the Mother Superior.'

'Did she? That old nun? I never knew that. But if she was a regular visitor there, it would have been an obvious place to try, and I assume the detective would have done so.'

Incarcerating herself in a convent was just the sort of thing one might have expected of Clare Vavasour, Hugh thought, and he saw why that would be an evidently more acceptable answer to Emily than the fairly obvious explanation – that she might have been having a child by this

194

man Gautier. He added gently, 'They are good women at the convent. If she had gone there, they would not have kept it secret.'

'Mother Mary-Emmanuel would have known, but she can't be alive, she was over seventy, then.'

'There you are then. It was a long time ago, Emily,' he said gently. 'A long time ago.'

When she had left, Hugh picked up a manila envelope-folder containing a manuscript from a new author that he had promised Gerald he would deliver to Edmund Sholto for an initial reading. He found his panama and his shooting stick and whistled for his fat old spaniel, Alice.

As he came out of the door, he saw that Emily had stopped to have a few words with the gardener, and he waited until she had finished talking to him and had walked through the wicket gate that led towards Leysmorton. When she disappeared from sight, he walked in the opposite direction, down the drive of Steadings towards the main gates, but halfway there took a path that led through the woods on either side.

Go with her to Madeira, eh? The idea had its attractions. Hugh had from time to time met British expatriates and had no desire to become one of them – but don't waste these last years as we've wasted the rest, his sensible self told him. It's not as if there will be lingering reminders of Emily's marriage there. Her husband never lived with her in that quinta. Paddy Fitzallan's last days had been spent in a sanatorium up in the mountains.

He had tried to conceal from her the great pull

of the heart her suggestion had given him. She was willing for them to be together, at last. But as he had told her, it needed thinking about. He had detected a certain hesitancy, which he hoped was due to the thought of abandoning Leysmorton once again. Did she really want to live permanently in Madeira, now that Fitzallan was gone? But for the two of them to live at Leysmorton with that fellow Stronglove and his sister still in occupation wasn't to be thought of . . . and Steadings now belonged to Gerald, and he, Hugh, was an appendage. Leave, and give the boy's marriage a chance? Yes – if things had not already gone too far for that. He slashed hard at some nettles encroaching onto the path with his stick. Damn Stronglove, damn Stella! Gerald deserved better. At the same time, he could pity Stella: so unhappy, so wrapped up in herself, spoiling her looks with her anger at her own unhappiness. Gerald was a good son – good publisher, too, knew how to sell books, especially if he could become less inclined not to take risks. They had had a slight difference of opinion over the novel the Drummond boy had written. The manuscript had been a lot better than this one he was taking to Sholto, against his own judgment. But people liked anything these days, and perhaps Sholto would see something in what Hugh thought of as modern trash, and would recommend it to Gerald, with some editing, as a saleable commodity.

A pity, he had sometimes thought over the years, that his memories of Emily couldn't be so strictly edited. It had not been a thought he had ever entertained for long.

The night she told him she loved Paddy Fitzallan and had consented to marry him, the world had crumbled around Hugh's ears. Bewildered, hurt and stiff, he could not bring himself to argue and plead, but his equable temperament had deserted him and for a few seconds he had astonished and shamed himself by wanting to shake her and shout that she should open her eyes, couldn't she see Fitzallan was taking advantage of her? But rage against Emily was something he couldn't sustain. What he wanted was to punch the fellow on the nose and knock him down – demand of him how such a cad could think himself good enough for such a star as Emily? But he had not sunk so low as to argue with someone for whom he had such contempt.

Instead, he cursed himself for not having seen what was going on under his nose, and then wondered if he had not subconsciously suspected it, and had refused to acknowledge it because next to Fitzallan he had always felt himself stiff-necked and wooden, arousing untenable feelings of inferiority. Beside that jackanapes he must have seemed a very dull dog.

He also despised Anthony Vavasour for being so spineless as to allow the marriage, when he had known she was all but engaged to Hugh, but wisely kept this opinion to himself. Nothing formal had ever been said between him and Emily after all. It was his own pride which had made him believe there was such a rapport between them that there was no need to rush into formalities.

To the devil with it, he'd thought, lashing himself with the raw pain he felt. She was not the only

197

girl in the world. Within a year he had married Lavinia. She had been a good wife, they were as happy as most married couples, the only flaw in their marriage being that after Gerald, there were no more children, something he'd minded more than she had.

After that letter he'd written on Anthony's behalf, telling Emily that Clare had vanished, he had continued to hear from her at regular though infrequent intervals – firstly, that she and that husband of hers had left India – it wouldn't do, things had not worked out for him there, his father had died, the tea plantation had been a failure before they got there, the troubled Indians he intended to write about were offended at the idea of a Britisher – even an Irishman – thinking he could sort out their problems, feeling against British rule was still too strong. There had followed Egypt, and the exporting of antiquities, then selling Jaffa oranges from Palestine, ostrich farming in South Africa and some God-forsaken scheme in Armenia, where the Turks from across the border were intent on genocide. From all of these places came occasional newspaper articles written by Paddy which Hugh came across from time to time. He supposed they were well-intentioned, but he knew them to be lightweight, written from the fringes of whatever conflict interested him at the time, innocuous in comparison with those written by bona-fide foreign correspondents. He could not have made any profit from it – but that, Hugh thought with a touch of cynicism reserved only for Paddy Fitzallan, would not have mattered, considering the money he had married.

By now, he had reached the stile that led to the road, with Sholto's cottage fifty yards away. It was still warm, but this exceptional summer was nearly over; the hedgerows foaming with cow parsley and wild roses were giving way to the dying flame colours of autumn. He took off his panama and mopped his brow, flipped away the flies, and as old Alice flopped down, panting, indicating it was time for a rest, he settled himself on his shooting stick and allowed himself to remember.

Paris. Notre Dame. A table outside a pavement café near the Pont Neuf on a sunny day. The *bouquinistes* lining the quays doing their usual leisurely trade, where he had just picked up a translation of the vagabond poet Francois Villon's 'Ballade' and opened at random. *Where are the snows of yesteryear?* he read, as waiters balancing a row of plates along their arms rushed past him, and the *flâneurs* sauntered along the pavements, in the nonchalant yet acutely aware manner only Parisians could assume.

He had been on a walking holiday in the Dolomites, reliving, as he did every year, the time he'd once spent there with two friends just after graduation, this time revelling in being alone for three weeks of long, solitary tramps over the mountains in tweed plus fours, with bread, cheese and a book in his pocket, staying at small, welcoming hotels, sleeping and eating well. Now he was back in civilization, having stopped off for a long overdue meeting with a business associate. The business concluded, he was now sipping coffee and a *digestif* after lunch and thinking rather half-heartedly of his return to England later that day, once more in a conventional suit and stiff collar, his mind still full of lakes and mountains.

Lavinia had never shared his enthusiasm for that sort of holiday, saying it was a man's recreation, but that if he insisted on going, she could always spend a few weeks with her sister in Tunbridge Wells. He was a little ashamed of the relief he'd felt at being able to satisfy his need to be alone for a while, and it had tinged his holidays with a feeling of guilt. But Lavinia had died two years ago and this time he had been unencumbered by any such emotion. He was tanned and fit and for once reluctant to get back to family, work and publishing. As the bells of Notre Dame sounded the hour he realized he would need to move soon to catch his travel connections, but the sun shone, the air smelled of French cigarettes and good food, and from one of the cafés further along came the jaunty, wheezy lilt of accordion music. The heads of several appreciative Frenchmen turned towards a woman walking gracefully towards the river. He debated whether or not to have another *pastis*.

The woman had paused to lean on the stone parapet by the river, a small, slim figure in dark blue. He looked at the back of her, the lustrous dark hair, the fashionable hat, then hurriedly threw money onto the table and walked towards the railings. For a moment he, too, stood there and stared across the Seine, then as the woman turned to go he faced her.

'Emily.'

200

'Hugh!'

She had been too far away to get home in time for her father's funeral. So many years since they had last met, but she was just the same, the carnation flush to her cheeks, the wide brown eyes, and this time the smile was only for him.

He had sent a cable home to say that he was unavoidably detained and let them make of it what they would. She had three weeks earmarked for shopping, sightseeing, amusing herself, while Paddy, refusing to allow his worrying state of health to stop him, had gone off on some hare-brained escapade she was not quite clear about. Of those weeks he remembered only the joy, not the details. Presumably they had eaten and drunk; he knew they had walked the city, visited museums and art galleries, all the things one did in Paris, only he could scarcely remember anything they saw, except for the Monets. He had known, half an hour ago, that she too had remembered them. During those three weeks they hadn't talked much – really talked, or discussed their future – how could they? They both knew she was not going to leave her husband. His health was deteriorating – and besides, duty, loyalty, promises were not so easily broken in those days, a tenet he upheld then, and still did.

They parted – something else he had erased from his memory – and afterwards they had continued to write to each other, but still infrequently. Not love letters, but innocuous missives which anyone could have read. And now, when he had ceased to expect it, here was the prospect of being together. His heart began to beat wildly, like a young man's. Or an old man's about to have a stroke. Calm down, he told himself as he eased himself off the shooting stick.

Nothing was without its complications. For now, here was this other damnable business.

Seventeen

'Don't think I'm unsympathetic, Novak.' Superintendent Brownlow sat back in his chair, steepling
his fingers and looking sorrowful. 'You're playing
on a sticky wicket and I understand the difficulties. But we're not getting on very fast, are we?'

In the beginning, it had been understood that
no one had expected results in this case immediately, or even at all. An unidentified skeleton,
lying there for years – the circumstances hadn't
left much room for optimism. Brownlow's attitude now was irritating, though Novak could
understand his anxieties. The man was highly
ambitious and it wasn't all that long since he had
stood in Novak's shoes, a mere inspector, and he
was still having to justify to his superiors his
elevation to superintendent, acting puffed up yet
jittery about his association with the great and
the good. Both he and Novak knew that this
investigation had to come together soon, or be
abandoned, but Novak couldn't see the latter
going down well with Brownlow, much less the
powers that be he was so eager to impress, who
had yielded to the string-pulling in the first place
to bring Scotland Yard to the investigation.

'We've had very little to work on, sir.'
Brownlow's mouth pursed. 'But I think we can
say we've moved a few steps forward.' Briefly,
he recounted the details about the money found

in Sholto's workshop, which at least elicited a grunt of interest.

'They're matters that require careful consideration,' Brownlow conceded.

'And we've also managed to make contact with one of the men Sholto served with.'

Willard, doggedly working his way through the army demobilization records to which they had eventually been given access, had traced Sean Hennessy, an Irishman now living in Peckham and married to an English girl, and together they had gone to see him. Hennessy remembered Peter Sholto well. In fact, they had been pals, had gone side by side through some of the bloodiest battles of the war, and were together right until the time Peter had disappeared.

Hennessy had good reason to recall the last conversation he'd had with Sholto, since it was one he'd had to repeat more than once to the military police who had chased up his apparent desertion. Mainly because it had happened on the seventeenth of March, St Patrick's Day, the first one after the armistice, and the Irish contingent in the regiment had been all set to make a night of it. Sholto had promised to return in time to join in the high jinks and had asked Hennessy to cover for him in the meantime. He'd left camp in the afternoon, hitching a lift to the nearest town in a lorry that delivered supplies to the cookhouse. You could have knocked Hennessy down with a feather when he didn't return. He was sure the lad had never intended to go AWOL, though like everyone else he had been sick with resentment and impatience for his release from the army.

Hennessy, however, also told them that Sholto had had a letter that day, which he'd said made it necessary for him to make an immediate sortie over to Netherley, on the other side of the county. It wasn't anything that would justify asking for leave on compassionate grounds, but it couldn't wait. What was the urgency? Hennessy had asked – he would be home for good, sooner or later, wouldn't he? But no, he had to go there and then. There was something he had to do, something he had to retrieve, straight away. Retrieve? Yes. Hennessy had laughed. Sholto had used words like that – he'd had an education, and his dad had been a schoolmaster, hadn't he? – though he'd refused to give any further explanation. Well, young Peter had never been one for giving away too much about himself.

'I'll tell you this for the truth, though. If I was a betting class of man, I'd wager it was something to do with a girl, maybe someone he'd left in the lurch, or something after that manner. He had a photo he always kept with him, like we all had these lucky mascots. I'd me half-crown that saved me from a bullet, still keep it with me.' He had pulled a battered piece of silver from his pocket to demonstrate. 'This girl now. Maybe Peter had wakened up to his responsibilities, grown up while he was in the army. I saw it happen. War makes men out of boys, God help us all.'

Hennessy wouldn't go further than that. He'd been sick to hear Sholto had been murdered, and he wasn't prepared to dish any dirt on him. In Willard's estimation it had been an odd sort of friendship between the young chap and the older

Hennessy, but Willard hadn't been in the war. Novak had seen odder friendships, comradeship forged through having spent terrible years of their lives together. When you'd lived, slept, eaten and fought alongside each other, in the unspeakable conditions of the late war, when you'd stood shoulder to shoulder, up to your waist in mud and blood, facing the enemy, your guts churning, then a bond of loyalty was formed that no one but those with similar experiences could ever understand. In this case, mistaken loyalty might have kept Hennessy's lips buttoned, but both he and Willard had been inclined to think that he knew no more than he had told them.

'At least we now know why he went missing,' Novak said to Brownlow. 'Something in that letter he got made it necessary for him to risk defying the authorities in order to make a quick visit to Netherley.'

He wasn't entirely happy with what he surmised must have happened: Sholto leaving camp on the supply lorry to the nearby town – a train to Luton, more accessible than Kingsworth Halt – and then what? Too far to walk to Netherley in the time available. All the same, he had got there by some means.

Brownlow listened to everything, but with a thinly veiled impatience. He nodded, while his eyes slid to the big clock on the wall as it neared eleven – though Novak knew from past experience that he had not missed a thing, and would have facts and figures at his fingertips, ready to throw back at him, verbatim, if and when necessary. He straightened his tie. A meeting with the top brass, he'd said. The Assistant Commissioner, no doubt. His Majesty even, Novak shouldn't wonder. Finally he pushed his chair back as a signal for dismissal. 'Well, play your cards right with this one, and you'll do yourself a bit of good. I've had my eye on you for some time, Adam, and I'll be keeping it there. Best of luck then, but get a move on, there's a good scout.'

When Brownlow used Christian names it was time to be wary. 'Thank you, sir. We'll do our best.'

So it had been Brownlow who'd got him into this, Novak thought, as he shut the door behind him. Had his eye on him, had he? He took this with a pinch of salt. It was what spurred you on, being told that, but promotion, my eye! In his experience, promotion came by stepping into dead men's shoes.

The trouble was, however, that Brownlow was right, in one sense. Progress still wasn't quick enough.

At the moment, it came down to who had sent Peter that last letter, the contents of which had apparently made it necessary for him to take the risk of absenting himself without permission. Who was it from? That girl in the photograph, causing Sholto to wake up to his responsibilities, as Hennessy had suggested? Unless he'd suddenly begun to worry over that cache of banknotes left in the box. But since it had been sitting there all the time he was in the army, that didn't square with any sudden need to return home. And in any case, it was to Leysmorton he had gone, not to his old home where the money was hidden.

Back in his office, Novak twirled a pencil between his fingers and leaned back until his chair was on its two back legs, a habit that drove even the unflappable Willard mad. It helped him to think, however. And now he found his mind going over and over the conversation he'd had with Edmund Sholto until finally, something clicked. He let the chair fall forward and reached for his notes, and yes, there it was, that mention of the notebooks Peter used to scribble in. It hadn't seemed important at the time, and probably it wasn't important now. Nothing but doodles, he'd told his father, sketches and notes of the old furniture at Leysmorton House he so admired, yet he'd been secretive about showing it. He couldn't have blackmailed Stronglove – or Stella Markham – without some form of tangible proof . . . was it conceivable he'd kept something of the sort in one of those notebooks? If so, he would not have destroyed them as Edmund Sholto had surmised. Novak paused, pencil in mid-air – was it possible there had been something incriminating to himself in them? And that he'd hidden them, not at home but in one of the dozens of hidey-holes likely in a rabbit warren of a house like Leysmorton? He puffed out his lips. Possible, but a long shot. Maybe worth a try.

The following day, back at Netherley, Novak tried out the short cut from the village to Leysmorton House, the route Sholto was likely to have taken in order to avoid coming across any of the villagers.

The river wound lazily between poplars and

willows, its banks edged with pink balsam and cow parsley, a pretty enough scene if he hadn't been forced to watch where he put his feet so as not to fall from the stepping stones into the river, though he guessed it was hardly deep enough to do more than wet his feet. The greater danger was a broken ankle from slipping on the smooth and irregularly spaced stones. It would have been dark by the time Sholto arrived and this way would be a hazardous undertaking, however familiar you were with it. After negotiating it, crossing the meadow and stepping through that gap in the wall, had he then been intercepted and met his death before he could get to the house? In this clearing where Novak now stood?

Even he, less susceptible than most, felt a shiver as he stood with his hands behind his back, surveying the scene. It was that great tree, he decided, its immense girth, its weird structure, composed as it was of numbers of trunks fused together, the fissures and hollows between, that made the place so eerie, the drooping branches and sombre foliage casting a brooding, church-yard shadow everywhere.

He was so absorbed – or else she walked so lightly, making no noise – that he wasn't aware of Lady Fitzallan until she emerged into the clearing, and for a moment, as he stood in the shadow of the tree, she didn't see him, either.

She stared around in wonder, as if this might have been the first time she had come here since the spot had been cleared of the years of accu-mulated debris. Novak's men had meticulously obeyed instructions to sift through the pile of wood and rubble covering the skeleton so as not to miss any tiny bones or fragments, any tattered shreds of clothing or other pieces of evidence which might have lain concealed, and they'd made a thorough job of it. The bricks had been removed and stacked neatly by the gap in the outer wall from whence they had originally come. Later, someone, a gardener Novak supposed, had finished the job by burning the rotten wood and weeds and raking over the soil. There was still a circle of fire-blackened earth in the centre of the clearing, though around its edges new grass had already begun to grow. Around the immense old yew whose rough, scaly trunk he now leant against, the earth was bare except for a carpet of browning needles that had fallen since, and the huge gnarled roots protruding through it.

'Inspector Novak!' She stepped back as she saw him, but waved away his apologies for startling her. 'I was miles away and didn't see you.'

'Looks a bit different now, hmm, this place?'

'You have saved us a lot of trouble, clearing the bricks like this.'

'And now it's cleared . . .?'

'Oh,' she said vaguely, 'have the wall bricked up again, perhaps? Return it to how it used to be when my sister and I used to come here as children. We had that little play house in the tree, a long time ago. Clare loved this spot before she . . . before we both . . . went away.' She drew a steadying breath. 'As you know, I've lived abroad for most of my life.'

'And your sister, too?'

'No. Clare died.'

210

'I'm sorry.'

Emily looked away and then she gave an odd little sigh and said suddenly, turning towards him, 'She went away without any explanation and they never found what had happened to her, neither the police nor the private detective my father hired. They assumed she was dead, but I knew she wasn't, not then.'

'How did you know that?'

'She didn't write, but she used to send me birthday cards – anonymously, but they could only have come from her, so yes, I knew . . .' She held her arms tightly round herself, as if she were cold. 'Well, it's old history, interesting to nobody but me now.'

He had heard the story of the sister's disappearance from Nellie Dobson, but not this part of it, and he hadn't thought any more of it, but now a thought, fleeting and elusive, came to him. Not a time to try and capture it, though. He prized himself away from the tree. 'I'm afraid I shall have to leave you now, Lady Fitzallan. I'm supposed to see Miss Heeren shortly.'

'Poor Marta. Don't be too harsh. This business has been a shock to her. I believe she and this boy, Peter, were very close.' She hesitated. 'May I ask you a question first, before you go?'

'Go ahead.'

'After so much time, do you think there could be any possible chance of finding out what happened to my sister?'

'Lady Fitzallan, I'm trying to investigate a murder that happened three years ago, and the trail's as cold as Christmas.'

'Even though I think I may have found some-thing that might throw some light on why she left?'

He still shook his head, but she took a piece of folded paper from her pocket, as though it were something she carried about constantly, like a talisman. 'This is a letter I've found. It's written in French, but I can tell you what it contains.'

'My mother was French.'

'I'm sorry, that was clumsy . . . I myself wasn't able to read it properly without help, but your French must obviously be better than mine. Would it be too much of an imposition to ask you to take it, and read it when you have time?'

He smothered his irritation as he thought what to say. He couldn't refuse to read a letter, though it was a distraction he could do without. 'You do realize there is absolutely no possibility that we – the police – would be interested in opening this case?'

'Of course. But you could give me your opinion on what I might do.'

Reluctantly, he put the letter in his wallet. 'I'll let you know what I think, but don't hold out hope.'

When Novak presented himself at the back door of the house, Nellie Dobson had her coat on and was spearing her hard felt hat with a long hatpin. A little girl with copper-coloured curls was standing on a chair and having her coat buttoned up by Marta Heeren, to whom she gave a sloppy kiss as she was lifted down. 'I liked doing the elberberries.'

'Elderberries.' A rare smile crossed Marta's face as she passed a hand over the curls. 'Thank you for helping, Violet. Run along now and I'll see you next time.'

Marta turned to Novak when the door closed behind them. 'Well, Inspector?' Her face had resumed its stolid, unreadable expression.

'A few words please, Miss Heeren, if you can spare the time.'

'Come into the little parlour.'

'Oh, here will do very well.' He liked the old-fashioned kitchen, so big it was still cool despite the heat of the day and the sizeable fire necessary to heat the range and the recently used flat irons, now upended and cooling on the hearth. The smell of freshly laundered linen mingled with a rich scent of baking pastry.

'As you wish,' Marta said. 'Please sit down.' She appeared measurably calmer than the first, and last, time he'd seen her, and quite in command of herself, and in fact didn't wait for him to begin his questions, but took the initiative. 'You no doubt want to talk to me about Peter. I was upset when you gave us the news, but that's behind us. I'm not about to burst into tears again. You can go ahead.'

He admired the self-control she displayed. He did not believe she had shaken off the grief he'd seen so easily.

'At this point, I'm mainly trying to get hold of some idea of what Peter was like, what he did. One of his interests was woodworking, I'm told.'

'His only one. He got ideas from some of the pieces in this house, sketching and measuring

213

them. I let him wander round whenever he wanted. He was upset at how much some of it had been let go – in fact, he offered to do a few small repairs, and he made such a good job you'd never know they'd been mended.'

'I've seen some of his own work. He used his grandfather's tools, didn't he?'

'That's right. Some are still here.'

'I have an idea his father would like them.'

She stared. 'He should have asked. Wait, and I'll get them.'

She returned within a few minutes with a strong canvas tool bag, containing several chisels and other tools, their wooden handles polished with long use.

'Thank you, I'll see Mr Sholto gets these,' he said, seeing she was not offering to return them herself. 'One more thing, Miss Heeren. I believe you used to write to Peter regularly when he was away?'

'Not so very regularly. Once a month, in fact. I always wrote on the first.'

'That must have been a comfort to him; letters from home were much appreciated.'

'I'm not much good at knitting scarves and socks,' she said drily. 'It was the least I could do, to put pen to paper now and then.'

'No young ladies to write to him?'

'He never told me if there were.' A spot of colour appeared on both cheeks.

'I'm told he kept a photograph of a girl with him always.'

'Well, it was no one I knew anything about,' she returned sharply.

He was not sure whether he believed her, but

felt he was in danger of losing her by pursuing that line. 'He left camp on March the seventeenth, after he'd received a letter which caused him to take leave without permission. Could the letter have been from you?'

'I told you, I always wrote at the beginning of the month.' She fell silent and then said stiffly, 'Edmund Sholto lied about his son being killed. Why, is quite beyond me.'

'Mr Sholto thought his son had deserted, Miss Heeren.'

The colour on her cheeks intensified, but she didn't answer.

'It would seem as though he came straight here after leaving camp. Why do you think he would do that?'

She said colourlessly, 'I've no idea. He knew the house was empty, and would be until after Easter. In my last letter I asked him to come and see us then, because my brother's eyesight had worsened considerably, and I thought he might give Peter his old job again. And that's all I can tell you.'

There was the sense of shutters coming down. This was a woman who buttoned up her feelings, a childless woman who lavished her frustrated affections on other people's children, such as little red-haired Violet, and he didn't doubt Mrs Dobson had been right about her feeling the same affection for Peter.

'Thank you, Miss Heeren, that'll do for now.'

He picked up the heavy tool bag and, sliding a hammer through its leather handles, slung it over his shoulder as workmen did, and headed

215

towards the police house in the village, where he was to meet Willard. When he reached a convenient low wall, he balanced the bag and opened it. He moved the tools to one side and yes, there underneath were two notebooks: tattered and well used, an untidy mixture of scribbles and jottings mixed in amongst carefully executed drawings and detailed measurements of various pieces of furniture, with accompanying notes, pencil-written in a small, tight handwriting. Both were full and the leaves between the covers bulged with random scraps of paper on which quick, rough sketches had been made. But nowhere did he find anything that seemed remotely like a lever to blackmail anyone.

He had agreed to keep Constable Pickles up to date with the investigation, as a matter of courtesy more than anything else, though he suspected Pickles would actually have preferred to remain in blissful ignorance, to pretend that a murder hadn't occurred on his patch, where he'd been constable for most of his working life. He was on the verge of retirement and wanted nothing more than a quiet life in the place where he was more valued as a rich baritone in the church choir than as an enforcer of the law. A policeman's duties were not exactly onerous in Netherley. Trouble of a criminal nature was rare, murder unknown. Until now.

Tea was being served, with scones and Madeira cake made by Mrs Pickles, and Willard was already sitting back with an empty plate before him and his cup waiting to be replenished. 'Tell the inspector what you've just told me, Albert.'

216

Pickles, in his shirt sleeves and weskit, rubbed his hand over his face. 'I never thought anything of it till now.' He was a heavy man, grizzle-haired round the edges of his pate, bald as an egg otherwise, with a prominent Adam's apple.

'Thought anything of what? Good cup of tea, Mrs Pickles, just what's needed when you have a lot to discuss,' Novak said to the constable's wife who, having brought in reinforcements by way of a fresh pot, and having poured a cup for Novak, was hovering with interest near the door.

Pickles took the hint. 'All right, Mary.' He waited until she'd unwillingly closed the door behind her before he began, 'Well, there was this here bicycle, see.'

The constable was a long-winded narrator, but it finally emerged that about three years ago a bicycle with a buckled front wheel had been found in a ditch on the Kingsworth Road. It was only now that Pickles knew they were looking for anyone who might have been seen in the village on a certain night that he had connected the two events. 'Mystery how it got there, though not why it had been left. Nobody could have ridden that machine with the wheel as it was. That road's cruel with flints and it was just on that sharp bend. I thought hello, somebody's hit a tree and come a cropper.'

'When was it found?'

'Middle of April, thereabouts. Any rate, it was when old Jed Carter went along with his bill hook to finish laying Farmer Beale's hedges. Should've been tackled afore then, on account of the new growth, but he'd been laid up with rheumatics.

217

He came on it in the ditch. Might have been there some time, of course, though it hadn't yet started to go rusty.'

'Nobody saw anyone ride through the village?'

'No. Nor saw anybody going away. Always thought whoever it was must have walked on to Kingsworth, myself, and taken Joe Offord's taxi, though I never did hear tell of that from Joe.'

'Not likely you would,' Willard remarked. 'It doesn't look as though he walked anywhere, except across the stepping stones towards the big house.'

'You reckon it was young Sholto then?'

'It's possible he got a train as far as Luton, so now it looks as though he most likely half-inched that cycle to ride on here. It would be dark by that time, that's why nobody saw him.'

'One mystery solved then,' Pickles said with satisfaction.

'What happened to the bicycle?'

'You'll have to ask Kingsworth. I reported it to them and they came and took it away. Might still have it. If it was young Sholto, it won't have been claimed, will it?'

'No, I don't reckon it will, Albert,' said Willard drily.

Novak had come to a decision. 'Do they have rooms at the Drum and Monkey, Constable?'

Pickles scratched his head, 'A couple, maybe, but I don't rightly know if they'd be available. Mrs Gaunt, the landlady, only has herself to run the place since she lost her husband over in France. You thinking of putting up there?'

'It's time we were here on the spot, I think.'

So far, there had been no justification for it, though it had meant a good deal of to-ing and fro-ing between here and the city in an official motor – justified because of the infrequency of trains to Kingsworth Halt, and thence by that village's only taxi to Netherley, with the inconvenience of doing the same on the return journey.

'We'll have a word with her and book the rooms from tomorrow if we can.'

'Brownlow ain't going to like that,' Willard remarked.

'Superintendent Brownlow doesn't have to waste hours a day getting here and back. Besides, think how chuffed he'll be at not having to authorize a motor. That should square it with him.'

Eighteen

'Now, look here,' said Gerald. 'Let's get one thing clear.'

Val, summoned to Steadings, stood in front of Rosie's father, feeling like a schoolboy brought before the Head for some misdemeanour. He had never heard, or imagined he would hear, that tone from Gerald Markham.

'I don't care – or not much,' went on Gerald, more mildly, 'if you break your neck on that contraption you've bought, but I won't have you breaking my daughter's as well.'

'It has a sidecar,' Val ventured after a moment. 'The three wheels give it stability,' he added, without much conviction, because he had not intended to test that, only to drive with extreme care with Rosie as a passenger, even in a sidecar. He'd known she would never be allowed to ride pillion. Or anywhere else, it seemed now.

'It matters not to me, young man, if you tell me it's as stable as the Rock of Gibraltar. My daughter is not to ride on that motorcycle. I hope that's clear.'

'Yes, of course. I'm sorry. Only she was so keen.' In case this should be seen as trying to shift the blame, he added hastily, 'But I shouldn't have agreed, sir, and we'll do as you say.'

'I sincerely hope you will.' Gerald gave him a long, considering look. 'Rosie can be very . . .

persuasive. But at the moment she doesn't know where she is, you know. Lost without her sister, in the mood to try anything once. But I know my Rosie, she'll find her feet – and meanwhile, keep an eye on her for me, there's a good chap, and we'll say no more – but no motorcycles. Now, sit down. Drink?'

'Er – thank you.' Disconcerted by having to climb down about the motorcycle and by having to admit that her father was probably right about Rosie's present mood – though he didn't think the assumption about missing Dee was at all near the mark – Val sat and accepted the drink. Scotch, in heavy crystal glasses. He rather wished Gerald hadn't said that about keeping an eye on her. The implication being that there could never be anything more than a chummy boy and girl friendship between them, which was only too patently true. He was no Hamish Erskine, heir to all that money, he reflected bitterly, no catch for someone as spiffing as Rosie Markham, even though Gerald was unlikely to be as set upon such things as her mother, Stella. He took a sip of the excellent whisky, sat back and tried to seem at ease.

This was Gerald's private sanctum, a small room that mirrored Hugh's den on the other side of the front door, another masculine room, though unlike Hugh's this one displayed sporting prints and photographs of cricket teams. Did they all have their separate hideaways in this house? If so, Rosie's must be the tack room where she had nailed up her gymkhana certificates and rosettes. He wanted to smile at the thought.

Gerald settled back in his chair, glass in hand,

relaxed now in his rumpled weekend tweeds and with an air of having got something unpleasant off his chest. It suited him better to play the genial host than the heavy father.

Val had always found Gerald good-humoured and easy going, and he knew Rosie adored her father. He suspected he was a countryman at heart, more at home when he was riding to hounds, fishing or shooting, and that he had fallen into publishing by default, following family tradition. He knew the Peregrine Press was a much respected publishing house – Gerald himself was also well respected in the profession. He left every morning at eight and didn't return until six. He obviously worked hard and gave a lot to his work, though he didn't love books as old Hugh did.

'How's your next book going?' he was asked suddenly.

'Sir?'

'You *are* still writing?'

'Not much.' Not even to Gerald – shrewder than he'd estimated – would Val admit that he was writing at a furious pace, often well into the night. The climate of Leysmorton, as quiet and peaceful as if half-asleep or under a spell, its whole air of a faded past, suited his mood very well. This was a very different book, his anger purged by the writing of that first one, *Mars in Scorpio*, and sometimes he dared to hope it might turn out to be a better and more balanced one, too.

'Well, don't be discouraged by one rejection.'

Cautious words, non-committal, but Val's spirits rose. Maybe there had, after all, been something

222

worthwhile in his first attempt at authorship, even though Gerald had not felt able to publish it.

Later, in one of the unused Leysmorton stables – unlike Steadings, nobody living in this house rode horses now – he stood next to Rosie as they both gazed at his recent acquisition. Next to the showy two-tone black and cream Lanchester that Dirk owned and Marta drove, the motorcycle looked like a poor relation, which indeed it was. It had passed through the hands of many owners, had seen war service in Flanders and bore the scars – of that and of its myriad encounters with rough roads and other unsympathetic surfaces. Its sidecar was battered and its paintwork had been retouched and overpainted until its skin was as thick as that of a rhinoceros. Val put away his oily rag, wiped his hands and patted the saddle. He loved it like a brother.

'I'm sorry, Rosie, he won't hear of it.'

Despite the open door, it was very close in the stable, and the smell of motor oil and petrol was strong. Rosie pushed back her hair. 'I expected he wouldn't, but it doesn't matter. I hope he wasn't too rotten to you.' She spoke with less than her usual cheerfulness and Val looked at her more closely.

'Of course he wasn't. But I was looking forward to taking you for a spin or two. We could have gone up to the Downs and seen that famous view you're always talking about.'

Her expression took on more animation. 'If you want to see it, we could still go there. Mother hardly ever rides Blanche lately and she needs the exercise.'

'Except that I couldn't ride Blanche – or any horse if it comes to that.'

Rosie looked at him incredulously. 'You mean you don't ride?'

'I mean I can't. Horses never featured much in my upbringing. Couldn't afford it.'

A tide of colour suffused her face. 'Oh, Val, how could I? I'm so awfully sorry. Please take no notice of me, I'm always putting my foot in it. I speak without thinking. I'm afraid I'm never going to be a woman of poise and sophistication, like Dee, or Mother.'

'Don't change, Rosie. I wouldn't like you if you were poised and sophisticated.' Especially if you were like Dee or your mother, he thought, as he looked into her candid eyes. She was nearly as tall as he was. He searched her pale face and saw the band of freckles across her nose, and worried at the absence of the sweetest smile in the world. 'What's bothering you, Rosie?'

'Nothing. Why should there be?'

'Come on, that's prevaricating.'

She laughed shakily. 'If you mean I'm telling lies, you're wrong.' She pushed a strand of wayward hair back, copper-gold where a beam of sunlight coming through the stable door caught it. 'It's just that – oh, everything's so beastly!'

'You're still upset by that wretched skull you found?'

'No – yes, well, partly . . .'

'Come on, buck up, you'll see the other side of it soon enough. "Alas, poor Yo—"'

'Don't you dare!'

Val looked contrite. Normally she would have

laughed with him. 'I'm sorry, you're right, it's not a subject for joking. It was tasteless.'

'Yes. That skull was – once it was Peter.'

Silence fell. He wiped his forearm across his face. 'Jehosophat, it's hot in here!' With sudden decision he took her arm and propelled her outside into an atmosphere scarcely less oppressive. The heat had built up over the last week and the day was humid and heavy. He had to brush the dust off the seat set against the wall with his handkerchief before they sat. The paint on the stable doors had blistered in the heat. Even the weeds in the cobbled yard were wilting.

'You said "partly". What's the other part of what's upsetting you, Rosie?'

'I'm sorry. I can't tell you, it's nothing, not really.'

'Don't be a juggins. You can tell me anything. I'm not easily shocked. Cough it up.'

'No, I can't, Val – I can't tell *anyone*. Especially you.' She was on the verge of tears.

He sat patiently while she struggled with them. In the end, he said, 'Just as a matter of interest, why does it happen to be especially me you can't tell?'

She shook her head. 'It's too shaming.' Then all of a sudden she gave in. 'I – the truth is, I eavesdropped on a conversation and you know what they say about eavesdroppers. They never hear any good.'

'About themselves, usually. When was this?'

'Oh, when I was very young . . . years ago.'

'Years ago. And you believe it still matters?'

'I rather think it might, now. But it wasn't about me – in fact I didn't really understand *what* it was

225

all about, not then. Not properly, anyway. But the inspector, Novak, he *did* say anything at all might be relevant, didn't he?'

'Then it was something about Peter Sholto you overheard? Peter himself was talking?' She nodded. 'And who was he talking to?'

She poked with the toe of her shoe at a feathery weed growing between the cobbles and presently it broke off. A sweet smell of apples rose from the bruised stem.

'Well?'

As he spoke, she looked up. There was something about the set of his jaw she didn't recognize.

'It was Poppy, wasn't it?' he said.

Novak was beginning to regret the decision which had made him smooth-talk Superintendent Brownlow into agreeing, albeit grudgingly, to him setting up a temporary headquarters at the Drum and Monkey. Last night, Mrs Gaunt had given them a stodgy rabbit pie and treacle sponge for supper. Breakfast, as cooked by his wife Hannah, had always been Novak's favourite meal, one that kept him going for most of the day, but Mrs Gaunt, a well-built, bustling woman who belied her name, had no such skills. After spending a hot, airless night in a room whose window frame had been painted shut, and a bed with a lumpy mattress and pillows like rocks, the greasy breakfast she offered did nothing to improve his temper.

He abandoned it and went a for walk, leaving the stoical Willard, who lived alone and seemed to notice nothing wrong with the fatty bacon and swimmy eggs, to finish without his company.

Walking along the village street, the sun already hot and the houses throwing deep shadows across the road, he nearly missed the little shop that sold groceries – and almost everything else by the look of it. He went in and picked up a packet of Huntley & Palmer's digestives and half a pound of Cheddar to keep hunger at bay, and walked further along the street until he found a grassy bank of the river where he slung off his jacket, mopped his brow and threw himself down. He ate some of what he'd bought, then began to pace about while he thought about his next move and about that letter Lady Fitzallan had given him to read, and why she was pushing him in directions he didn't want to go. All this was an irrelevance he did not need. Emily Fitzallan seemed to him a sensible and intelligent person who had seen enough of the world to be sanguine about its failings, and he wondered exactly what she had expected from his perusal of the letter. After reading it, he had drawn his own conclusions, which seemed to him to be the ones most people would have drawn: that what had happened to that young woman, Clare Vavasour, was no different to what happened to thousands of young women, particularly those exposed to temptation when away from home and the parental eye. And even more particularly to one who had mixed with the sort of arty young crowd who had thought it a scream to kick over the traces and shock the older generation with a so-called Bohemian lifestyle, encompassing free love and all that nonsense – a world that had been unknown to her younger sister.

He was surprised that Emily hadn't been prepared to accept this obvious explanation, and puzzled that she really thought it possible the mystery of her sister's disappearance could be solved after nearly half a century had elapsed. He would not have thought her so naïve. She had told him that Clare had been beset by doubts about her future as an artist, that many of her friends had tried to persuade her to keep on with her training at the Slade. She herself had never met any of these people her sister had associated with in her new world. It evidently comforted her to believe that the dilemma was about her return or otherwise to art school, rather than the result of a disastrous liaison with this young fellow from France.

He broke a biscuit and threw the bits to a passing swan, who inspected it, found it not to its liking and glided disdainfully away. 'Please yourself,' he said to the retreating back. Wrapping the rest of the cheese in its greaseproof paper, and screwing up the top of the biscuit packet, he went back to the Drum and Monkey to collect Willard and receive a reproachful look from the landlady. The woman had two children and, like so many other women whose husbands hadn't returned from the war, she was making the best of a difficult situation on her own. He felt sorry for the barely touched plate of food he'd left, and gave one of her children sixpence to run along to Leysmorton with a note, informing Lady Fitzallan that he and Willard would be along within the hour.

After telling her the conclusions he'd reached, he left her in no doubt that the police would never

228

consent to reopen any enquiry, certainly not on the flimsy evidence of that letter – which was no evidence of anything, if it came to that. And that any further private enquiry would almost certainly be unproductive.

'Yes, I know,' she replied, almost absently.

He exchanged a look with Willard, the same thought occurring to both. If she'd anticipated the outcome, why had she brought the letter to his attention? He couldn't make out what she wanted him to say.

'Where did you find the letter?' Willard asked.

She explained that it had been among some old drawings of Clare's, and Novak asked if they could see the place.

Showing no surprise at the request, she led the way upstairs, along a corridor and down some steps into a small, airless room tucked away between floors, set up as an artist's studio. She waved towards a large chest of drawers, a heavy piece of old furniture in dark oak. 'This was where Clare kept her work. I'd been looking through some drawings and after I put them back, I found the letter on the floor and thought it had probably fallen out of one of the sketchbooks where she'd put it.'

There were four small drawers, two each side, surmounting two larger, deeper drawers. Willard lifted out the smaller ones. They were all tidily stacked with sketchbooks, but it wasn't their contents that interested Novak. After emptying each of them in turn, he upended them, while Lady Fitzallan looked on without speaking. It wasn't until the fourth and last of the smaller drawers that he came upon what he had expected to find. He nodded and pointed to the small dab of hardened, resinous substance on its undersurface, and then took out the folded letter from his wallet, with the yellow smear that appeared to correspond with it.

'Looks as though someone glued the letter underneath the drawer, and the glue eventually became brittle and perished, so that when it was opened, the letter shook loose and fell into the one beneath.'

For a time she didn't say anything. 'Yes. It does look like that,' she agreed. 'All the drawers were heavy and I had to jerk them to open them. But why should Clare have wanted to hide it there?'

He didn't reply, waiting until she put forward the suggestion he was waiting for, the one he thought she had wanted him to make. 'Though perhaps Clare didn't, perhaps it was someone else,' she said at last.

'Why should anyone else be in possession of your sister's letter?'

'Well, they say Peter Sholto used to poke around. Maybe he found it.'

'And why should he want to hide it, if he did?'

'That's the question, of course, isn't it?'

She had been a step ahead of him. She had known all along the police would never agree to concern themselves with the long ago disappearance of her sister – but if it should appear in any way to be concerned with Peter Sholto's murder, that might put a different complexion on things. He mentally saluted her. But at the same time, he was grateful that the letter and the presence of the glue had been brought to his notice. Because he was asking himself the same question she had asked. He scraped the blob of hardened glue from the drawer and put it into the envelope he'd brought with him, asking if they might keep the letter a little longer.

Willard took the envelope from him and left. If this was cabinet-makers' glue, it wouldn't exactly prove that young Sholto had put it there, but it would go a long way towards it.

Nineteen

The day had grown steadily hotter and even the short walk from the claustrophobic room that had been Clare Vavasour's studio had caused Novak to break out in a sweat. He looked forward to another night in his room at the Drum and Monkey without enthusiasm. No need to return just yet, he told himself, not unwilling to take a moment off on one of the seats below the terrace, while he thought over the last half hour and got things straight in his mind. Automatically feeling in his pocket for his cigarettes, tapping one out of the packet, the scent of roses wafted deliciously towards him just as he was about to light it. For a moment he breathed in the perfume and for some reason the urge to smoke left him. He looked at the cigarette, speculated, but finally abandoned it.

Flinging an arm along the back of the seat and leaning back, he saw the house there in front of him, its red-brick outlines limned against the strange, almost lurid light of the afternoon, its low eaves and sloping roofs, its twisted chimneys, the walls clothed with that invasive creeper which had turned scarlet over the last few days, giving it a picture-book appearance. This old house, everything in it dating from the year dot . . . funny how it got a hold of you.

He had grown used to it, for all it was a house of ghosts: those of the soldiers who had lived

232

here, wounded in mind if not in body, of the sad daughter of the house who had mysteriously disappeared, and not least of the victim, that boy for whose death he hadn't yet found a reason. But old ghosts should not be allowed to inhabit the present. Nor to cloud his thinking. He closed his eyes and a low rumble of thunder was followed almost immediately by the first heavy drops of rain beginning to fall on his face.

As he grabbed his jacket, he looked up at the livid sky. This was not going to be a sharp shower, soon over. Making a run for it to the village was out of the question. He had covered the first few yards back to the house when he heard a whistle. Looking round, he saw young Drummond, with Rosie Markham a little in front of him, beckoning him and pointing in the direction of the stables towards which they themselves were running. He sprinted and they all reached the stable yard together, and were inside the door, only slightly damp, just in time to avoid being soaked as the downpour began in earnest.

The only natural light inside came from the upper half of the stable door which had been left open, and through a murky skylight set into the roof, and Val now busied himself lighting a Tilley lamp sitting on a rough workbench set up against one of the walls. As the lamp threw more illu-mination into the shadowy interior, Novak saw the stable was now used as a garage. He made out the shapes of a showy automobile, cream with black coachwork, and behind it a motorcycle combination.

Rosie sat on the running board of the Lanchester,

shaking drops from her hair and rubbing her face with a handkerchief. Val propped himself against the motorcycle, while Novak, by default, leaned against the workbench. 'We'd only just left here when the rain began,' Val explained. 'We were actually on our way to find you, so it was lucky we saw you.'

A streak of lightning lit the stable, followed by another roll of thunder. Novak waited for one of them to say what it was that had caused them to shout for him: he didn't think it was simply to offer him shelter. And finally, it was Rosie who spoke.

'I don't wish to overdramatize a situation that may not mean anything,' she began stiltedly, as if she had prepared this approach in her mind, then bit her lip and after a minute went on more naturally. 'The thing is . . . well, the thing is, I think there's something you might like to know – but please, before I begin, I have to say that I won't say anything at all unless you *promise* my father won't hear anything about it. Not ever.'

He looked at her with raised eyebrows. So what had *she* been up to, this fresh-faced, wholesome young lady? 'I can't promise anything. But if it has nothing to do with this investigation, then of course I won't mention it.'

She looked only slightly relieved. 'Well, I'm not sure if it has.' She glanced towards Val, who had his arms folded across his chest. It seemed as if he had no intentions of taking part in this conversation, but he nodded and she went on, 'I was only about eleven or twelve, you see. I may not have remembered it properly.'

234

'I find children often remember things very clearly indeed, Miss Markham. Things they would rather not recall, sometimes,' he added encouragingly.

'You're right, I have tried to forget, but I haven't been very successful.' The light was not good, but that didn't prevent him seeing how pale she was. Her hands were twisting the damp handkerchief into a ball. Suddenly she went on in a rush, 'I overheard a conversation, you see. They were in the library and I was outside on the terrace. It was Peter Sholto and – and Val's sister, Poppy,' she hurried on, carefully not looking at Val. 'She was staying with us at the time and he was asking her to do something for him. It was a private conversation and I should have gone away, but when I heard who they were talking about – I'm afraid I stayed where I was and listened.'

'So who was it they were talking about?'

She was silent for so long he thought she'd taken fright at having begun this, but he'd underestimated her. She took a deep breath. 'They were talking about my mother, that's why I stayed. And maybe,' she added, in a burst of shamefaced honesty, 'maybe because I was a bit jealous of Poppy at the time. He was awfully good-looking, you know, and to be truthful, I had a bit of a crush on him, although he was so much older than me.' She had flushed to the roots of her hair, but she went on bravely, 'They were quarrelling – well no, not really quarrelling, I suppose, but he was pressing her to do something she didn't want to do and she was getting frightfully worked up about it.' She began to tear at the handkerchief. 'He was asking her to look in my mother's desk,

235

to see if she could find any letters from—' She faltered.

'From Mr Stronglove, perhaps?' he prompted.

'Actually . . . yes. But how could you know that?'

'Surmised,' he replied diplomatically, and was relieved that, after a moment's hesitation, she didn't pursue it.

'Oh well, it doesn't matter. Yes, from him. He was always sending notes across from Leysmorton, to my father, as well as my mother – Peregrine Press publish him, you know – but the ones Peter wanted were the ones he said Dirk had sent to my mother. Poppy used to help her with her letters and he was ever so insistent, pressing her to look in her desk. She said no, not possibly, she couldn't do that, and then he said something about there being other ways . . . I think he meant spying on my mother, watching where she went,' she finished. 'He told her if she did this, they'd soon have enough money to get married. I'm afraid, in the end, she gave in and said she would.'

'I see. I assume by that they were engaged, then? Was it her photograph he kept with him, all through the war?'

'Poppy's photo? I don't know, I suppose it might have been—'

Val, unable to stay silent any longer, interrupted violently. 'If it was, she certainly hadn't given it to him! He was really spoony on her, but he wouldn't accept that she wasn't in the least interested in *him*. The truth is that he wouldn't leave her alone, pestering her and following her around and generally making a perfect nuisance of himself.'

236

'And yet – according to what you heard, Miss Markham, she agreed to do what he asked?'

Another lightning flash was followed by a deafening thunderclap, while the rain fell in a seemingly unstoppable grey curtain into the yard and drummed onto the skylight. Val stood up and began to pace about unnervingly. He stopped at last and said, 'You have to understand, Inspector. Neither of us, my sister and I, had any money. We'd been left near penniless, we had nothing!'

Novak's enquiries about Poppy after his visit to her shop had revealed a little of the extent of the brother and sister's penniless state. Which wouldn't have seemed penniless to most people of his acquaintance, but it was all relative, he supposed. If you'd been brought up to expect certain standards, perhaps what they had to go on with seemed paltry to them – but was that reason enough for Poppy to agree, against all her inclinations, and probably her upbringing, to do what Sholto had asked?

'But that isn't what happened,' Val went on. 'She might have agreed – I don't say she did, but she *might* have done – simply to get rid of him, but I happen to know she never did what he asked, or any such thing. They had been very good to her, Rosie's family. We're very distantly related, you know, and although I myself had never met any of them until Dee's wedding, Poppy had stayed with them often. She wrote and told me what had happened and that she'd have to find some acceptable excuse to leave Steadings, because she didn't want to seem ungrateful. It was the year she left school and she had absolutely

237

no idea what she was going to do with the rest of her life, except that she didn't want to spend it with Peter Sholto. Besides—' He stopped abruptly. 'Besides, she was in love with someone else.'

'My brother, David,' Rosie said quietly. 'Only I don't actually think David was in love with her. He liked her, terrifically, but—'

'—but he wasn't ready to marry anybody,' Val said. 'Or that's what I gathered from what Poppy said in her letters. She wrote to me a lot, that last summer. She was very miserable.'

They stared out at the rain. 'Has – has this helped, Inspector?' Rosie asked, at last.

'In the end, it always helps to know as much as we can find out about a murder victim. Thank you for telling me this, Miss Markham.'

'You'll keep your promise, you won't tell my father?' He inclined his head. 'I was only eleven, but I wasn't a fool, you know,' she added, unexpectedly. 'I knew such things went on, even then. After I overheard that conversation, well, it didn't come to me in a flash or anything like that, it was just that it became impossible not to see what was going on between Dirk and my mother.'

'Your father won't learn about them from me.'

'Oh,' she said, 'it's not that. Dad's no fool, either. He doesn't like Dirk, and maybe there's a reason for that, I don't know. But don't let him know who you heard this from. He mustn't know it was me, that I sank so low as to listen to a private conversation, he would hate that.' Unexpectedly, her smile returned. 'He only loses his temper about once a year, but I'd rather be elsewhere when he does.'

Mrs Gaunt's repertoire was seemingly not extensive. That night's supper was rabbit pie again, this time followed by plum duff. Hardly appropriate food for a day such as today, but the coolness that followed the storm had taken off most of the heat, and both men had been hungry. Willard had tucked in and even Novak, having eaten nothing since his cheese and biscuit breakfast supplement, had done his best. Now, in the small parlour at the back of the pub where they ate, away from the noisy tap room, Willard sat upright in a wooden Windsor chair, folded his hands across his stomach and instantly went to sleep.

The meal had no such soporific effect on Novak, although he, too, felt overfed. At home – in the unlikely event he'd managed to get home in time for a family supper – Evie would be climbing on his knee, clamouring for a story from one of her fairy books before bed, Hannah would be quietly sewing or knitting, eleven-year-old Oliver would be fiddling with his home-made crystal set, finally driving them all mad with the incessant crackles coming across the ether. In the end Novak would remonstrate, but mildly. He always tried to hide his secret pride in his clever son. He sighed, put aside thoughts of domesticity and picked up his notes.

Fountain pen in hand, he flicked through the scant pages, only kept for the necessary facts he must report back to Brownlow. Impressions and conjecture he preferred to keep in his head.

PETER SHOLTO. Weekly boarder at his school, only home at weekends and holidays. Not academically inclined at school. Shone in the handiwork and woodwork classes, but since this had largely been regarded as something to keep the boys occupied in their spare time, it was not overencouraged.

Edmund Sholto had confirmed that the glue Novak had scraped from the drawer was indeed the same sort of fish glue that Peter had used in his cabinet-making. Glue came in slabs, and had to be heated before use. After that, getting it to Leysmorton before it hardened again might have been a problem but, recalling the tools he had kept at Leysmorton, Novak felt pretty sure there would have been a glue pot somewhere on the premises.

That his other activities included blackmail was now clearly evident, reinforced by what Rosie Markham had reported overhearing about the notes that had passed between Stronglove and her mother. Novak's fountain pen nib spluttered as he wrote: *N.B. See Poppy Drummond again. Soon.*

It was clearly blackmail money, almost certainly contributed by Stronglove, and possibly Stella Markham, too, in that laburnum wood box, though it still puzzled Novak that Stronglove, who had ridden out other scandals, would submit to threats by Sholto to keep an affair quiet. Of course, it would have been a tricky situation, living in such close proximity to Stella, who had married into a family that had always been closely linked to Leysmorton. And did either of them, Stella

240

or Stronglove, have such means at their disposal? Stronglove lived a comfortable existence at Leysmorton, and though he presumably earned his living as an author, it was a big house to keep up. How dependant was he for that on Emily Fitzallan, his cousin? *Query: Stronglove Lady F's heir?*

STELLA MARKHAM. Pretty much an unknown quantity, so far. Aloof, didn't involve herself in village affairs. Friends among the 'county' set. The family Daimler that took Gerald to the city each morning came back and was at her disposal, apart from the few times her father-in-law needed it, until it was time for the chauffeur to return to pick up Gerald. During the war, she had sat on one or two committees, concerned with sending parcels to the troops etc., and called it her war effort. Sometimes she drove to London with her husband, occasionally stayed there for one or two days alone.

Was Stronglove's pre-war move to London a coincidence? After a moment he added, *Relations between Mrs Markham and her daughter Rosie strained, for obvious reasons. N.B. Arrange to see Gerald Markham at some point.*

Screwing the cap back on his pen, he did his favourite trick of rocking the chair on its back legs and letting his thoughts wander. None of the facts he had written down were new, but now, from somewhere, a shape was dimly beginning to take form.

Willard opened his eyes and said, as if he had never been asleep, 'Thinking there might still be another notebook, wondering where it might be?'

241

Novak's interest in Sholto's notebooks had become peripheral. He had been letting his thoughts take him in quite a different direction, and he answered Willard absently. 'What? Oh, off and on, George. Off and on.'

'Have you considered that old tree?'

'What old tree?'

'That massive yew. Plenty of room inside that. Better than somewhere in the house. And that's where he was found, wasn't it?'

Novak blinked. He wasn't envied his sergeant by his fellow inspectors. Mostly, they didn't know what to make of him, and Novak himself had felt that way, too, at the beginning of their partnership. But three years' working together had changed that. Willard might do a pretty good impression of a zombie at times, but it was more due to a one-track concentration, and it often gave him a distinct advantage. Even so, how could he have known that Novak had, at that very moment, been thinking back to that moment in the clearing under the yew, when Lady Fitzallan had given him the letter, and that vague idea he'd had, that he hadn't paid sufficient attention to since it had first stirred?

'Don't know about that, George. Why would Peter Sholto have known about any hollow in the tree?' he asked. It wasn't often Willard had flights of fancy like this.

'I reckon everybody round here knows. Took it into my head to look in the church this morning. There's a village history on sale for sixpence, written by the vicar, with a page or two about Leysmorton. That tree's a bit of a legend. They say it's thousands of years old. Wouldn't do any harm to have a look-see.'

At that moment, the door opened to admit Mrs Gaunt. 'Somebody to see you, Mr Novak. It's Nellie from number eight.'

'Mrs Dobson? Ask her to come in, will you?'

'She won't come in, she wants to see you outside, in the back. On your own. I see you enjoyed *your* pudding, Mr Willard.' She flashed a reproachful glance at Novak, who'd been defeated by his portion.

'Rather too much for my London constitution, Mrs Gaunt.' Her expression said what she thought of London constitutions.

Mrs Dobson was waiting for him in the yard, among the upturned beer casks stacked there.

'I didn't want any of that lot in the tap room to see me talking to you. It'd be all round the village in five minutes. We'll be quieter out there.' As she spoke she was walking to the end of the yard, past the hen run and a lethargic, yellow-eyed old collie at the end of a chain outside its kennel. It barked once as they passed, then returned to its torpor. Maybe it had had the remains of his rabbit pie and a helping of plum duff for its supper. The wicket gate at the end opened onto a footpath beside the river that ran behind the row of cottages. Occasional seats of one sort or another had been set up, but no one else was out there, taking advantage of a sunset like a Turner painting. Mrs Dobson perched on a rough seat made of a plank balanced on two sections of tree trunk and he sat down at the other end.

'I hear Albert Pickles has been asking again

243

about that old bicycle that was found in Farmer Beale's ditch,' she began straight away. 'Left there on St Patrick's Day, it turns out, is that right?'

'Maybe. Why – do you know anything about it?'

'Not me. It's that Wilf Thready, my Ivy's chap.'

'He saw the cyclist?'

'No. He doesn't know anything about any bicycle. But it's on account of what day it was that he remembers. Or thinks he does.'

'And what's that?'

'He'd been down to Kingsworth for band practice – he blows the trumpet in their village band – and having a drop too much into the bargain with that Irish family that lives there, if you ask me. Celebrating St Patrick's Day, or that's what he said. Anyway, he swears he saw something funny when he was coming home. He'd cycled home from Kingsworth, and a wonder *he* didn't end up in a ditch, the state he was in, never mind the way he came. Silly fool had cut through along that old lane.'

'You've lost me. Which lane is that?'

'The one we call Courting Lane. It runs off the Kingsworth Road, round the back of Steadings and Leysmorton, nothing more than an old cart track and more bumps and holes than a tinker's kettle. You'd break a leg soon as look at it and nobody with any sense uses it – except some of the young 'uns, for obvious reasons.'

'And he saw . . . .?' Novak asked patiently.

She sighed. 'He reckons he saw lights on in the house.'

'Just a minute, hold on, Mrs Dobson. Are you telling me this because you think Mr Stronglove and his sister could have been down here on the seventeenth of March?'

She stared. 'No. I know they weren't. Miss Heeren *had* been here, but it was a few days before. I know that because I was there helping. The house was still topsy-turvy and we made a list of things that needed to be done, what to buy to restock the larder and so on. I left them and went home and I heard the motor go past my house about an hour later.' She stopped uncertainly.

'Yes?'

'Wilf reckons he saw something else. He *says* it was a motor car, under the trees, by the Leysmorton wall. But it was black as your hat that night, and the state he was in, could have been anything, one of Farmer Beale's stray cows, anything. In any case, it wasn't *their* motor. It was black or some dark colour, which was why Wilf couldn't hardly see it.'

The light colour of that Lanchester in the garage would certainly have stood out, even in the darkness.

She said, 'It's not often I lay much store by anything Wilf tells me, but this time – I think he did see it, or something just as queer – but you'd best try and talk to him yourself, if you can get any sense out of him, that is.'

'Thank you, Mrs Dobson – you and St Patrick. I think he's smiling on us. That's twice he's given us a lead.'

After she'd left him, he watched a swan as it glided by, possibly the same one who had disdained his biscuit offering, followed by its mate and their grey-brown brood, changing course and

245

gliding across a golden path made by the setting sun, towards the other side, to where the willows dipped into the water. Ripples followed them until they disappeared. The evening was very still.

He suddenly became aware of a heron, perching on a low branch, silent and immobile as if carved from stone. How long had it been there? He knew they could wait patiently for hours, and could eat just about anything. He hoped this one was not waiting for a chance to get one of those cygnets, but he was afraid it was.

Twenty

Hugh had chosen the time carefully: early morning, when Rosie would be safely out of the way, exercising her horse. Ten to one he would find Emily out here alone, even so early – here, or in the neglected hothouses she was trying to get back up to scratch with the aim of once more producing peaches, figs and grapes for the table. It was as though she felt she had to make up for the lost years

She was there, kneeling on the path, doing something to a lavender bush. 'Nearly finished this. I'll be with you in a few minutes, Hugh,' she said over her shoulder.

He stood watching her capable fingers move among the purple blooms, deftly selecting shoots, taking cuttings with a sharp knife and putting them into a small, lidded glass jar she pulled out of the pocket of the loose smock she wore. 'Why are you doing that? Putting them in the jar, I mean.'

'I don't want them to wilt before I can pot them up.'

'Oh,' said Hugh, from the depths of his ignorance. He stood there watching, thin, upright, spruce and feeling too well brushed. How many other women did he know who would dispense with gardening gloves so as not to hamper their efforts? None, but then he knew few women interested in poking about in the earth at all.

After a while she straightened and secured the lid of the jar. 'There, that's enough, I think,' she said, dusting her hands off on her smock and then removing it, revealing to his amusement a tailored skirt and soft silk blouse. She looked immaculate as ever.

'Come and sit down.' She stood up nimbly and he took her arm and she let him walk her past that crumbling little fountain that never failed to irritate him mildly – damn thing, always in the way, smack in the middle of the path – and into one of the so-called sentry boxes, where they seemed doomed to have all their significant conversations. She sat expectantly, waiting for him to begin.

'Well, Hugh,' she prompted at last. 'What's all this?'

He still hesitated. It was one of the few times when he didn't know what to say. Untrue – he knew well enough, but he didn't mean to speak at the wrong moment and appear an old fool. Caution, the watchword for the elderly, was the word.

As it was, she made it easy for him – what was it about women and that sixth sense they seemed to have been born with? – by remarking, as though the lavender bush, and not his reluctance to speak, was still on her mind, that her gardener in Madeira, Domingo, had the greenest fingers she knew of when it came to cuttings. 'But then, everything grows in Madeira. Push a pea stick into the ground and it roots.'

Though this was going faster than he intended, for he hadn't meant to embark on this particular point until he'd got the other thing out of the way, he couldn't miss the opportunity. 'Just as well. I shan't be much help, as you've no doubt noticed. Never been my line, gardening. Don't know a dandelion from a dahlia, I'm afraid. But I'm willing to learn.'

She suddenly became very still. 'Does that mean what I think it means, Hugh? You and I, in Madeira?'

'If you're still of the same mind. Not too much of an old dodderer, am I? Too late to make such a change?'

'Of course it's not too late, we can both dodder together. Oh, Hugh!' Her face alight, she put out a hand towards him and then drew it back, remembering she'd been grubbing amongst the plants. He caught it and held it just the same, and raised it – to the devil with grubbiness! – to his lips. Not grubby at all, in fact. It smelled of the flower-scented sachets his mother used to put with her linen. For several moments they sat in a bemused silence while he tried to marshal his thoughts on what else he had to speak of, which might well cause that smile lifting the corners of her mouth to disappear for ever – for him, at any rate.

'You have thought about this long enough? Are you sure? You won't miss – everything?' she said seriously then, waving towards Steadings, his home for all of his life. 'Your family, and everything else?'

'No. That is yes, of course I'm sure. I shall miss them all, naturally, but not as much as I would miss you if you went alone. By now, it's us who matter, Emily. But what of you? You and your Leysmorton, hmm?'

'My Leysmorton,' she repeated. 'My dream. Hugh, I sometimes think the Leysmorton I knew was in another life. I can't live in a dream, I want the reality.'

'And you think the reality is Madeira?'

'Of course,' she said, rather too quickly, he

thought. She took his hand, wrapped his fingers around her own. Was she being just a little evasive?

'There'll be rather a lot of arrangements to make before we can leave,' she reminded him eventually. 'For you, at least. You'll have things to see to, people to tell—'

'Oh, fiddlesticks! Nobody to please but myself. I can leave tomorrow – or next week, at least.'

'Not quite as soon as that! Actually, I don't want to leave until Poppy has finished whatever else needs doing in the house – and I would like to see this awful business settled, too,' she finished soberly.

He didn't need to ask what awful business she meant. Peter Sholto's murder was still upsetting everyone. He didn't feel it would be politic to mention what had occurred to him more than once: that it might never be settled. The police weren't magicians. 'I saw Inspector Novak and that big sergeant of his as I came in. They seemed to be making their towards the clearing. I thought they'd finished with all that.'

She frowned. 'They don't have to ask permission every time they want another look at their crime scene or whatever they call it, if that's what they're doing. I suppose they know their own business.'

'Not getting very far, are they?'

'Probably not. But Novak, the inspector, he'll chug on like a machine until he finds what he wants.' After a moment she said, 'I showed them that letter I found, Hugh. From Christian Gautier. They – the inspector – seemed to think Peter Sholto had found it before me and had deliberately hidden it.'

He hardly registered the last part of what she said, after that mention of the letter. He hadn't needed to make a confession since he was a schoolboy admitting to smoking behind the cycle shed at school, and it was proving more difficult than he'd thought, but they couldn't start a new life together with this still unsaid. Choosing his words, he said carefully, 'The other day, when you showed me that letter, you said you had known Clare wasn't dead. I suppose you meant to say you were convinced in your mind she wasn't?'

She fixed her wide brown eyes on him. 'Yes, that too. But it was only when the birthday cards stopped that I really knew.'

'Birthday cards?' he harrumphed.

'Yes, Hugh. The ones you posted.'

At many times in his life Hugh had felt like Atlas, holding the world on his shoulders. People had always depended on him, and he had not objected to that because he had always genuinely wished to help and liked the world to sail on an even keel. Now he, the experienced, respected head of the Peregrine Press, who had shared so many burdens, shelled out money, calmed down stormy board meetings, soothed difficult authors when their latest book was not selling well, had rarely felt more helpless or foolish in his life. 'I should have credited you with more intelligence.'

'There was no one else who always knew where I was living,' she reminded him gently. 'Aunt Lottie swore she hadn't sent them on, and Papa certainly wouldn't have.'

'Well. You will at least let me tell you how it happened? I don't want you to get upset but – hear me out, and then you can judge. Will you do that?'

* * *

251

When he had received that letter from Clare Vavasour, out of the blue, his first reaction had been one of anger.

He had never taken to Clare. It was in the nature of elder sisters to be bossy and overbearing, as he knew very well, but he always felt that Clare managed to get Emily to do what she wanted in a way that was manipulative. In fairness, his connection with the two girls had been slight. He had been away at school, and in the holidays he had been more interested in following manly pursuits – or those that were open to him as a young boy – and had scorned the company of girls, his sisters included. Later, when they had all grown up and he had fallen in love with, and then lost, Emily, and when Clare had done her disappearing act, he had, like everyone else, assumed the worst, and was sorry for the negative feelings he had had towards her. At that time, though, so soon after Emily's marriage, he was still too raw from her rejection for it to be uppermost in his mind, and as the months went by Clare was relegated to the back of it. The letter had completely discountenanced him. Posted in London but with no return address, she had asked him to forward to her sister the birthday card she enclosed. She knew that he, Hugh, would have her address, and was certain that he would for Emily's sake do as she asked. It was an impassioned and rather dramatic letter, begging him not to reveal that the card had come from her, or his part in the deception. She wrote that she had gone away for reasons she would never be at liberty to reveal, she was sorry for the upset it must have caused everyone, but she wanted her dearest sister to know she was alive and well.

For a while he cursed her and the certainty with which she had assumed he would do exactly as she asked him to. Why couldn't she have the decency either to let them know, openly, that she was alive – or at least to let them forget her? Had she no idea of the pain and anguish her thoughtless action had caused? At first he had been inclined to throw away the letter and forget all about it. But it nagged him. Who was he to decide, he asked himself, knowing how devoted Emily had been to her sister, that she would not be comforted to have even this hint that Clare was still alive? After a long argument with himself, and against all his inclinations, he had posted the card. And the other cards, which came every year, slotted into ready-to-be-addressed blank envelopes, enclosed in one sent to him at Peregrine Press, without any further word from Clare. When they had ceased to arrive he had assumed she must have died, and it had seemed too late, too futile, to explain his motivations to Emily. In view of what he had learnt later he was glad he hadn't. By then, he had more than an inkling of what her life with Paddy Fitzallan had been.

She listened to what he had to say without interruption and didn't answer for some time after he had finished. 'Thank you for telling me that, Hugh,' she said at last.

He detected no condemnation in her face. She only looked pale, and sad, and somehow exhausted. But then he recognized the glint in her eyes that betokened the beginnings of a smile, and saw the tiredness disappear. 'Really,' she said softly, 'how could you have imagined I couldn't work something like that out for myself? I knew you'd sent them from the first, or at least after I'd thought about it for a while. I don't blame you, I never have – I suppose you thought you'd done what was best for me, as you've always done, dear Hugh. And after all, it doesn't matter now.'

He felt as though the weight of the world had rolled off his shoulders and crashed into the nothingness below. Before he could say anything else, heavy footsteps on the path caused them both to turn their heads, towards the two policemen who were approaching.

To reach the dead hollow in the very centre of the great yew tree, it was necessary to duck under the branches, some of them sweeping right to the ground, before wriggling a way between the secondary growths that had formed around the parent trunk and then, by the tree's strange alchemy, become fused and twisted together as they grew to form a whole. Now its outer circumference, Novak estimated, must measure as much as thirty feet, probably more.

'In you go, George.'

'Me?' Willard patted his girth. He was not built for wriggling.

'You suggested it.' And one of them had to try it. He wasn't, Novak thought, going to find anything anyway.

With a grunt, Willard took off his bowler and his jacket, drew in as much of his stomach as he could, and began to ease his bulk through the twisting configurations. He swore picturesquely as his braces caught on a snag and twanged, and again as he dropped his flashlight. Further grunts and oaths accompanied his progress until at last Novak heard a muffled shout. 'Something here – aargh!'

A minute later, the sergeant emerged backwards, his tweed rear-end covered in twiggy debris, his hair dragged forwards from his bald patch, his face red. He held a limp bundle of fur between his thick fingers, like something contaminated, then chucked it into the clearing and stood up, rubbed his hands down his trousers and mopped his face.

'Well done, George.'

'Well done, my eye. It's nothing but a bloody dead animal.'

Novak peered closely. Gingerly, he picked it up, feeling the bones beneath the disintegrating animal skin. But why should a dead animal carcass have a leather thong tied around it? The leather had hardened and he used his penknife to cut through it. The fur fell open, exposing the tattered scarlet silk lining of what appeared to have once been a wide fur collar.

The two men stood gazing down at what lay inside: the collection of tiny limbs, a naked torso, and a head with dull, matted blonde hair. Even Willard looked shaken.

Novak picked up an arm, to which a hook was attached at the shoulder end, pushed his finger inside the armhole of the small bisque torso and felt around. But the doll's interior workings, which enabled the articulation of arms, legs and head by means of stringing between the hooks, could not be located. He recalled the trouble he'd had when the elastic in Evie's celluloid doll had similarly snapped or perished.

Willard, as usual, had little to say. But he had smoothed his hair back to its usual strategic position, and his colour was returning. 'Well, well,' Novak said. 'Only this – no notebook?'

'No notebook,' said Willard, mortified.

'It's Hildegarde,' Emily said, recoiling from the thing in Willard's hands. 'I called her that after our horrid governess, Miss Jennett.'

'Is that why you dismembered her?'

'Goodness, I didn't do that! Though I didn't like her very much.'

'The doll, or Miss Jennett?'

'Well, both. Hildegarde wasn't my favourite doll. The mechanism inside never worked very well, so the head would come lose. Clare didn't like dolls at all and she used to push her into the toy cupboard out of sight. And when I opened the door the head would roll out.' She pulled a face.

'And you didn't hide it in that big old yew tree?'

She stared. 'The Hecate tree? That was what we used to call it. Heavens, no, why should I? When I got married, I gave all my dolls to our old nanny and asked her to give them away. Is that where you found it – inside the tree? What on earth were you looking for in there?'

'It doesn't matter now, we didn't find it.'

'It has something to do with the murder, hasn't it?'

'Probably not. It's been there a long time.'

Emily tore her glance away from the macabre remains. She had been so preoccupied that she

256

hadn't noticed, until she heard Marta asking, 'What have you got there?', that she and Dirk had joined them.

But Marta lost interest, as usual, in anything that didn't concern her. 'Oh, a doll,' she said, peering at what Willard was holding. It didn't seem to occur to either of them to enquire why a policeman should be holding a dismembered doll in his hands. 'Well, if you'll excuse me, I have things to do.' She retreated and Stronglove, tipping his hat, followed, using his cane more like a fashionable accessory than an aid to walking.

Emily looked at the remains of the doll again. The unblinking eyes stared unnervingly. Why hadn't Nanny Kate, as she promised, got rid of all the dolls? But perhaps she had – all except Hildegarde, left unnoticed in the cupboard. Or was it possible that Clare had already taken it, and left it in the Hecate tree to cast some sort of spell? Like the one she had cast on Miss Jennett, long gone, long forgotten by then, surely?

Born to all the conveniences of living in London, Novak found the lack of transport available in Netherley trying to his temper. No tube to carry you where you wanted to go. No buses to hop on. Shanks's pony, round here, unless you hitched a ride on the carrier's cart or borrowed PC Pickles' bicycle.

Today it was Willard who had the task of riding over to Kingsworth to see if he could pick up anything more about the bicycle found in the ditch. 'Think of the exercise,' Novak told him.

Willard grinned amiably. 'Get me ready for another of Mrs Gaunt's pies, I suppose.'

After he left, Novak walked over to Leysmorton once more with the hope of catching Poppy Drummond, having been told she was expected there that morning. He was lucky, arriving almost at the same moment as she did, accompanied by the obliging young man who seemed prepared to ferry her about wherever she wanted to go. Seizing the opportunity, he asked to speak to her and she agreed at once. The decorating job at Leysmorton now complete, she had, she said, only come down to cast an eagle eye over the decorators' finished work – and presumably to present her final bill. 'We can go into the library, I expect.'

The young fellow, Archie Elphinstone, tactfully backed away. 'Heard there's good fishing in the river,' he remarked, and took himself off to inspect, while Poppy led the way into the spruced-up library.

Novak had expected a flat-out denial from her of that overheard conversation she'd had years ago, or at any rate a refusal to talk about it, and he approached the subject carefully, but in the event she seemed to have accepted the inevitable. Of course she would have been prepared. There were telephones installed here at Leysmorton as well as in her London shop, and her brother would undoubtedly have informed her of the conversation that had passed between himself, Rosie Markham and Novak. He thought it probable that Val would also have tried to smooth over Rosie's part, because if Poppy had taken exception to her eavesdropping, she wasn't showing any resentment.

'You have to understand,' she said rather defiantly when he began to question her about it, 'I was pretty

258

desperate for cash. I couldn't do what my friends were doing, go anywhere they went. It costs money to keep up appearances, you know, the country weekends where you need such masses of clothes, the holidays in the South of France, and the rest. All the girls I knew had their own dress allowances for marvellous clothes and things, and I hadn't a bean. If I could have found work, I would have done so, but I wasn't trained for anything. None of us were, before the war.'

'I understand. It was a temptation.'

'Yes. And I'm afraid I – well, I gave in to it.' She coloured slightly. 'At least, I passed on to Peter one or two notes that Dirk had written to Mrs Markham. But when he gave me money for them, I felt sick at myself, and in the end, though you might not believe me, I gave it back to him. Truly. I mean, they'd been so nice to me, all the family. Even Stella – well, I suppose Stella was different, but she was David's *mother.* I told Peter I couldn't do his dirty work any more, not for *anything.*'

'I don't imagine he was very pleased at that.'

'Furious at first! But then he just shrugged and said it didn't make much difference in the long run, he had far bigger fish to fry.'

'What do you think he meant by that?'

'He wouldn't tell *me* that, would he? I was only the girl he thought he could get to do whatever he wanted – even to marry him.'

'Which you were not inclined to do.'

'Not even *vaguely.* I thought him attractive when I first met him, and so he was in a way. Frightfully good-looking – and he could be quite charming. Perhaps I gave him the wrong idea, I don't know. But later I felt he was becoming – well, creepy. He had a chip on his shoulder about what he called "rights" – by which he meant money, being born to privilege and all that. He believed Karl Marx had the right ideas.'

'Is that why he believed he had a right to blackmail Stronglove – for ever?' Novak asked drily. 'To fund your future together?'

'If he did believe that, it would have been awfully stupid of him, wouldn't it? To have been so sure of me for one thing,' she added with some spirit. 'But he *wasn't* stupid, you know, far from it. And he had something up his sleeve. He was planning to make a trip abroad.'

'Where exactly abroad?'

'He shut up like a clam when I asked him and wouldn't say where.'

'Could he have mentioned Grenoble at any time?'

'*Grenoble*? Skiing and all that?' She shook her head. 'No, I think I might have remembered that – though after I had told him I wanted absolutely nothing more to do with him, I gave up listening. There were more important things going on by then, the war starting, for one . . .' She was very still for a moment, then said, 'Which meant, anyway, that I did get myself a job, after all.'

'War work?'

'You could call it that. If I'd been the sort who didn't faint at the sight of blood, I'd have gone for a nurse – most of my friends did that. As it was, they gave me a job at the Ministry of Food, copying lists of provisions to be sent to the troops, filing, addressing envelopes, *desperately* important things like that.' She grimaced. 'Ah well, somebody had to do it, I suppose. And then, after the war . . . well, Lady Fitzallan's husband had died and left Val a little bit in his will.'

She saw his raised eyebrows and explained, 'Our father had been a friend of her husband, Sir Patrick. It was hardly anything, really, but Val insisted I had it as capital for my business – I thought I might have a flair for interior decorating. And it did go well at first, but now . . . I'm thinking of selling my share, and Val will get every penny back, such as it is.'

Novak looked around the library, now back in functioning mode. 'I should think twice about that, Miss Drummond. You've made this room look . . . so much nicer than it was.' It was the best he could do, though he knew it was inadequate to describe the difference – how welcoming it was now, its gloomy aspect dispersed and what must have been its original grace restored.

She looked surprised that he should have noticed at all, and then smiled, evidently very pleased. 'Well, perhaps I won't give it up entirely. The thing is,' she said, playing with a silver bangle on her wrist, 'I'm probably going to get married. How brave of me, after all these years as an old spinster, don't you think?'

He said gravely, 'I hope you'll be very happy.'

'Thank you. Archie – you met him outside – he's top-hole, really. I'm frightfully fond of him.' A sparkle came into those beautiful eyes and she laughed. 'Actually, Leysmorton is nothing to the house I shall be living in – if I *do* get married. It's an absolute *mausoleum*. Archie's lived there

261

alone, poor pet, with a heap of simply *gruesome* ancestral furniture ever since his parents died – so it will be a challenge, if nothing else.'

It sounded, for all the ifs and buts, as though her proposed marriage was a *fait accompli*. He hoped that wasn't the only reason she was going to marry that nice young chap.

Willard was in front of a pint of bitter, thirsty after his cycle ride to Kingsworth police station and back. The bicycle had never been claimed. But he had also collected the information telegraphed down by Superintendent Brownlow, who had spared a couple of men to seek out and verify information Novak had already extracted from Stronglove. Although it had been three years ago, he could nevertheless give a good account of what he had been doing on that particular day. On the seventeenth of March, he had said smoothly, when asked, he had been present at an inaugural meeting of established writers – novelists, poets, journalists, who were intending to form an association to help and encourage younger writers and artists. Since he had signed a register of names, among them Mr George Bernard Shaw and other literary luminaries, his alibi seemed unassailable. The same evening, he had departed for a week's visit to friends in Brighton. 'And a certain lady confirms he stayed with her,' Willard commented drily.

'Does she now?' After a minute or two, Novak said, 'Supposing Peter Sholto *was* there at the house that night. Doesn't necessarily mean he was killed then. He could have camped out there for days. The tinned food and such Mrs Dobson had been stocking up for them could have kept him going for the age of a duck.'

'True enough. He seems to have known the place inside out, so he wouldn't have had any difficulty gaining access somehow.'

'All the same, you wouldn't have thought he'd have let lights be seen. And what about that motor?'

If Wilf Thready – although every bit as gormless as his mother-in-law made out – was to be believed, *someone* had been there on the night of the seventeenth. Someone careless about the lights – or confident enough to believe it didn't matter if they were seen?

'Well, what else do we have here on our friend Stronglove?'

Brownlow's report also stated that his ophthalmologist had refused, on ethical grounds, to divulge information on his patient – which he was quite within his rights to do, the superintendent hadn't failed to point out. Nor had army records provided anything more than Stronglove himself had told them. When he had enlisted, his poor eyesight had prevented him from being accepted for a combatant role in the army, though it hadn't stopped him from being directed, due to his excellent language skills, into intelligence work, mainly as a translator. He'd been able to continue in the same capacity right until the end of the war, so his sight couldn't have been so bad.

'By what he said, he was still making trips to the village for cigarettes, over those stepping stones. How much do you have to be able to see, to bash someone on the back of his head and bury him under a heap of rubble?' Willard asked, then sighed. 'More than he can now, I suppose, unless he's faking it.'

'I don't think he is. I'd say his condition has deteriorated rapidly since then. He'd have been physically capable at that time, maybe – still is, I should think – but there's a world of difference in being able to see with the aid of those damned glasses and being able to drive from London to commit murder – *and* conceal it. Won't do. Even if he didn't have an alibi.'

Even if he did find Stronglove arrogant, even if he detested the way he was scornful and impatient of everyone he regarded as less intelligent than he was himself, even if he had every motivation for getting rid of young Sholto.

'So that rules out our chief suspect,' Willard said gloomily. 'Our only suspect. There's nobody else within striking distance, is there?'

Novak said nothing for a while. 'Maybe we're on the wrong tack altogether, George. Time to try another one.'

Twenty-One

Edmund Sholto was working in his back garden, but the knock on his front door was clearly audible. Visitors were rare, especially ones who announced themselves with the loud, double rat-tat that sounded threatening even from where he stood, and he knew it would be the police again. It was with a feeling of dread that he made his way round the side of the cottage to the front door.

Novak, his hand already raised to knock again, swung round when he appeared. 'Mr Sholto. We've come to return your photographs – and Peter's tools. They were still at Leysmorton.'

'Thank you. Please come in.' They followed him indoors and Willard held out an envelope with the photographs. Edmund looked down at his dirty hands, still holding the bunch of radishes he had just pulled. He swallowed, his mouth dry, and indicated a drawer, asking the big sergeant to drop the snapshots in. 'Thank you. Er, my neighbour, Mrs Baxter, has made me some lemonade. Like some? It's very good.'

'That sounds like a perfect idea on a hot day.'

In the kitchen he took his time over washing his hands and collecting glasses and the jug of lemonade from the cool cellar. After pouring some for himself, he swallowed one of his pills and washed it down with a long slug before returning to the parlour, feeling a little calmer.

Novak was again taking an interest in the pictures on the wall. 'Nice place, this, by the looks of it. Cornwall, you said?'

'It's a small fishing village near Penzance. You don't have to look far to find paintings of it, amateur or professional – artists are around every corner there.' He waved them to take a seat, set the glasses down and began pouring lemonade from the stoneware jug.

'Your wife?' asked the inspector, suddenly fixing his interest on the photograph of Morwenna on the mantelpiece. He sat down, took a sip of lemonade and said, 'What really brought you here to Netherley, Mr Sholto?'

Edmund's pulses jumped. What was going on? Steady, he warned himself. 'Nothing more than what I already told you. A need to get away, somewhere different, make a fresh start.'

'The choice of St Albans couldn't have had anything to do with its relative proximity to Leysmorton?'

He could feel sweat breaking out on his brow but didn't dare bring out his handkerchief to wipe it off. 'Leysmorton? What could that have to do with it? I'd never heard of it until I moved to this village.'

A bee, trapped in the window, buzzed angrily, trying to find escape. No one took any notice of it. Novak said, 'You told me a lot about Peter, Mr Sholto, but you didn't mention the young lady he was interested in.'

Edmund blinked. 'I didn't know there was one! I suppose he knew several young women – the Markham girls, and their friends for the most

266

part . . . but I never heard of anyone special.' In fact, he thought, I might have been glad of something that would have diverted Peter's attention from other things.

'He never spoke of Poppy Drummond?'

'Poppy Drummond?' For a moment the name genuinely puzzled him, until he remembered who she was, that girl who had stayed at Steadings before the war. 'The sister of that young fellow who's working for Stronglove, you mean? No, he didn't.' He found the idea slightly bizarre.

'We've been told he carried her photograph everywhere with him – and that he was hoping to marry her.'

'*Marry her*?' Edmund smiled. 'You must be mistaken. Peter was in no position to marry anyone. And I can tell you there was no photograph with what the adjutant called his personal effects, when he returned his things to me.' His smile froze as the thought came to him: *but there wouldn't have been, would there?* If Peter had in fact been in the habit of carrying a photograph around with him, it must have suffered the same fate as everything else on his person after he was killed. Edmund's gorge rose again at the sickening reminder of his son's body slowly rotting under that pile of rubbish.

It took a moment before he was able to speak. 'I didn't know anything about her and Peter, and I have to say I find it hard to believe. He would have said something.' *But would he*? Edmund knew that it was all too likely Peter might have kept this quiet, too.

'Miss Drummond herself has confirmed this.'

267

There was a pause. 'What are you driving at? What has all this to do with my boy being murdered?'

'Maybe nothing. But I'm hoping we might find whether it had or not if we clear up one or two things first. Remember the sample of glue Willard brought you the other day?'

Speaking for the first time, the taciturn sergeant reminded him: 'Which you confirmed was what your son used for his woodworking.'

'It appeared to be the same sort, yes. It's common enough, what most cabinet-makers use – and anyone else for that matter. I couldn't say any more than that. Why?'

'It was used to attach something to the underside of a drawer. This letter, in fact,' Novak said, producing it. 'Have you seen it before?'

'A letter? The underside of a drawer?' His heart began a slow thud, so heavy he felt it must be visible under the thin cotton of his shirt. 'And presumably you think it's something that concerns me?'

'You're a schoolmaster, I suppose you might read French, Mr Sholto? Good, then perhaps you'd like to look at it and tell me whether it does or not.'

He took another long pull of the cool lemonade. The sweat was so thick on his forehead that this time he was forced to wipe it away before fishing for his reading glasses and accepting the letter. As he read it through, he was aware of Novak's deep-set regard, of the sergeant's silent attention. 'I'm afraid I can't understand all of this,' he said at last, as he came to the end.

268

'Enough, I suspect, to know that it *does* concern you?'

There had been no mention of his name, but somewhere, reading between the lines, they had presumably found some connection. He folded the paper and then leaned back. His hand was trembling. With an effort of will, he managed to steady it, wishing they would go away, wanting nothing more than to be left alone.

Novak let the silence continue until at last Edmund was forced to ask, 'Where did you find it?'

'It was with some old drawings and sketches Lady Fitzallan's sister did many years ago. Peter apparently hid it there.'

'Peter did?' Edmund attempted incredulity. 'If I thought it meant more to him than it does to me I might be inclined to believe you. What's it all about?' He thrust the letter back at Novak. 'Who is this Christian?'

'He was an art student from Grenoble who tutored the young Vavasour girls at Leysmorton for a time – Emily and her sister Clare. His name was – or is, if he's still alive – Gautier. Does that mean anything to you?'

Edmund shook his head emphatically. 'No.'

'Well, even if you don't know the sender, I think you certainly knew the woman this is addressed to, Mr Sholto.' Edmund didn't answer and Novak went on, 'I think you know it was your mother. She was Clare Vavasour, wasn't she?' The silence was even longer this time, and Edmund actually felt the blood draining from his face. There was nothing you could do to control that sort of reaction.

269

'You swear you haven't seen this letter before?'

'Never. How could I have done?'

Suddenly aware of the bee's frantic buzzing in the confines of the small room, he levered himself up from his chair and cupped his hand carefully around it, guiding it to the open pane where it flew off, released. Feeling a reaction out of all proportion to the effort, he sat down heavily. 'What has all this to do with my son?'

'Well, I think Peter discovered the letter when he was poking about among the furniture at Leysmorton, going through the drawers where some of Clare's work was stored – maybe he was even looking for it, or something like it, that would provide him with the means he wanted to exert pressure on someone. Maybe he just came across it accidentally and put two and two together. Or maybe he already suspected your reasons for coming to live in this part of the world – for one thing, to be near Leysmorton where your mother had grown up. But let's be frank. I think it's more probable you were in it together, that you'd told him about the fortune that was waiting to be claimed – your mother's, his grandmother's share of the Vavasour inheritance. Even though you were illegitimate, there were grounds for thinking there might be a moral if not a legal claim. On Lady Fitzallan, whose heir at present is Dirk Stronglove.'

Silence once more, while Edmund searched for what he could possibly say.

'No,' he said at last. 'It wasn't like that, not at all. I grew up knowing nothing of any inheritance. My mother would never speak about her

270

family, who they were, whether they were rich or poor. I didn't even know what her maiden name was. Before I came here, I had never heard of Leysmorton House and the Vavasours, and how wealthy they were reputed to be.'

'And when you did it was like a fairy tale come true? Oh, I know coincidences do happen, Mr Sholto, but I don't believe in ones as large as this.'

'You may believe what you like, Inspector,' Edmund said wearily. 'I'm telling you the truth – which is precisely what I told you before, about why I came here. I'll admit that this part of the world drew me because I had somehow picked up that it was around here my mother had been brought up, but I had no idea where. And the only coincidence is that I came to this village by having met Hugh Markham, through my bookshop.'

'That really won't do, Mr Sholto,' Novak said mildly.

'Then I don't know what else to say.'

'I think there's a lot more you could tell us.'

For a long time, Edmund sat without speaking. Novak, arms folded across his chest, waited. The room was heavy with the heat of the day and Willard ran a hand round the side of his collar. At last, his shoulders sagging, Edmund spoke. 'Very well.'

He made himself sit very still for a moment or two longer, then he stood up and walked across to the drawer where he'd asked Willard to drop the snapshots, and from it he removed a pencil sketch, framed in gilt, handling it almost reverently. 'I have never spoken to a soul about this before, I swore I never would, but . . .' He held out the sketch.

271

Novak looked at it with interest before passing it over to Willard.

Willard said, 'This is Lady Fitzallan as a girl, isn't it – and her sister?'

'It was the only thing my mother had kept of her previous life; it always hung on the wall of her bedroom. It was her most cherished possession. I hung it on the wall when I came here until Hugh Markham saw it one day. I noticed that for some reason the sight of it had quite upset him, though he denied that it had. When I later learnt there was another drawing like this of the two girls, I thought it best to remove it.' He stopped, overcome with the effort, but then he pulled himself together and went on, gesturing towards the letter Novak still held. 'So my father was this Christian – Gautier, you say? From Grenoble?'

Novak repeated what he had already said to Emily Fitzallan. 'The chances of you finding him are slim, non-existent, I'd say.'

'Finding him? Oh, but I haven't the least desire to do that. Ethan Sholto was the only father I ever knew. I loved him and respect his memory more than ever I could respect anyone who deserted my mother as this man appears to have done.'

'You'd better tell us the rest.'

'Yes, I had,' he replied, after a moment's further debate with himself. 'Then maybe you'll see what I mean.'

Once launched, he found no difficulty in speaking freely. In fact it seemed to be a release, much like the cessation of pain after a carbuncle had been lanced, or a rotten tooth drawn.

272

In the oddly assorted marriage of his parents, it had often seemed to him as though the man he called father, though only fifteen years older than his mother, was more like his grandfather. A short, dark and dour Cornish tin miner from St Just, a widower who had married his mother when Edmund was seven years old, Ethan Sholto had nevertheless been a significant presence in Edmund's life, although it wasn't until after his death that he realized just how much he had loved him. When he was young, he had thought him hard as the ore he mined, and maybe he was, in a way. That was what had got him part-ownership of the mine.

'He was a wealthy man then?'

'Comfortable, no more. It was only a small concern. But he died suddenly, without making a will – like many more, he thought there was still plenty of time to do that – and everything went to my stepbrothers, the children of his previous marriage. Which was fair enough by me. He had put me through college and by then I was married, working as a schoolmaster and earning my own living.'

'How did your mother come to choose Cornwall as a place to live?'

'I don't know. She never spoke about her past life, but she knew several of the artists painting down there at that time, so I suppose that's why she went to live among them. They had a fairly free and easy lifestyle, not judgemental. A woman with a baby and no husband wouldn't be condemned by them, and if they'd known anything about her previous life, they never said so to me. She met my father, Ethan Sholto, and he braved local opinion to marry her. I always called him my father, I always shall. Not this unknown man who fathered me.'

No one said anything for a while, until Novak said, gesturing towards the framed sketch, 'Tell us how you learnt about the other drawing of your mother.'

'It was Peter who found it. He came across it at Leysmorton one day just before the war, and borrowed it to show me. He was full of excitement, saying he had found his grandmother. When I saw it I was stunned, because there was really no question about it. One of the girls was undoubtedly Clare, my mother. The pictures were a companion pair, and I had the other.' His eyes closed, momentarily reliving that moment of shock. 'That, I'm afraid, was when Peter started talking about making a claim on Lady Fitzallan. He wouldn't listen, even though I told him categorically that I would have nothing to do with anything like that.'

Novak regarded him steadily. 'Not for yourself, maybe,' he said, 'but it would have been a different proposition, surely, if you were thinking of your son's future? Are you sure you didn't in fact encourage him to go ahead? It would have been only natural if you had.'

'Except that I did not,' Edmund said shortly. He said nothing more for some time, weighing up whether he had not already said too much. At last he said, 'Besides, there was something else, something Peter didn't know.'

'Go on, Mr Sholto.'

274

He looked at the photograph on the mantel. *Forgive me, Morwenna*. When he could, he said, 'He was determined to go ahead, with or without me. But what he didn't know was that he had no claim without me. He was not Lady Fitzallan's grandson. He was in fact in no way related to the Vavasours. Peter was not my son.'

Silence.

'My wife and I could not have children, but then her brother died in a fishing boat accident, and his wife, Peter's mother, lost her will to live and threw herself from the cliffs into the sea. It was the natural thing for us to take the child and bring him up as our own.'

'That's a tragic story.'

'Too tragic, we decided, ever to tell him – which I see now was a mistake, but . . . hindsight is a wonderful thing. He was only three years old, and he very soon forgot his parents, and never questioned the fact that we were not his true mother and father. Then Morwenna, my wife, died. Peter was growing up, it was a small community we lived in, and I began to be afraid he would sooner or later hear talk, that he would never forgive me if he learned I had kept the truth of his birth from him. I see now it was a monstrous thing to do. If Morwenna had lived, she would have known what to do, but I . . . As it was, I decided to move. Peter never knew he wasn't my son.'

'And you couldn't bring yourself to tell him, even in the light of your own upbringing, when he began to talk of those false claims?'

'My circumstances were entirely different. Ethan

275

Sholto never pretended to be my real father – and there was my mother to consider. There had to have been a strong reason why she had suffered poverty by cutting herself off from her family. She had been at pains not to let them know about me, nor me about them, and nothing would have made me go against her wishes – even if I'd had the slightest inclination to involve myself in a sordid, long-drawn-out and expensive lawsuit. But Peter wouldn't listen. It became an obsession with him. He even had some foolish notion of going out to Madeira and appealing to Lady Fitzallan, though in view of the difficulties – the war had just begun, for one thing – I couldn't imagine how he envisaged getting there.'

But Peter had known how. And as soon as Edmund had opened the laburnum box and seen those banknotes stashed there, he had surely known what they were for. He said sadly, 'As the boy saw it, she had unfairly come into what should have been my mother's share of their inheritance along with her own, and had a moral duty to put things right.'

'In my experience, morality has little to do with it when it comes to money,' Novak remarked.

'Be that as it may, I forbade him to do any such thing. For the reasons I've given – and for another. I had no idea what sort of person Lady Fitzallan was. I still don't – I've never met her.'

'It didn't occur to you to make yourself known to her – relieve her of the anxiety about her sister? It's preyed on her mind all these years, you know.'

'How could I have known that?' Edmund knew he sounded stiff-necked, with the same sort of

276

stubbornness his mother had shown all her life, though he had had a deeper reason for avoiding Emily Fitzallan: he was afraid of awakening memories and perhaps having to defend what Clare had done. He said, 'She found that letter, you say. Does she – does she know who I am?'

'After finding it, I'm sure she has accepted the reason for her sister's disappearance was because she was having a child by Christian Gautier. How much else she has deduced, I don't know. But I suspect you won't come as a great shock to her. Lady Fitzallan is a very astute woman. And I would think it very likely,' he ventured, albeit with the air of a man who feels himself on shaky ground, 'that she would like to meet you.'

A variety of emotions chased each other through Edmund. At last, he sighed. 'Well, it was Peter's wish we should meet, so for his sake I will see her, if only to let her know I am not seeking to claim anything from her.'

Twenty-Two

Driving home that evening, when they reached the junction where the road sign indicated North, Gerald Markham's chauffeur suddenly made an exclamation of annoyance and put on his brakes. Traffic and milling crowds blocked the road ahead, with no possible chance of getting through, while the automobiles, carts and vans already piling up behind them prevented any possibility of turning back to find another route. 'Another demonstration, looks like,' he remarked, switching off the engine. 'Nothing to do but wait, Mr Gerald.' He sat back, arms folded in resignation.

Gerald, not resigned at all, thought of the tiresome dinner party he and Stella were due to attend that evening. If he was late, Stella would not be pleased. 'Where are the police? They should be keeping it under control.'

'It's a women's demonstration – garment workers, by the look of the banners, Mr Gerald. The coppers are sympathizing, shouldn't wonder. Out on strike theirselves not so long since, weren't they?'

'What's the world coming to, Deegan?' Strikes and lockouts, was there no end to it? There had even been trouble down at one of the printing works that employed only old, trusted craftsmen, last month.

'It's the war. Stirred something up in everybody.

278

Jack was as good as his master in the trenches, so why not out of it?'

'Why not, indeed?' They both knew it was no more true now than it had been then, but it was reassuring to pretend. 'But I wish they hadn't chosen to try and prove it just here.'

Normally, Gerald enjoyed these little exchanges with his father's old chauffeur, and thought Deegan did, too. 'Chip off the old block you are, Mr Gerald. Just like your father,' the older man often said, an idea Gerald had liked, and quite agreed with. Until the bombshell the old man had exploded last night. Gerald couldn't imagine himself even contemplating what Hugh was proposing to do. Not even at his father's age, with nothing to lose, as Hugh put it. Up sticks and off to Madeira – with Emily Fitzallan! Both of them prepared to leave England on a permanent basis, though with the caveat that since the Peregrine Press had been Hugh's whole existence, he was not about to relinquish his interest entirely. He had promised he would come over at least once a year for board meetings. The surprise to Gerald was that Emily, with her evident passion for the old place, was prepared to leave Leysmorton again. He hoped they were not making a mistake, but his own cautious nature told him that they might be.

But then he grinned as pure pleasure shot through him, imagining what Stronglove's reaction would be to the other piece of news Emily had confided, that she was changing her will. Not that she was cutting Stronglove out entirely. She would, she announced, see he was well provided for, but she wanted to see continuity, to see Leysmorton House go to someone who would love it and its garden as she did. When Gerald, stunned, had at last taken in the astonishing fact that she proposed to leave Leysmorton, eventually, to Rosie – *to his daughter, Rosie!* – the idea had pleased as much as it had astonished him. He rejoiced for Rosie's sake, of course – but the thought of Stronglove out of his life filled him with unalloyed delight.

People thought Gerald a soft touch. They underestimated him, which was foolish, but that was how he liked it. He knew when to act, and wasn't afraid to do so when necessary, though in his own time and then not openly. He preferred to work behind the scenes. He had done what he had to do once before, in the case of Peter Sholto, and saw no reason to regret it.

But now, without the need for Gerald having to do anything about it himself, the Stronglove situation might be solved.

When at last they drove into Netherley, he checked his watch yet again. Still time for a quick one before dressing. Hopes of that vanished, however, when he reached Steadings and found that inspector chap who was investigating the Peter Sholto business sitting on a chair in the hall. Stella was nowhere to be seen.

'I was hoping to see Miss Markham,' Novak said, 'but I'm told she's out riding, expected back shortly, I understand, so I thought I'd wait.'

'Oh, she'll be out giving young Drummond his lesson. She's teaching him to ride – which I suppose is safer than that motorcycle contraption of his!' her father said easily. 'Hello, Alice, old girl!' He bent to pat the fat old spaniel who had appeared and now flopped down at his feet.

Novak had in fact known Rosie would not be at home and had timed his visit precisely to accommodate this. He hadn't been able to come up with a better way of meeting Gerald Markham without making an appointment, which he didn't wish to do, but the times of Mr Markham's regular departures from home for his office, and his return, were open knowledge to everyone in the village. As it was, he was uncharacteristically late, and Novak had had to hang around here, hoping Rosie would not return before her father did. 'Just a small question to ask her,' he murmured, hoping he wouldn't have to say what it was.

'Well, I'm sorry you've missed her.' Gerald hid his irritation with a smile. 'I'm afraid we are dining out and I'm already behind time, so if you'll excuse me . . .' He had the look of a man who regularly wined and dined well. An affable, genial fellow, with a rubicund, outdoors sort of face, slightly incongruous somehow with his smart city clothes. 'But I shouldn't advise waiting for Rosie. Time is expandable, when she's out riding.'

'Well, I dare say I can see her tomorrow.'

Her father nodded, but the smile became less warm. 'Inspector, I know you've your job to do, but I really don't appreciate this hounding of my daughter.'

Novak's brows rose. 'I'm sorry you see it as hounding, sir. Miss Markham has been very willing to help us in our enquiries so far. Very helpful.'

281

'What has she been saying?' Quick colour mounted, over and above his natural freshness. 'What has she – in fact, to be blunt, what have any of us – to do with this business of yours?'

'You all knew the victim, sir,' Novak pointed out mildly. 'Your children in particular. He was a visitor to your house.'

'The victim,' Markham repeated. Suddenly he looked sadder, and older. 'Yes, Peter was David's friend . . . what an end, what a waste. At least my son died for his country.'

There was a moment of silence. 'What would you say if I told you Peter Sholto probably died because he was blackmailing someone?'

'Blackmail? Peter?' He stared at Novak, then he said abruptly, 'Look here, I need a snifter. Been a long day. Would you like one?' Novak thanked him but waved the offer away. 'Well, come in here while I have mine.' He entered a door to one side of the hall, leaving Novak to follow him into a masculine study with sporting prints and team photographs adorning the walls. The old spaniel padded behind them and collapsed in a heap on the hearth rug, her big, soulful eyes watching their every move. It was dim in the room but Markham made no attempt to switch on a lamp as he crossed to a side table and poured himself a substantial measure, lit a cigarette and stood in front of the fireless grate. He did not invite Novak to sit, the implication being that the talk should be brief.

'Who, then, was he blackmailing?' he enquired at last.

'I'm not at liberty to say, sir. But do I need to? Don't you already know?'

Markham's knuckles were white as he gripped the glass. He was white around his mouth, too, and there was a dangerous glint in his eye. Novak understood what Rosie had meant when she'd said she didn't want to be around when her father lost his temper. Gerald said, 'I don't think I understand what you are saying.'

'We have reason to believe Peter Sholto might have been blackmailing your wife, sir.'

'That's an outrageous suggestion!'

Novak didn't rise to this. 'Did you send a letter to Peter Sholto just before he disappeared?'

The reaction was not what he expected. Markham suddenly subsided into one of the leather chairs and waved Novak to the opposite one. 'Perhaps you'd better sit down.' He gulped at his drink and said, tiredly, 'All right, I don't know how you know, but yes, I did write to him. I'd heard he was due to be demobbed and I wrote and told him that I wanted to see him as soon as he arrived back in Netherley.'

'Presumably you wanted to talk to him about the blackmail?'

'About that, yes . . . you're quite right, he *had* been obtaining money from my wife, I'm afraid. He didn't answer my letter. Then weeks later, out of the blue, he telephoned me – calling from Leysmorton. I was astonished – stunned! I knew the place was locked up, though I'd no doubt he knew how to get in. He said we should have that talk I wanted right there and then, he would wait for me to go over. It was just before dinner, and after some hesitation, I agreed. He was waiting outside the door when I reached

283

Leysmorton and we said what we had to say out there.'

'Why outside?'

'There were lights on in the house, but as he didn't make any move for us to go inside, I suspected he had someone else there with him. I was glad enough to keep our conversation to ourselves, however, without anyone else overhearing.'

'Go on.'

'I called his bluff and told him his sordid little game was over. That I knew what it was all about, that the affair was finished and he could say goodbye to any more money from Stella – or from Stronglove. He said if that was all I wanted to see him about I needn't have bothered, all that was an irrelevance now, he'd have all the money he wanted soon enough. I'd no idea what he was talking about. I could only assume he meant blackmail money from other poor fools.'

'How long had you known about your wife and Stronglove?'

'Oh,' he said tiredly, 'I suspected before the war. I happen to love my wife, in spite of everything, and I care about my family, so I said nothing, hoping it would blow itself out, like Stronglove's other affairs. I had no idea that Stella was being blackmailed, though, until I discovered a valuable piece of jewellery I had given her had been sold, despite her very generous allowance. I said nothing to her, but I was able to work out what had happened for myself. I had never liked Peter Sholto, I thought him crafty, and something about the way Stella

284

had always reacted to him made me put two and two together. But then the war put a stop to it. Both he and Stronglove went away and I thought that was the last of it. Until, when peace came, I heard Stronglove was planning to return to Leysmorton. Peter, of course, would be demobbed and would also be coming home, and I was afraid the whole business would start up again. That was why I wrote to him. When I saw him, I told him to his face that his nasty little scheme had gone flat and warned him to keep his nose out of my wife's affairs in future, or I'd let the police know what was happening.'

'What did he say to that?'

'He laughed.' Markham had grown taut with anger. 'He said, "No, you won't do that, I think. Too much risk of all your fancy friends getting to know. A slur on your precious family name. Sniggers behind your back whenever you—"' He passed a hand across his face, as if to wipe away a distasteful memory. 'Well, he was going on to say a lot more, but I didn't stay to hear . . . I turned my back on him and left him standing where he was.'

'You're sure you didn't threaten him further?'

'What would have been the use, with someone like that? I simply left him and came home.' With an effort he prised himself from his chair. 'It's not a particularly elevating story – but now, if that's all . . .'

'Before I go – this all happened on the seventeenth of March, did it not?'

He looked puzzled. 'I don't remember the exact date.'

285

'That was the day Peter Sholto absented himself from his unit.'

'Then I suppose it might have been.'

'Did you send him a second letter?'

'No'

'What did you think when you heard that he had apparently been killed at least six months earlier, just before the war ended? When you had actually seen and talked to him a few days previously?'

For a moment he said nothing. 'I'll tell you what I thought. I knew it wasn't true, of course, but as far as I was concerned it couldn't have been better news. If he was supposed to be dead, he couldn't bother us any more. If he wasn't, the same thing applied. And now, Inspector, I'll leave you to find out which of his enemies dealt with him.'

'Oh,' Novak replied, 'we know who did it. What we don't know – yet – is how.' He, too, stood up. 'I think you're right about not waiting for Miss Markham. I can always see her in the morning, and Mrs Gaunt will have my supper waiting. No, don't bother, I'll see myself out, sir.'

'You're very late, Gerald. You do realize we're dining with the Sydenhams?'

'Don't remind me, Stella. I hadn't forgotten that! But there's still plenty of time.'

'Only if you hurry like mad.' She looked annoyed, but then she shrugged. Her fingers plucked through her jewel case, selecting a small pair of emerald earrings he had given her on her last birthday.

'Let's cancel,' he said suddenly. 'I'm very tired, and I don't think I can face Pamela Sydenham tonight.'

'Don't be ridiculous, Gerald.' She screwed a green jewel into her ear-lobe.

In two strides, he was across the room, gripping her shoulders from behind and staring into her face as she sat in front of the looking glass. She winced as his grip tightened painfully. 'I have been ridiculous for too long,' he said, 'but not any more. It's time you and I talked and got things straight. It's too late for anything but the truth between us, Stella.'

Twenty-Three

At last it was out in the open, no longer a secret. His affair with Stella was finally, irrevocably, over.

Dirk smarted as the last half hour played itself over and over, like a needle stuck in a gramophone record. Gerald – *Gerald Markham*, of all people – storming over here to confront him, lecturing him with that insufferable air of righteousness. That stuffed shirt actually having the effrontery to announce that he was speaking for Stella! When in fact it wasn't difficult to see what was really happening: Gerald delivering an ultimatum and forcing the issue, laying down the law and forbidding his wife to have anything more to do with Dirk – which diktat Stella would have had no choice but to obey, and probably no inclination, either, thought Dirk bitterly, at last accepting the inevitable. He crashed his fist impotently against the desk. Now, when the threat of exposure no longer existed, Stella had to go and admit everything about their affair to her husband! He wondered what else she had told him.

Stella. Finish. Finale. Their affair had finally run its course, and he was affronted to find how much pain it caused him, though he had always known that she would never leave her husband. Gerald represented too much that was paramount in Stella's life: money, comfort, status, the opinions of the set she moved in. At first he had never imagined their casual affair would last so long, would turn into something much more important – for him, at least – would even survive the separation of the war and be rekindled after it. Or perhaps he had known subliminally that it could, and that was at least one of the reasons why he'd fought against his desire to return to Leysmorton, after the war had forced a break on them, his intuition telling him it would be a mistake. His previous affairs had always been relatively short-lived, easily dismissed, but this one was different, and more dangerous. Yet he *had* returned. And then had come a great lifting of the weight that had lain on his shoulders for four years, when Sholto's father, for reasons best known to himself, let it be known that Peter had not survived to see the end of the war.

It was not only the prospect of restarting things with Stella, however, that had brought him back. Despite himself, Dirk had a nostalgia for this old house where he had grown up, ancient creaking timbers, draughty stone passages and all. But primarily, he considered a famous author such as Dirk Stronglove had a right to live in, and eventually inherit, such a fitting setting as Leysmorton. He had never dreamt that right would ever be challenged.

Even before life had unfairly thrust the disaster of his failing sight on him, he could have found his way blindfold around every corner of Leysmorton, so familiar was he with the whole of this great house and its garden, his home since he had been a babe in arms. He could still find his way tolerably well around it now, without making too much of a fool of himself, without blundering into anything or falling over and thus bringing someone rushing forward with officious offers of help, which he hated above all things. People who didn't know him had difficulty in believing the extent of his blindness. They did not even guess that it was so bad now he could barely distinguish even the words he himself wrote.

He wasn't, as everyone thought, putting off the advised operation because he was afraid of the uncertain outcome. He *knew* what that would be. *Knew* – with utter conviction, without any shadow of doubt – that, operation or not, one day he would be completely blind. He had always been cursed by this intuition, second sight, clairvoyance, call it what you will. As a twelve-year-old boy he had foreseen that his mother, Florence, would die of the pleurisy she had contracted. He had been forewarned of the tragic end to that business of Marta's. And he had known that Peter Sholto would die. Throughout his life he had had these unshakeable convictions of what was to happen.

And he had never been wrong.

There were other discomforts that went with his condition: a sick vertigo and the headache that today was blinding. He had difficulties in sleeping. The lotion Marta had concocted to bathe his burning eyes with was soothing, and the pills she rolled for his headaches sometimes helped, though little more. So what was the point in going through with it? Operation or not, very soon he would be completely blind.

Meanwhile, there was Marta. What of her future? What was he to do about poor Marta?

The police would be back, inevitably, and he had to act before that.

He reached out for the Chinese tobacco jar that stood on his desk. Lifting its lid, he let the contents slide through his fingers for a moment before picking up a small handful and stuffing it into his pocket. He then pulled a sheet of writing paper towards him and, unscrewing his fountain pen and bending his head until it almost touched the paper to see better, he began to write.

When the police came, Dirk was in the small dining parlour with Marta, who had just crossed the room to draw the curtains.

The darkness outside made a mirror of the window, and for a moment she stared at her reflection: a dowdy, unattractive, middle-aged woman, her doughy face expressionless. With a sharp tug, she pulled the curtain across to shut out the image and went back to sit with Dirk at the table, where only the wine and their half-empty glasses stayed after the remains of supper had been cleared. She lifted the bottle, a sweet purplish wine akin to port, to refill Dirk's glass, but he covered it with his hand.

'No, I've had enough. This elderberry stuff of yours is enough to knock out a horse. Any more will only make my head worse.'

She put the bottle down. His eyes were half-closed and he had let his chin drop to his chest. 'You should go to bed, Dirk, get some rest.'

Even as she spoke, the sound of the heavy

knocker on the front door reverberated through the house. They looked at each other and the blood surged to her face. She left him and hurried to answer it. 'It's not a good time,' she told the two policemen. 'My brother has been having a bad day, he has a very severe headache.'

'I'm sorry to hear that, Miss Heeren,' Novak said. 'But it's important we see you both now.'

Grudgingly, she let them in. When they entered, Dirk looked up. 'Marta. Some of your coffee for these gentlemen, perhaps? I suppose it's Peter Sholto again?' he asked in an exaggeratedly resigned note.

'Not for me, thank you,' said Willard, waving away the offer of coffee.

'A glass of my wine then.' Without waiting for an answer, Marta produced two more glasses and poured a substantial amount into each.

'Yes, it is about Peter,' Novak said.

'He always liked my home-made wines,' Marta remarked, refilling her own glass and then, despite his earlier refusal, Dirk's too. 'Go on, a little more won't hurt you.'

The hair of the dog? wondered Novak, noting the pallor of Stronglove's face, the tense frown between his brows. The alleged headache, no doubt. He sipped cautiously from his own glass. Syrupy sweet, but with a heck of punch, probably. These home-brews were deceptive. He took a moment to wonder if Marta, too, had been at it already. She looked suspiciously bright-eyed, and a dull, unbecoming flush was on her round face. It might be a clue as to how Marta Heeren got through her day. He sensed that she could

292

have had more to give to the world than worrying over a brother in the way she would have worried over a troublesome child, living in someone else's home, doing nothing more exciting than growing herbs and vegetables.

Willard, too, sipped, raised his brows at the taste, put his wine aside and then opened his notebook.

Novak began, 'Let me start by going over what we've gathered together about Peter. Correct me at any time if you think we've got it wrong.'

Stronglove fingered his wine glass. The light from the oil lamp on the table gleamed on his dark features; he looked like some devilish, predatory insect, his eyes hidden by the thick, distorting lenses of his spectacles. 'Go on.'

'As we've established, his abiding interest was in old furniture. But it seems not to have been the only thing he was interested in.'

Moments passed before Stronglove spoke. 'Perhaps you'd care to be a little more explicit.'

'To put it bluntly, he was showing an unhealthy preoccupation with your personal affairs, Mr Stronglove, isn't that so?' He didn't answer. Marta began to speak, but Dirk put a heavy, detaining hand on hers where it lay on the table. Novak watched them. 'All right, let's not beat about the bush. Let me tell you that we have the money you and Mrs Markham paid out to keep him quiet about the affair you were having. You should have gone to the police over that.'

He made no attempt at bluster. 'Has Mrs Markham admitted this?' Not getting an answer, he shrugged and asked, 'Where did you find the money?'

'That doesn't matter. You don't deny the affair – or the blackmail?'

'I don't suppose there's any point. You seem to have made up your minds. Anyway, it was finished with, all that, before he died.'

Novak doubted whether this was the truth. 'That wasn't his only reason for threatening you, was it?'

'That, I'm afraid, is purely a matter of speculation on your part.'

'Not entirely. As I understand it, you have reason to believe you are Lady Fitzallan's heir, that you will inherit this house and quite possibly her fortune as well.'

'What has that to do with Peter Sholto?' he said stiffly.

'Quite a lot, Mr Stronglove. I have something here that he believed gave him an even stronger hold on you. And I suspect you believed it, too.'

'Please don't speak in riddles. It's exhausting.'

'I'll try to be more plain. Have you seen this letter before?' The thin paper rustled as Novak showed the Gautier letter, opening it carefully because its recent handling was beginning to threaten disintegration.

'No.'

'I think you know what it is, though. Peter told you he had discovered that he was the grandson of Lady Fitzallan's sister, and he had a letter that would go far to substantiate his claim when he made one on her estate. I suggest he was blackmailing you over that, too. Wills can be changed.'

Stronglove suddenly reached out an unsteady hand and took a large gulp of wine, spilling it slightly as he put the glass back on the table, not deigning to answer.

'You must have felt very relieved when his father told everyone he was dead. But you already knew that, didn't you? You were here when he died, the night of March the seventeenth.'

'I never saw him, after the war.'

'As we've told you, no one was here that night,' Marta put in.

'I don't think that's so, Miss Heeren. Lights were seen in the house.'

'But if Peter *had* come here, as you say, wouldn't that account for it?' Stronglove reached out to top up his glass, which did not seem like a good idea in view of his intense pallor and the nervous tremble in his hands he didn't seem able to control.

'Whoever that witness was,' Marta said woodenly, 'must have been mistaken. We left the house two days before that, and didn't return until the end of April.'

She might have been even more dismissive had she known just how unreliable that witness was, but before she had the chance to question their identity, Stronglove added, 'And in case you had forgotten, I have what's known as an alibi for March seventeenth.'

'Indeed you have, sir. A meeting, followed by several days in Brighton. But the meeting you attended began at six and ended at eight. Plenty of time to get here and back to London in time to get the last train to Brighton. I might add that on the same night, as well as the lights, a motor was seen here at Leysmorton.'

It was not only Stronglove's hands which were trembling now – it ran through his whole body. He looked agitated. He put a hand to his chest, as though he were having difficulty breathing.

'Are you not well, Mr Stronglove?'

'No, he is not!' Marta cried, springing up. 'I told you before you started all this—'

'Marta, don't, I'm well enough . . . don't say any more.'

'I will, Dirk! The whole of the village could confirm that we weren't here that night,' she said wildly. 'Everyone would have known if we had been. A motor going through Netherley is enough to alert everyone.'

'But not,' Novak said, 'if you had skirted the village and arrived here by means of that back road, the one they call Courting Lane, that runs along the back of the house. I believe you drove along the lane – a hazardous undertaking, I might say, considering the surface, and—'

'Yes, indeed, have you *seen* the state of that lane?' Marta interrupted scornfully. 'No one with any sense would risk driving down there.'

'Not unless they were a skilled driver. And you've driven on worse roads than that, haven't you, Miss Heeren? It's nothing to the roads in France, when you drove an ambulance full of wounded men.' She could not fail to know what he meant: appalling roads made worse by shell craters, often filled six feet deep and more with Flanders mud; under enemy fire, in pitch darkness, trying to avoid the worst of the craters as well as abandoned, shattered machinery and vehicles, and sometimes the bodies of men already dead, lying where they had fallen.

At that point Stronglove gave a groan of something like despair, and made a tremendous effort to speak. He took off his spectacles and this time left them off. The effect of his dark eyes, black as coal in his white face, was alarming. 'Marta . . . too late for lies . . . Yes, we did come back that night . . .' He was gasping, unable to form a proper sentence. 'I killed Peter . . . hit him . . . the poker . . . written all down, my study . . .' He stood up, staggered dizzily and sat down again, almost missing the chair, retching a little. His skin looked clammy and grey and his lips had a leaden tinge. A thin trickle of vomit escaped from the corner of his mouth and he tried to pull his handkerchief from his trouser pocket to wipe it away, only to collapse, falling forward over the table.

Marta gave a sort of sobbing scream. 'He needs a doctor! My God, you've killed him with all this – he's had a stroke!'

Willard, galvanized into action, took over. In two strides he was bending over Stronglove, feeling his pulse. After a moment, he looked up and shook his head. Novak took hold of Marta's arm. 'It's too late, Miss Heeren. I'm sorry. I'm sorry, but I'm very much afraid Mr Stronglove is dead.'

Her face almost the colour of his, she stood like one turned to stone, staring petrified at her brother, the handkerchief he had reached for hanging half out of his pocket, and at what had been pulled out with it – a trickle of small scarlet berries that lay scattered on the floor.

'What are those, Miss Heeren?'

'Don't touch them. They're yew berries. He's eaten some of them deliberately. He did it to save me.'

The blank stoniness that had come over Marta after that last despairing utterance had given way to an agitated restlessness, as they gathered in Dirk's study. Emily, arriving back a few minutes ago after dinner at Steadings, had walked into a situation she still couldn't comprehend. 'Let me get you a drink, Marta. Take those pills the doctor's given you and you'll feel calmer.'

'It's nonsense,' Marta said suddenly, addressing Novak as if Emily hadn't spoken, jerking a hand towards the sheet of paper, the 'confession' Dirk had written. 'It's not true.'

'I know it isn't, Miss Heeren,' Novak said. 'I know. It's not worth the paper it's written on. Of course your brother couldn't have killed Peter Sholto. Physical constraints apart, he wasn't even here, was he? He was on his way to Brighton. It was you who murdered him, arranged it all.'

The words made no impact. She seemed to have forgotten, or obliterated from her mind, what she had said when she had seen those berries, scattered like drops of blood across the carpet.

Emily looked up in shocked protest. She had been told that Dirk had killed himself by eating yew berries, chewing not only the harmless outer red flesh but the deadly inner seed as well. Shocking enough in itself, but now, it seemed, Novak was accusing *Marta* of murdering Peter Sholto. She felt out of her depth, someone who had no business to be here. She scraped back her chair.

298

'Leave if you wish to, Lady Fitzallan,' Novak said shortly, as if she'd spoken her thoughts aloud. 'I'd advise you to remain, however – there are things you need to hear. If you do stay, please try not to interrupt.' She sat down again rather abruptly. Willard nodded reassuringly at her and turned a page of his notebook.

Novak turned back to Marta. 'Is there anything you wish to say, Miss Heeren, about your brother's confession?'

'Confession!' she repeated scornfully. 'Dirk was ill, he didn't know what he was saying.'

'Tell me about the night Peter Sholto was killed.'

'I know nothing. We weren't here.'

'Very well, if you won't tell me, then it's up to me to spell it out.' Novak paused and then began patiently to go over the version of events he believed to be the truth. 'I think Peter Sholto, when he was due to be demobbed, let you know that he was not about to relinquish his claim to be the grandson of Clare Vavasour.' He turned round at Emily's involuntary exclamation, ready to silence her, but the shock had robbed her of speech, or even the volition to get out of her chair and leave the room. He gave her a steady look, then turned back to Marta. 'The war had put a suspension on his blackmailing activities, but you knew that when he was demobbed, he would start again. So you wrote and told him that you, too, had discovered – *and destroyed* – the "proof" he had told you he'd found and hidden.'

An oddly contemptuous smile sat on Marta's face, but he went on, 'In fact that was a lie, you had never even seen it, but it was enough that he might be afraid you had. But he didn't react as you thought. He immediately absconded without leave in order to confront you. When he arrived here, he telephoned you in London, didn't he? You didn't expect that, but in fact it suited you rather well – your brother was off to spend the weekend in Brighton, which left you free to deal with the situation alone.'

'You believe *this*! You know *that*!' The scorn was oddly reminiscent of her brother. 'How do you know anything?'

The truth was, Novak *didn't* know, but he was sure that was more or less how it had happened, and that was the line he was going to take. 'Your brother had been buying him off, not to press the claim. In actual fact, had Mr Stronglove known it, there was no danger to his inheritance from that quarter. Peter had no rights, legal or otherwise, to any of his grandmother's inheritance. He need not have worried.'

'*What*?' The smile left Marta's face. She looked suddenly dazed.

Unrelated facts, fears, suspicions were whirling with dizzying speed through Emily. That letter from Christian Gautier, its implications . . . a child . . . Dirk's unexplained visit to her in Madeira – was that to find out if Peter had already been in contact with her? Had Peter's death been planned, even then? But Novak had said Peter had no claim . . .

'Do you understand what I'm saying, Miss Heeren?'

Marta's glance had become unfocussed. 'You will never be able to prove anything.'

300

'In that case, we shall have no alternative than to use Mr Stronglove's signed confession.'

For a moment her chin lifted in defiance and it looked as though she might be going to challenge him, but she held tightly onto the arms of her chair, breathing deeply, while the spark went out of her, as if a light had been switched off. At last she said dully, 'It doesn't matter. Nothing matters now.'

'Then tell me what happened.'

For a moment her old stubbornness appeared. Then her tongue flickered out to moisten her dry lips and she began to speak in a flat monotone. 'We share a garage in London with a neighbour, an American. He was visiting in New York and he'd left the keys of his flat and his motor with us. It's a black Siddeley. When Peter telephoned, I drove it here.'

She stood up and began a restless pacing, moving round the room, touching familiar objects. After a moment she went on. 'He was waiting when I arrived. He said he hadn't eaten anything since breakfast, so we went into the kitchen and I opened a can of soup, and while it was heating up, I poured him a glass of my wine.' An unpleasant sense of self-congratulation broke through as she added, 'He drank it straight down – he really should have known better. I poured him another and he drank that down, too. And then he . . . just fell asleep.'

'What did you put into it?'

'Oh, nothing much,' she said, giving him a sly look. 'He was slumped in his chair and – it was easy. I came up behind and hit him over the head.'

'You hit him over the head with the poker. Just like that.'

'No,' she corrected. 'The flat irons were on the hearth, as usual. I used one of them.' She looked directly at Novak and now her eyes were brimful of malice. 'He deserved it.'

Emily closed her eyes against the horror she was hearing. Why, she asked herself, why? She opened her eyes and found Marta staring at her, those round eyes unnaturally bright, like polished pebbles, and when she spoke it was almost as though she had heard Emily's silent question. 'I used to love Peter, you know. But when somebody does the sort of thing he was doing to Dirk, you begin to hate them. All the more, for once having loved them. It was what he deserved,' she said again.

'Marta—'

Novak said, 'Peter's body was found a long way from the house. How did you get him there?'

She passed a hand across her eyes. 'I don't remember. Oh yes – in my wheelbarrow, of course. I put him by the yew tree. The ground was too hard to dig, but I did cover him up.'

She was a strong woman. It would have been difficult, but not impossible, for her to do as she said she had done – lay him on the ground and throw the bricks over him, tussle with the old tree house planks.

Her pacing had brought her to Dirk's desk. She looked wild and disorientated, gazing down at it until all of a sudden she said, quite clearly, 'It was the doll, wasn't it, that made you suspect me? When I saw you showing the doll to her.' She nodded in a dismissive way towards Emily.

'*You* put Hildegarde there?' Emily said. 'Why?'

'Does it matter?' she returned impatiently. 'It was only a doll. I opened a cupboard and it fell out, all arms and legs and bits and pieces.' She laughed again, then the confusion returned. 'Poor baby!' she went on. 'I didn't have a shawl so I wrapped her in that fur tippet – little babies should be kept warm . . .'

Something very dark had entered the room. Emily's scalp crept. Marta was looking, and sounding, more than a little mad. 'She never felt the cold, or the sun, you know. They took her away, my baby, my little dead baby, and they wouldn't tell me where her grave was. But this time I found a place myself, one where babies would be safe.'

Emily tried to smother the horror she felt. 'A safe place in the Hec—in that tree. Why, Marta?'

'What? Oh, Nanny Bunting was always going on about how her dear little girls used to play there, how Clare used to hide things in it. They were very pampered children, you know, Inspector,' she said spitefully. 'Spoilt. Allowed to do what they wanted. Pretty clothes their mama brought home from London for them, all the toys they wanted. They left a whole cupboard full of dolls behind.' She shook her head, then added in quite a normal voice, 'I – I wasn't myself at the time. But I still had Dirk, didn't I? And then he killed himself to try and save me, when I only did it for him.'

Novak knew what he had to do, the words he had to say, but for the moment, hearing the desolation, looking at the woman before him, he couldn't bring himself to utter them. Willard coughed. And Novak began, 'Marta Heeren, I—'

She laughed again then, shockingly, a harsh, grating laugh, and without warning she kicked the desk chair over violently and then, panting, her hand lunged out and the heavy, cut-glass inkwell was knocked over, ink spreading across the green leather surface, and everything else on the desk was swept to the floor. Except for the Chinese tobacco jar which teetered on the edge while its lid rolled off and the yew berries Dirk had left in it spilled out.

For a moment there was a stunned silence, then quick as a flash she bent and scooped up a handful. But before she could get them to her mouth, Novak's hand was round her wrist. There was a long silence as little by little they trickled to the floor, and after that she said, 'Take me away from this place. I never want to see it again. I have nothing left now.'

Twenty-Four

'This was where she worked, then?'

He walked around the little room, focussing on every detail, and Emily sat on the window seat and watched him, liking what she saw. A careful, scrupulous, kindly man, Edmund Sholto, she thought. She saw white hair that had probably once been fair, a pale face, his eyes. Half an hour ago, he had been a stranger to her, but the green-gold of his eyes had given her the truth. She had wanted to say, 'I would have known you anywhere. You have your mother's eyes. Tell me about her. Tell me all about Clare.' But it had been too soon to say that, just then. She was only too grateful that he had agreed to come and see her.

This first meeting had been painful so far, in view of the circumstances: the tragic death of his son, the appalling events surrounding it, the police enquiries and everything that had emerged out of them, leading to the revelations about Clare. They had circled around both subjects, neither wishing to hurt the other, and now, all that surmounted, they were left in an awkward hiatus.

It was Emily who took the first step, a literal pace towards him, smiling and extending her hands. 'For your mother's sake, I hope we are going to be friends. We are the last of the Vavasours, you know.'

'My name is Sholto, Lady Fitzallan,' he said evenly.

305

With no hesitation she answered, 'Of course, and mine is Emily, Edmund.'

They regarded each other gravely. Then he smiled. 'She would have preferred me to call her Clare, too, though I never did.' He slid a hand into his pocket.

Emily looked at the snapshot of Clare, wearing a loose smock and an unfashionably long skirt, her hair inadequately bundled under a wide straw hat. She was standing before her easel in a flower-dotted meadow with a paintbrush in her hand, and the photographer had caught the rapt absorption on her face. No longer the young face Emily remembered, but still, in her thirties, recognizably Clare's.

'I was lucky,' Edmund said lightly. 'As I snapped her, she realized what I'd been doing and that was the end of it. She would never have her photograph taken, and she ordered me to destroy the negative, but I wasn't going to get rid of the only photos I was ever likely to have of my mother.'

Emily could not take her eyes off the snapshot. Clare. The same slightly defiant tilt of the head, the same concentrated frown. Her eyes misted over, and he allowed her to recover herself while he leaned against the desk, his arms folded, and gently went over the story he had briefly told Novak – of Clare's life among her artistic friends, her marriage to Ethan Sholto, a good man and a hard worker. She listened avidly, wanting to know all the details that would enrich what she already knew.

'Life must have been very difficult for her, supporting a child. How did she live, Edmund?'

'Until she married my father we were poor, yes, But she worked hard and scratched a living by

306

selling sketches and watercolours to shops that sold those sorts of things to tourists, and painted other things solely for herself. What she did sell didn't bring in much money.' He stopped, looking at her intent face, her wide eyes. 'I don't want to distress you.'

'Oh, please, go on,' she urged. She was greedy for more, for every detail of Edmund's early life with Clare in that small Cornish fishing village – which she noticed he always spoke of as 'home' – of the man he called father, and above all of Clare herself.

'There's a school for painters and an art gallery at Newlyn, which isn't far away, set up by Stanhope Forbes, the artist. Her friends used to exhibit their paintings in the gallery, prior to submitting them to the Royal Academy, but she could never be persuaded either to show or submit hers, although I know now that she'd nothing to be ashamed of in her work – to the contrary, in fact. It was all part of the secrecy that pervaded her life, but everyone thought she was mad, including my father, though he never really understood art or even pretended to. But it made no difference. She went on selling what she called potboilers to the tourist shops as she always had, getting practically nothing for them and infuriating everyone with her stubbornness. The money didn't really matter by then, of course.'

Emily showed him the sketchbooks and every-thing else Clare had left behind, including all those obsessive depictions of the Hecate tree, and then went back to sit on the window seat, leaving him to look through them. Only one thing had she removed: the pen-and-ink drawing of the dark goddess herself – removed it and burnt it. She still didn't know whether Clare had left her obsession with magic and Hecate behind, or passed it on to Edmund, and that particular drawing, which still disturbed her so much, was something she didn't want him – or anyone else, for that matter – to see.

Eventually, he came to stand by her at the window with the sheaf of drawings in his hand, gazing straight towards where the old yew stood, looking at it with some amusement. 'Some size, isn't it, that funny old tree? Interesting, though. I guess that's why she had to draw it so many times. She was compulsive that way – she'd draw something a dozen times or more, simply to get it right. I like these drawings of it, though – may I keep one or two?'

That funny old tree. Not 'the Hecate tree'. Spells, magic, witchcraft, none of it meant anything to him. Clare had not, then, passed on her obsession. Had the trauma of finding herself with a baby, unmarried and virtually penniless, knocked all that nonsense out of her, as Nanny Kate, all those years ago, had said was needed?

'The drawings are all yours, Edmund. Please take them, and everything else, if you wish.'

'Then this seems like a fair exchange.' He lifted a bulky parcel from the carpet bag he had brought with him, spreading out on the chest of drawers half a dozen small framed watercolours. 'Some of her later paintings.'

Emily didn't have the expertise to judge whether they would be classed as beautiful works of art by those who knew about these things; for her they did have beauty, and revealed a tenderness, unexpected and astonishing in Clare, which made her heart turn over. She saw at once they were more mature and assured than the few earlier paintings she had selected, and the subjects more varied and interesting: fishermen in oilskins and sou'westers, a fishing fleet setting out to sea at twilight, a small lighthouse in the distance; brown sails, wet sands, barefoot children playing in rock pools, crab-pots and fishing nets spread out to dry; a glinting sun, a light over it all that was almost translucent. 'Thank you, I shall treasure these. They're – lovely,' she said, inadequately.

'Many people thought so. But because she was so adamant about not selling them, neither shall I. The rest I have can hang back on my cottage walls now,' he said wryly. 'I took them down when Hugh showed too much curiosity about the sketch I had hanging there of my mother.'

'Yes, I know about that. So she took that with her, then. Its companion is in my bedroom here.'

'Then we shall both have one.' He hesitated. 'He was a proficient artist, the man who did them.'

She nodded.

'My father, it seems.'

She said nothing for a moment. 'Yes.'

'What was he like?'

'Your father . . . was a charmer.'

'Was he? The only time she ever spoke of him to me, it was with scorn – though probably as much at herself as him. She could never forgive herself for that one lapse.'

'I can believe that.' Clare would never have admitted to having fallen from grace, not even – or perhaps especially – to her nearest and dearest. How had that happened to Clare – to *Clare,* of all people? Allowing herself to be taken in, seduced? Yet somehow Emily could not admit romantic feelings had been involved, any more than she could erase the memory of Clare's eagerness – wilfulness, if you like – for the pursuit of new experiences. Whatever it was, it had shamed her into secrecy for the rest of her life. If Clare's rebellious spirit would ever allow shame. Contrition, maybe. The wish to protect her son from disgrace? Or another, more compelling reason?

The truth didn't always come in a flash, or even through reasoned, patient seeking out. Sometimes it happened gradually without one being aware of it, seeping into one's consciousness until it lay there, waiting to be acknowledged. A certainty that this was how it had happened, an acceptance of hurt . . .

'Lady Fitz—Emily, are you all right?'

'What? Oh, yes.' Indeed, she felt as though she had been asleep all her life and had only just woken up. 'She sent me birthday cards every year, you know. When they stopped, I knew what had happened.'

'She was ill for such a short time, just a few weeks, and then she died peacefully in her sleep.'

'Were you left alone?'

'No, my father was still alive, Ethan Sholto, the man she married to provide me with a father. He was a good, honest man, you know, a chapel goer, but they suited each other well. It wasn't a

310

husband she wanted, really – she never had much opinion of men as a whole, and he – he only wanted a companion, but I do think they were—' He broke off.

'Happy?'

After some consideration, he said, 'I'm not sure that happiness was something you'd ever associate with my mother. But I think she was content with what she had made of her life and she kept rigidly to her own code of behaviour – which was very strict,' he added ruefully. 'She would probably have made a good nun, had she been of a religious turn of mind.'

If Clare's gods had not been of a different order, taken up when she was young and easily swayed. Talk of Hecate, the Otherworld, dark magic and arcane lore had been heady stuff for the sort of impressionable young girl she had been. The sort of mumbo-jumbo that had drawn her to the yew.

Yet the old tree had duality, Anthony had always said – properties of good and evil. If you believed that, it was possible to believe, as Marta Heeren had, that it had sheltered Peter's body after his death, that her pitiful secret would be protected deep inside its hollow heart.

Ever since Marta's arrest, thoughts like that had been haunting Emily.

'What will happen to her?' she had asked Novak.

'She won't hang,' he had replied after a while. 'They won't hang somebody who is not altogether sane.'

Mad? Sad, deluded Marta?

He had held out his hand. 'I'll say goodbye.

I'm going back to the Smoke, where I belong. I don't want any more cases like this.'

So Novak wasn't just a detecting machine. She had felt his sympathy for Marta, and saw she had misjudged him, taken face value on his appearance. 'Thank you, Mr Novak,' she had said, shaking his hand. 'Thank you for giving me my sister back.'

Epilogue

The chief emotion Emily had felt at abandoning the idea of permanently residing in Madeira was relief, and she knew instinctively that Hugh felt the same. It had once seemed to both of them like the solution to a problem, but that no longer existed. Now, Leysmorton was waiting for them, to occupy and cherish it, until in due time it would be passed on to Rosie.

He tucked her arm under his, and clasped her hand as well, as if he wasn't going to let her go again, not this time. On her other hand, that held the basket, her shiny new gold wedding ring gleamed. Absurd at my age, she told herself, not believing it for one moment, as they walked in the winter garden on this crisp, cold day, on their way to gather holly to decorate the hall at Leysmorton, for their first Christmas together.

The garden was not at its best in December, the disadvantage of having so many roses. Roses are not beautiful in winter. Nothing more than a boring bunch of twigs, Clare used to say. But worth it for the promise of later glory, Anthony would reply. It almost required a suspension of disbelief to have faith that, looking so dead in their winter dormancy, they would ever awake again to all that beauty . . .

Hugh said suddenly, 'Do you remember Bertie Featherstone, by any chance?'

'Who? Oh, Boring Bertie, the soldier? Of course. He was such a fool.'

'Yes, but he got a VC fighting the Boers.'

'Bertie did?'

'Lost an arm. I hadn't seen him for years, but I met him at my club one day. I gave him lunch.'

'What made you think of him now?'

He shrugged. 'Oh, you know, no particular reason. As one does.'

They walked on a little, then she said, 'Memory's a funny thing. Where it starts, where it ends. What you know, what you think you know . . .' She didn't finish, and he wondered . . . Sometimes, he thought Clare had not been the only secretive one in that family.

Bertie Featherstone, invalided from the army, had been glad of company and in the mood for reminiscence. They talked about people they had known and Paddy Fitzallan's name had come up, Hugh had forgotten now in what context, but giving him an unpleasant jolt. Of course Bertie had known him – he'd known everybody. 'Married the Vavasour girl, didn't he?' he said. 'Landed in clover, marrying money. Always knew he would, lucky devil.'

Hugh had been incautious after pheasant and a shared bottle of Margaux. 'Depends how you look at it. Emily's hardly in clover, marrying him.'

'Emily? No, got it wrong, old boy. It was the other one he was running around

314

with, the arty one – when she could escape
that dragon of an aunt,' he guffawed.

After that conversation, occurring just before his meeting with Emily in Paris, Hugh was more convinced than ever that he'd been right to agree to Clare's request to forward those birthday cards. If he hadn't done so, he was sure Clare would have tried to find someone else who would, somebody who might have been less discreet.

He had sworn he would never tell Emily what Bertie had said. But sometimes, lately, he had felt almost certain that she already knew. Whether she had, and had perhaps forgiven, if not forgotten, he couldn't tell. But if that was the way she wanted it, he was not the man to raise questions.

She was releasing her hand and arm from his. 'Wake up, Hugh, and put those gloves on,' she said briskly, tapping him smartly on the arm. 'We're here.'

He saw they had reached the end of their journey, the copse where the holly grew, near the shadow of the great yew which had outlived Clare, would outlive himself and Emily, and might well outlive Leysmorton itself.